The Dust Roads
of Monferrato

ROSETTA LOY

The Dust Roads of Monferrato

TRANSLATED FROM THE ITALIAN

BY WILLIAM WEAVER

Alfred A. Knopf   New York   1991

THIS IS A BORZOI BOOK
PUBLISHED BY ALFRED A. KNOPF, INC.

Copyright © 1990 by William Weaver

All rights reserved under International and Pan-American
Copyright Conventions. Published in the United States by Alfred A.
Knopf, Inc., New York. Distributed by Random House, Inc.,
New York.
Originally published in Italy as *Le Strade di Polvere* by Giulio
Einaudi editore s.p.a., Torino. Copyright © 1987 by Giulio
Einaudi editore s.p.a., Torino.
First English translation published in Great Britain by William
Collins Sons & Co. Ltd., London, in 1990.

Library of Congress Cataloging-in-Publication Data
Loy, Rosetta, [date]
[Strade di polvere. English]
The dust roads of Monferrato / Rosetta Loy. — 1st American ed.
p.   cm.
Translation of: Le Strade di polvere.
ISBN 0-394-58849-5
I. Title
PQ4872.O98S77I3   1991
853'.914—dc20   90-53303   CIP

Manufactured in the United States of America

FIRST AMERICAN EDITION

CONTENTS

1 PIDRÈN 7

2 THE COSSACKS 42

3 GAVRIEL AND LUÌS 71

4 RUST APPLES 102

5 BRAIDA 130

6 THE DRAGOON JUNOT 158

7 GIAI'S VIOLIN 203

EPILOGUE 251

The Dust Roads
of Monferrato

The Great Masten

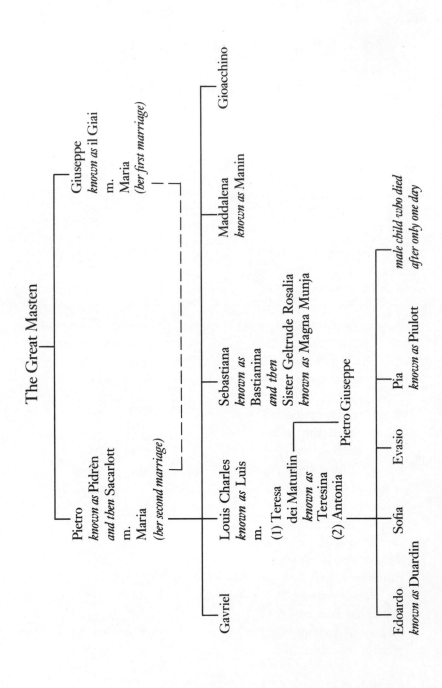

1

PIDRÈN

It was the Great Masten who had the house built, at the end of the eighteenth century, when he became a *particulare*, a man who had land of his own, oxen, cows, chickens and rabbits, and so many acres that he had to hire extra hands. He was in a hurry and he didn't bother much about the foundations, even though the house, with its yellowish façade, was anchored to the ground through the years, the long sequence of rooms, one after the other. A building of two storeys plus the attic with its low windows directly under the roof. The brick path ran from the house to the driveway that curved down towards the gate, while the barn and the stables extended from one side until they reached the road where the great wooden gate opened. There is no knowing what that road was called then; the house was the last in the town and, later, when another was built, it was on condition that there be a blind wall between it and the Great Masten's garden.

No one has ever found out the Great Masten's real name because the parish ledgers were burned during the first Napoleonic campaign. No doubt, he was a man who had grown rich thanks to the coming and going of soldiers, providing fodder for the horses and grain, first hidden, then sold for three times its value. And wine to get French and Austrians drunk, and Russians and Bavarians, Alsatians, during those endless wars that had coloured, as in a game of exchanges, the map of central Europe. All we know of him is that, working from sunrise to sundown, never letting up, in a few years he doubled the acreage, and that his legs were so long he could step across ditches without jumping. He married late, and of the many children he brought into the world only two sons grew to manhood: Pietro and Giuseppe. Pietro, known as Pidrèn, was later nicknamed Sacarlott. Giuseppe was so blond that, from childhood, he was called Giai, which in dialect means yellow.

His wife went first to join all those dead babies, buried in haste to the sound of the Tribundina, with a plain stone to indicate where. He, the Great Masten, fell under the wheels of a wagon one summer when the rain poured down so heavily that the Tanaro overflowed its banks and the fields were flooded before the corn had been harvested. They didn't even have time to toll the Agony, and during the funeral it went on raining and the relatives had to take shelter inside the church. The hail shattered a stained-glass window. Pidrèn and Giai decided to marry: they were twenty-two and twenty-one respectively.

A cousin, known as Mandrognin, told them about two young sisters who would also be good company for each other in the house. Two girls from Moncalvo whose mother was dead; they embroidered hangings and vestments for the church and sometimes, seated at the cushion bristling with pins, they worked at lace-making under the strict surveillance of an aunt from the Veneto, Luison. One of the girls, Maria, was a brunette; the other had that dull brown hair that some women try in vain to pass off as blonde. A colour so common in certain parts of the Monferrato region that it almost suggests an adaptation of the species: the colour of the land, the mud, the interminable mists.

The brunette, Maria, was beautiful; Matelda, on the contrary, her eyelids always lowered, talked with plants and seeds; and the vestments she embroidered were the most prized in all Moncalvo. On solemn occasions, when the priest held up the chalice, glints of purple and gold darted from the embroidered silk on his back. Some even said that Matelda

8

talked with ants and, on certain evenings, with her Guardian Angel.

Pidrèn and Giai both fell in love with Maria. They called in a painter, to decorate the ceiling of the living-room with four different views; in the other rooms they were satisfied with a few scrolls that might please the girl from Moncalvo. They planted a walnut, two pears, and some *rusnent*, rust apples. The walnut grew until it cast too much shadow on the house and it was later decapitated; then it spread out like a gigantic umbrella and became the focal point of the garden.

The dark girl from Moncalvo chose the younger of the brothers, Giai. And Pidrèn, who should have taken Matelda, went off in the train of a young French general, who was beginning a brilliant career in Italy. Ah, he's a *testa mata*, that Pidrèn, a strange one, refusing that Matelda, who, when she holds her needle, has the Madonna at her feet . . . and he'd rather go off with that Frenchman, that *Bonaparti* . . . But Matelda, who was embroidering an altar cloth covered with flowers and birds, and violet-winged butterflies, waited. Perhaps some voice, not entirely of this world, had advised her to be patient.

Not many things happen in the life of Giuseppe known as Giai. He plays the violin and this, to be sure, is an unusual activity for a man who has to take care of so many acres, partly vineyards and partly fields of forage and grain. He plays, his handsome profile bent towards his shoulder, he plays in the evening by the fire, he plays in summer under the shady walnut. The evenings are long, damp, luminous; his wife grows bored sitting there listening to those notes that, to her, seem to reply to the song of the nightingales; she loves no music except furlanas and the *currenta* because you can dance to them. Nobody ever takes her dancing, and if Giai has married the wrong wife, she has certainly married the wrong husband: his bow pierces the evening, gently torments it. Giai is a solitary, and if somebody turns up, he tells his wife to offer the visitor a drink, while he goes on playing. During the day he goes out into the fields with the cane that belonged to the Great Masten, but instead of ordering the sheaves to be covered in case a storm comes, instead of having the weeds cleared out of the canal, he stands and contemplates the hills. The rectangles of earth, brown, lighter brown, green, blond, almost white as milk where the plums and the cherries are blossoming in spring.

One evening he sat on the edge of the well and there he started playing the violin, looking at the stars reflected below in the round mirror of water. His wife took fright and ran into the house, weeping; he stayed there, playing, his feet dangling in the void, and when Mandrognin looked out into the garden, seeing that trunk emerging from the well, he thought the Great Masten had come back, never weary of watching over the land and the house.

What else is there to tell about this Giai, who died at thirty with his violin beside him, his curly hair that had so attracted the two Moncalvo sisters, his feet so delicate that they developed sores when he stumbled over the clods? He goes out into the fields more and more rarely, the harvest grows scanter every year and his grain, his grapes, even the millet, are always less than the crops of his neighbours. Similarly, his cows are often sickly and the calves are slow in growing. His wife is always trying to economize, doing sums over and over, mending his clothes, which he tears when, gripped by a sudden impulse, he scrambles over the ditches, through the bramble hedges. Following a sound, a light, the glint of water among the cane brakes. His wife looks at him: he is merry, laughing, handsome with that head covered with curls, and then her love returns and quivers in her throat like the first time ˙they were left by themselves, seated on the stone bench under the hazelnut bushes.

Her family back in Moncalvo scolds her, it's her fault, they say, that everything is going so badly. Why doesn't she at least have a child? But no children come, and she thinks the fault

lies with that violin, the strings that vibrate in the evening
beneath Giai's slender fingers. And when he comes to bed and
kisses her on the mouth, she sleeps, she is sleepy, sadness and
solitude have drained away even her soul. When she goes to
Moncalvo to visit, her sister follows her with her eyes as Maria
wanders among the rooms of her girlhood like a sparrow that
has lost its instinct of the seasons, seeking in winter the food
of summer. Neither of the two sisters knows that life at times
takes strange turns and to reach a place that once was easily
found, they must follow endless labyrinths.

Pidrèn meanwhile is in Lombardy, the Veneto, Mantua. He
even reaches Egypt and sees there the Pyramids and the
Mamelukes. He's at Marengo. From the top of the tower,
where he is to give signals to the troops, he looks at the peaks
of the Alps still white with snow, and the fields and the
vineyards laid waste by the battle. The house where he was
born is not far off, less than two hours on horseback, and not
much farther is the Moncalvo hill, where the dark girl once
lived, the girl he had so wanted to marry. Perhaps she, too,
can see the glint of the mirrors transmitting signals from the
top of the tower and she is wondering what will happen to the
grain, now trampled by so many boots, and the uprooted vines,
fires that raise grey pillars of smoke. She must already have a
child, he thinks, maybe two, a little girl for whom she makes
brightly coloured smocks. He can almost see his more fortu-
nate brother, coming home as she runs to meet him; maybe
she has put on weight, no longer has that waist that he used
to think he could clasp in one hand; perhaps in this brilliant
June sun she has washed her hair and now she is sitting on the
grass drying it, that hair so long it almost touches the ground.
Meanwhile the grenades shake the mulberry trees, uniforms
are spattered with blood, wagons break their axles on the rocks
in the Scrivia, as they ford the stream, the horses rear up and
the currents drag them off. *Ramener l'aile droite*, say the mirrors
from the top of the tower.

*

On that 14th of June Giai had gone to watch the battle from the hill towards Lu. The roads were deserted and it was a very clear day, he was seated in the shelter of a row of alders. He wasn't afraid of disbanded soldiers or even of the fires that crackled in the distance, scattering sparks that lighted other fires. Red, swift tongues that, in an instant, devour huts, trees, insects. The priest would want him to be in church, praying with the others, with Maria and Mandrognin, Scarvé, and all those who are sick with worry about the harvest. He prefers to sit up here and think about his brother, who is God knows where. Maybe in the midst of those fires, maybe among the white clouds raised by the mortars. But all of a sudden something incomprehensible, like a pin jabbed into the works of a clock, subverts the silent order of his body. His breath fails him; the heat, it's the heat, he thinks as his vision falters, those fires like stars in a firmament of smoke. His hands seek some hold, they slip along the trunk of the alder, his head strikes the ground hard.

Matelda, up at Moncalvo, has a start, the needle escapes her fingers and pricks her, Luison takes fright, seeing her so pale. Matelda is trembling all over, her head flung against the back of the chair, her eyes dull beneath her wan, protruding brow, faintly marked by the bones of the skull. As if she could see through Giai's body sprawled beneath the alders and senses the crazed beating of the heart. She sees the maze of the veins, the wrench of the viscera; and a groan bursts from her lips.

Giai feels nothing now, a little bloodstain has formed on the ground where his head struck. Up at Moncalvo Luison runs to fetch some vinegar, to jolt Matelda from her trembling, she calls, but on that day of battle everybody has other things to think about than Luison's cries as she looks for the vinegar. Giai's hat has rolled to the foot of the alder, his cherub head is now like straw, parched, his mouth is grey and little bubbles of saliva form there. A little more and he would have died, on that day, the 14th of June.

But instead, that was only a first warning, and when Giai

reopened his eyes he thought it was a spell caused by the heat, the emotion of the battle. The fires were dying out and now there was a great silence all around, the wind had dropped and the air was cool. He collected his hat and went home to drink a glass of wine, he told Maria he had had a fall and she washed his wound; the blood was still fresh and it dripped on his clothes. And a few days later they were all amazed when Matelda sent for news of Giai by way of Tambiss, an itinerant pedlar, who went around the area selling undergarments.

Maria touches the linen, smooth, delicate, you wouldn't even know you were wearing it. 'We're fine, we're all fine,' she says. '*Tucc?*' 'Yes, all of us . . .' She turns the underthings over again between her fingers; Tambiss smiles and winks. '*At pias?* You like them?' She flushes and drops them back into his basket. Silly stuff, something for a general's wife, for a duchess. Tambiss now is telling about Marshal Melas and his Austrians, who have abandoned their camps and their fodder. And the dead, dead everywhere, and those *franseis del diavu*, those French devils commandeer the wine from the cellars, raise the tricolour flag on the spires of the churches. They plant the Tree of Liberty.

Pidrèn is already well away, on his horse with the checked blanket and the worn saddle. His general was killed in the fighting and he waited outside on a bench while the glorious Desaix was laid on a bed and nothing more could be done for him, the soldiers came and went. Pidrèn wept, his head in his hands. Afterwards he didn't have time even to go by his home and embrace once again the brother he hadn't seen for years. No time and perhaps not even any wish to.

Tambiss recognized him as he was going by Serravalle, leading his horse by the reins. He had a bandaged arm and, who knows, maybe they would make him a colonel, even a general: 'With those *franseis* there's no knowing what can happen,' he says to Maria, and he tells how Pidrèn looked so handsome, like Napoleon in person, with the sabre clattering at his side. Standing in the kitchen, Giai's beautiful wife drinks in Tambiss's words, and he has to repeat the story two or three times, and where his narrative seems scanty he invents. Maria wants to know what the uniform was like, and the tunic, the spurs. 'And the hat?' '*Al'era sensa capè*, no hat: he had long hair, like a girl's.'

Gonda has come in with an armful of washing she has collected from the grass, Maria looks at her with glistening eyes. Pidrèn was at Marengo, she tells the woman; and as Gonda, in her surprise, drops the washing, Maria goes out, reaches the road and looks over there, towards Serravalle, the Alessandria plain, Marengo. Never has this countryside seemed so beautiful to her, with the shadows falling, purple, from the hills, the road white with dust where now she runs till she is breathless, till her dress is soaked with sweat, while the air, entering, fills her sleeves.

But Giai fainted again. Two, three times. And then one evening they hoisted him into the cart and the oxen plodded, stumbling among the clods. Mosquitoes bit him while he couldn't defend himself, a cart nail wounded his shoulder. He took to his bed and never got up again: from the window he sees the boughs of the walnut, the leaves that brush the windows turn yellow, crumple, the wind tears them off one by one, the sky, autumn-grey, appears among the few that are left. In the morning the fog drips slowly along the boughs through which the next house can be seen, above the blind wall closing the garden.

The room is big, the bed deep, with white sheets; Matelda has come down from Moncalvo to lend her sister a hand and she sits on a stool at the foot of the bed. She has stopped embroidering; her footstep is light, she has cool hands, plump, quick. From the bed, its sheets tucked in without a wrinkle, Giai follows her with his gaze, his head more and more like the head of Saint Sebastian, pierced with arrows, beside the altar. He doesn't play the violin any more, he keeps it close to the bed, shut up in its case, and the moths are already eating the red lining.

Matelda didn't marry and she will never marry now, now everyone calls her the *Fantina*, the Maid, and the nickname pleases her, it seems to her to give off a much sweeter sound. With the passing of the years her face has lost what little colour it had and her eyes are coming more and more to resemble those of certain portraits whose gaze is elusive: they see but never look. If someone comes to pay a visit, she silently slips out of the room, leaving a perfume of lavender and mint, and she goes down to iron Giai's linen, neatly folded in a basket. Maria rests her elbows on the table, where her sister presses the iron hard, and she wants to know what Matelda and Giai say to each other, always together in that room. Matelda shrugs, moves from stove to table, quickly changing one iron for the other, moistens her finger with saliva to gauge the heat, against her opaque skin all questions are lost, become as impalpable as her thoughts, the words that come from her lips say nothing.

Maria knows that she should take possession of that iron, wrest it from her sister's hand, and press Giai's shirts herself, then take them to his room, and slip them over that body that is growing thinner every day. And yet she doesn't dare; it's as if she no longer had the strength, as if that iron were so heavy it would break her arm. At night, when her husband falls asleep beside her, if she tries to caress him, to touch his hand, Giai slowly draws away. She lies there for a long time, her eyes open, looking at the flicker of the candle. The shadows.

She has much to do now, running the place, everybody tries to cheat her. Her features have sharpened, her eyes are bigger, the skin is drawn tight over her cheekbones. When she goes out into the fields, she binds her face so the sun won't ruin it, but something unripened, unexploded, rusts the splendour of her twenty-three years. Nobody can decide if she is jealous of her sister, always there with her husband, with those hands that, at every touch, give off a little shock. Maria's voice at times turns harsh, at other times it is light again as it was when she was a girl at Moncalvo.

Giai will die, indeed he should have died already, only a thread keeps him still attached to life, a thread bound to the fingers of Matelda, now called Fantina, who passes a cloth soaked in tepid water over his face, and shaves him, her forefinger collects the soap that slides down his cheeks, her face so close to his that Giai can feel her breathing, can peer deep into her irises dotted with little autumn leaves like certain plants that have grown in the darkness, they are so colourless. She combs his blond curls, now fine and sparse, she dries some last drops of water forgotten on his neck. Fingers that smell of lavender, that weep and smile, that say what the voice is unable to express. Giai never takes his eyes off her, doesn't miss a movement of hers, a sigh; and when she stops by the window, lost in her thoughts, he gazes at her form outlined against the walnut's boughs, her nape, the knot of her hair. Her back as it becomes rounder towards the waist. Who knows what that back is like, under the grey cloth of her dress, the little knots of the spine. At night Fantina sleeps in the room at the end of the corridor, and the bed is so narrow that she can't even turn over.

Three years it lasted, three winters with the stove burning and Fantina sitting on the stool doing nothing. Once, one summer, word arrived that Pidrèn would be coming back. It was a letter written half in French that talked about Prussia and Saxony and of a strange place called Einsieden. With a map borrowed from the priest the two sisters began looking for it, running a finger over rivers and plains, mountains coloured brown; but they could never manage to find that Einsieden. Outdoors, in the August heat, the exhausted leaves curl up and the wasps assail the first grapes ripening in the arbour; in his room on the floor above, Giai pulls the string attached to the bell hanging at the top of the steps, calling Fantina; by now he can't stay half an hour without her. Fantina lets her finger drop from the map where it was following the route of the mounted colour-sergeant, for the first time pain seems to lacerate her dull, paper skin and in her eyes, focused on Maria, regrets accumulate, the hours that have never been and never will be. Never together in the fields, never to kiss, to feel body against body. Never, never. To sit by the ditches and laugh, laugh with joy. 'Why didn't you take Pidrèn then. For God's sake, why didn't you?'

The beautiful Maria has a shiver of fear at that gaze. 'Me? Pidrèn?' she asks, in a faint voice. But Fantina has already turned her back; she runs up the steps, opens the door, from the bed Giai looks up: that day when, with his brother, he arrived at Moncalvo to take a wife, he was like the lark, crazed by the play of mirrors. Forgive me, Matelda, forgive me.

When Giuseppe known as Giai died they started looking for Pidrèn. Even the *Maire* of Casale took an interest, and the sub-prefect Monsieur La Ville, and Maria made the trip into the city several times, accompanied by her sister. It was winter and the snow settled on their cloaks, the buggy by now was so broken-down that there was no way they could protect themselves. Maria had a nasty cough but all the same Monsieur La Ville took a liking to her and immediately promised to see to it that Pidrèn came back. But when the sub-prefect received the sisters for the third time he still had no news and Pidrèn seemed to have dissolved on that map that Monsieur La Ville kept spread out on the table where he surely would have found Einsieden at once. But the sisters had forgotten that name, Einsieden. Monsieur La Ville paid Maria many compliments and invited her to come back again; before she left he gave her a silver snuffbox commemorating Napoleon's coronation. But the buggy now was no longer in condition to make even one journey and it remained in the shed next to the stable, waiting for a skilled carter willing to take it away in exchange for some wood.

Giai's room was shut up and Fantina took the violin in its red-lined case into her room. As for the land, it was decided to entrust it to Mandrognin while Maria would go on taking

17

care of the stables; and Fantina went back to embroidering. Every Wednesday Maria went to visit Giai at the cemetery accompanied by Gonda, who had always been fond of him and had held him in her arms as a baby. They walked along, one behind the other, and Maria carried flowers, and if she hadn't found any flowers she contented herself with a branch or two with red berries. At times Signora Bocca, who had a flourishing garden opposite the church, would allow her to pick the leaves of the two big magnolias by the gate. Hard and shiny, in the fog that threatened to swallow up Gonda behind her at any moment, those leaves seemed still darker to Maria. Gonda went to draw some water from the well and the caretaker, seated on one of the gravestones, went on talking about how beautiful Giai's burial had been with the sunshine and the doves, and how *malangrett*, how unfortunate, on the other hand, the Great Masten's had been. God knows how to choose, he would repeat, the day when people must die.

Fantina never went to the cemetery; in those three years she had spent in Giai's room she had consumed his every breath and, with his breath, his soul. What was now in the ground, she said, was nothing, less even than those empty larvae that you crush in the grass in springtime when the insects have flown away. Hearing some of the things she said, Gonda and Maria felt their blood freeze; in the silence that followed both seemed to hear Giai's violin when he played it on summer evenings. It was after one of these speeches that Maria decided to call Luison from Moncalvo to come and live with them again.

Luison didn't have to be asked twice. She had raised Fantina and Maria and had lived with them always, ever since she left her village, spread out like a handkerchief between Udine and Cividale, to come, a *furesta*, a foreigner, to live in Moncalvo.

She still remembered that journey, which had lasted over a week, the corn tall in the fields and the green vines sloping down among the furrows. The first cicadas accompanied the sound of the horse's hoofs and the cousin driving the cart had spent all his time criticizing the landscape, the hills, the houses, urging the uneasy animals to keep going, over the uneven terrain. Luison was twenty-five then and had thick, shining braids such as no one had ever seen at Moncalvo. Perched among her belongings, her furniture, covered with dust from head to foot: people had turned to look, wondering who on earth was that big girl arriving like Saint Cunegonda on her way to martyrdom. The farther the cart advanced into the town, the more tears Luison shed at the thought of her own land full of woods and ferns, where the water leaped, translucent, among the boulders; and she asked herself how her poor sister had been able to be happy in a place like this, among people so different. Her tears then became a flood of weeping when, crossing the threshold, she found the two little girls together on a sofa, their heads covered with scabs, a musty smell that took your breath away. One, Matelda, was just walking, and the other, Maria, swaddled up to her little chin.

Luison had been an apprehensive mother, sometimes frowning and sometimes jolly, she sang to the little girls the German songs she had learned from the soldiers who camped in the woods around her village, and she sewed dolls for them with all the scraps of cloth found in the house. Cloth from old aprons, threadbare sheets. She gave the dolls eyes and a red mouth, a big chin coloured like the apples in her country. Her brother-in-law wanted to marry her to put an end to the talk that had begun to spread through the town. He was still young, and to him it seemed only right to give Luison some acknowledgement, a position. But she wouldn't hear of it. She said she wasn't made for certain things, she didn't feel 'nature'. Men didn't repel her but they didn't have any appeal for her, either; she just didn't want them. All she wanted was her breadbin, decorated with painted flowers and birds, her cushion for lace-making, Maria and Matelda. Them, she let embrace her and kiss her; them, she allowed to slip into her bed, under the covers, to warm themselves with the warmth of her big body.

And if you took a good look at her, you realized that despite her firm shape, her strong back, she lacked something. When she washed her hair and the cascade of the undone braids hung down from the stone bench, she recalled certain heroines like Geneviève of Brabant who had spent some part of their life with wild beasts, more at ease among animals than with men. As if her keyboard lacked those notes that allowed music to be complete. And while the two girls could enjoy with great freedom the tenderness of her embraces, if anyone jostled her with an elbow or if a leg brushed hers under the table, she hissed through her nose the way cats do. Thus, while the sight of her with them on her lap could be moving, thanks to the shy and expansive sweetness of her gestures, the moment she straightened up or the girls slipped down from her knees, her body abruptly revealed the stiffness of the joints, the absence of fluid.

Now Luison is again with them, once again the breadbox, her furniture, always a bit older, have been loaded and unloaded, carried up and down stairs. Again her somewhat resounding voice breaks the silences of the evenings. Her willing hands nail the plank where a pane of glass is missing, and the money to buy it; those hands stir the polenta in the pot until it is smooth as cream, while she stands on a footstool to have more power, and sometimes, she sings. In that house with its great voids, she sings her songs, old songs of the Austro-Hungarian soldiers incomprehensible perhaps even for her, and they pass like a fluttering of birds.

Fantina embroiders, the cope ordered by Signora Bocca for the church of San Michele must be the most beautiful ever seen, and seated by the window of the living-room, she spends every hour of light at the frame. In the centre she has drawn a curly head and she embroiders the hair with gold thread, the eyes with blue silk. That, she says, is the head of the Baby Jesus, whereas the angels seen on either side are the Archangel Michael and his companion, the Archangel Gabriel.

Their faces cannot be seen because Fantina wants them with their backs to us, ready to ascend to heaven hand in hand. The Archangel Michael has a long red tunic, his hair loose over his shoulders, wings thick with feathers like eagles', and the silver sword is raised high while the lily of the Archangel Gabriel seems to sway, it is so slender, pervaded by glints of a pale lilac. And from the tunic his heels appear, delicate and thin with some tiny drops of blood.

Why the Archangel Gabriel should have blood on his heels no one can say, not even the priest, who breaks into cold sweats at the sight of the cope he will one day have to put on. The blood is there, Fantina says, because I saw it. Where, when, she doesn't remember, but she saw it. Perhaps, she goes on to say, it's because of the thorns and the brambles the Archangel encountered on earth when he came to bring the word to the Virgin Mary, and her eyes avoid the priest's, and sink, pale, beneath their lids.

It was a September afternoon. Fantina was embroidering, bent over, near the window, and the leaves of the pear tree drew shadows on the frame, the flies lighted on the ceiling the two brothers had had painted with four different views. Fantina had her feet firmly on the crossbar of the chair and she was talking about the apple crop; this year, she said, it should go better than last year's, unless hail came. Thinking she was talking with Maria, Luison had come in calmly, but then she froze in the doorway: Giai was standing there, one hand resting on the sill, and even though it was still warm, he was wearing his fustian suit and had a scarf around his neck.

He was so natural, Luison said later, that I would have started talking with the two of them myself . . . But now, on reflection, there was something strange about him: his hand. It was all scratched. Maria started to cry, the tears rolled down the wan curve of her cheeks, she knew what those scratches were and now that Luison was saying how beautiful Giai was, with his head bent, and that long scarf falling to his knee, she suffered at the memory but she also had a great yearning for him.

'It is not good to have any dealings with the dead,' the priest decreed. The thought that the cope, which Fantina seemed to embroider endlessly (it was to take her ten years), would come to him, made him ill. He felt that it would sear his back at mere contact. And yet such a cope had never been seen, where the reds are like rubies and the gold is almost blinding. The Archangel Gabriel's lily has petals that seem to dissolve at a touch they are so delicate, whereas the Archangel Michael's sword casts glints of sunlight. The priest sits down beside Fantina; the dead who go to purgatory, he explains to her, are there because they must expiate some sin, we all have our sins, but if they are then disturbed, they have to stay in purgatory hundreds and hundreds of years more.

The priest is still young, with a dark beard that he never has time to shave, he is drawn to this house all of women like a mosquito to water, he roams and stops, raises his eyes to heaven when Gonda approaches and interrupts him with her breath of rotting teeth. Fantina looks at him, impassive; she who has never been beautiful now has a flourishing appearance, her skin smooth and full, her neck rounded, she bends towards the priest, moistens her lips.

God! What tricks the devil invents! The priest springs up, stumbles over the chair, that cope on the frame exudes an odour of sulphur. Perhaps it is the gold, perhaps it is the silk. In the kitchen Maria is stirring the grape jam on the stove, her sleeves are rolled up, and the steam wets her hair, makes the black cotton of her dress stick to her body. 'And Pidrèn? No news of him?' the priest asks, his voice failing him. Even Luison, who is past fifty, as she helps Maria, allows glimpses of pure white, untouched skin.

Pidrèn is in Einsieden. He has learned a bit of German and maybe he'll marry the daughter of a rich tallow merchant. He has been engaged to many women, one in Amiens and one even in Seville, but it has never come to anything. And now, too, when he had thought of spending the rest of his life in this grey land of winds, with a river of pilgrims flowing through it, it seems to him that Einsieden is destined to be only a place of transit, a posting station. Best to tear from his heart also this milk-and-honey Margaretha with a house on the Platz where carriages of every description come and go, and dukes and princes alight in great dark cloaks, then go and prostrate themselves full length on the floor of the ancient Cathedral. Best to resaddle the horse with the checked blanket and hope for the great opportunity that will make him a general. The Tsar Alexander has broken with Napoleon and the Emperor is collecting troops throughout Europe, the Tsar is fabulously rich and there is talk of churches whose spires are covered with golden scales, and rooms panelled in lapis lazuli. The first man who breaks down the doors of the convents will find more riches than he has horses enough to carry it all away.

Sometimes he happens to think also of Giai and he imagines his brother has children already grown and there isn't time to cut all the slices of bread, or milk all the cows, and Gonda, older than ever, sings also to them the song of the *Pursè Soppin*, the lame pig. He no longer thinks about her, about Maria. He has forgotten her and he doesn't even understand how he could have suffered so much when she picked his brother. He doesn't know that Giai is dead, buried next to the Great Masten on a day of sunshine and white doves and in the house many rooms have been closed off and in the place of the broken panes planks have been nailed; and the silence at times is so deep that you can hear the gnawing of the termites.

At times. Because at other times, faint and just a bit shrill, Giai's violin can be heard once more. Winter has come and at certain hours Fantina becomes restless, she drops the golden threads of her embroidery. Maria pretends not to hear that sound, dark is coming on, and the farmhands with their families are shut up in the stables, she sits at the table to play *reversis* or *brisque* with Mandrognin, seated opposite. Luison is deaf and thinks that sound is the wind even if the fog, thick as it is, allows no wind to pass, not even a breath.

Mandrognin is in love with Maria but she cares nothing for Mandrognin or for any other man and she would now give ten years of her life to go back for just one day to the time when Giai took her face in his hands and kissed her mouth, or when he gathered her to his body as if their bed were a great white river. They have heard nothing more of Pidrèn, perhaps he also died, run through by some bayonet. Monsieur La Ville has gone back to Paris and his snuffbox has been laid away for some unspecified future generation. Perhaps a son of Pidrèn's, if one exists somewhere.

Mandrognin has made another mistake and Maria scolds him, he bows his head with resignation; and as he looks at her hands, ruined by the cold, he thinks that if she didn't raise her voice so often he might try to touch one of them gently. To volunteer for those jobs that she insists on doing, obstinate and clumsy. He has brought her half a cheese and Maria thanks him absently as if everything were her due. Because of her wretched life, because her young years are passing in such bitterness. But for Mandrognin things are all right as they are, it's enough for him to be able to look at her, knowing she'll eat the cheeses, in her enduring hunger. He sees her haggard face, her thin neck, the shoulders that betray her anxiety at the sound of that violin, a sound that hurts him, too; and he collects the cards hastily, takes a long time shuffling them. If only Maria doesn't go away, doesn't leave him alone here with Luison dozing in her chair, the fire dying. The dark corners, cold.

What happened to Pidrèn during the Russian campaign no one ever learned. No one ever understood how he came out of it alive and if, in exchange for survival, he had had to sell his soul to the devil. The portrait that shows him leaning on a plush armchair, the gold chain across his waistcoat, reveals no trace of his Napoleonic adventures. But that portrait was painted when he was already getting on in years and the tales of his exploits among the Mamelukes and in Westphalia had made the rounds of the Monferrato region more than once.

Of those places and of the battles he had fought there he kept memories that became increasingly rich in detail and nobody ever dared contradict him. He gave the first of his sons the name Gavriel after the comrade-in-arms who had saved his life at Wagram, and the second he had baptized Louis Charles because that was the name of General Desaix, whose death he had mourned, seated on a bench. The last son, finally, was called Gioacchino for love of Murat, who had looked into the eyes of the firing squad without flinching. It was even known that his betrothed Margaretha sang well and painted wondrous Easter eggs by moistening flower-petals with saliva. And if he didn't call his third-born, a daughter, by that name it was only out of respect for his wife. For many years he continued receiving letters from others who, like him, had followed the campaigns of Egypt and Italy, had fought in Spain. Letters that recalled battles, celebrating cities, brawls, horses.

But it was as if he had never been in Russia; if somebody happened to mention it, his eyes became lost in another direction, he knew nothing, and Borodino, Moscow, the Don, were places that belonged to another terrestrial sphere. Kutuzov? The sound of a language never heard. His body was covered with scars and each one had a name, they recalled, on his skin, forests and rivers, fields and camps. None recalled Russia, in Russia it seemed he had come through intact, like a devil through fire.

Almost immediately he was given the nickname Sacarlott (the *Sacredieu* of the French) because he became irritated easily, or more probably, because everyone stood in awe of him and if he suddenly came up behind them they flinched. Luison was the first to call him this, one morning when Pidrèn came into the kitchen as she was putting a hen to sleep, its head beneath its wing, a game that greatly amused little Gavriel in his high chair. Turning, she saw him from behind, and the chicken fell from her hand, breaking its neck. '*Sacredieu!*' Pidrèn cried.

He came back one evening in late March, it would soon be seven years since the death of Giai; the two sisters and Luison had long finished their supper. They ate early, at five, sometimes even at four, and the farther away harvest time was, the faster they ate because there was little on the table. The door was opened by Mandrognin, who had come to play cards with Maria, and he shut it again promptly. Pidrèn began pounding furiously and the more he pounded, the more they were frightened inside, until Maria looked out at the window; and even though it was not easy to figure out who that vagabond was, all skin and bones, his feet bound in rags, a sheepskin instead of a shirt, she recognized him immediately. And fainted.

In fact, in those seven years, without great remorse, she had consumed all of his share, both what had been set aside by Giai during his lifetime and what she should have set aside herself, in case Pidrèn ever came back. They had sold his land, his crops, his seeds, his livestock. Only Luison now kept her head, and she and Pidrèn had a dialogue all made up of rapid, concise news, yes's and no's. Then Pidrèn, slumped down, his head on the table, bemoaning his brother's death, abruptly fell asleep. So deeply that it was almost dawn when they managed to get him upstairs to bed, where he slept for three days in a row, clutching a loaf of bread to his chest.

He married Maria almost immediately. She didn't know whether she wanted him or not, but she didn't dare say anything because of that land, those seeds, that livestock she couldn't account for. He married her at five in the morning in the deserted church, dark, with two candles at the sides of the altar and the priest still unshaven. On her finger Maria already had a wedding-band, to buy one for Pidrèn they sold the sheepskin, which was of good quality. Luison prepared the polenta and

Mandrognin served as witness, with a fever scorching his brow. It was a fine day, and when they came out of the church Maria saw white doves and to her they seemed the same as the ones at Giai's funeral. The sun made the magnolia leaves glisten at either side of Signora Bocca's gate and the Signora, who always got up at dawn, was strolling majestically, followed by her little dog. But she seemed not to see them.

They settled in the room on the upper floor where the leaves of the walnut struck the panes; but Pidrèn would not have the bed that had been Giai's and they laid two mattresses of corn husks on some planks. And there, after such a long time, Maria made love again. But the man holding her seemed a stranger, someone who had come to rob her, like the others, and for the first month she did nothing but cry, as Pidrèn wanted to make love morning and night. After a month Pidrèn put on the new cotton shirt Luison had sewn for him and sent for Mandrognin to go over the books of the land, Maria washed her hair and loosened it, letting it dry in the sun. And as her hair dripped on the grass, Luison said something about how Mandrognin at the mere sound of Pidrèn's voice had been seized by a fit of shaking; and Maria burst out laughing. It was a cruel laugh, light, that vibrated for a long time in her throat. The first.

Within a year Pidrèn had bought not only a new bed but a whole bedroom suite in heavy walnut such as had never been seen in the town, except in Signora Bocca's house. The bed, made to stand against a wall, was like Napoleon's at Fontaine-bleau. Fantina left off embroidering the cope in order to make little shirts for Maria's first baby.

Gavriel was born at six in the evening, he was dark, and Pidrèn said neither that he was pleased it was a boy nor that the baby was very beautiful, as everyone else declared; all he said was: *As ciamerà Gavriel*, he'll be called Gavriel. And he went back outside to keep an eye on the milking. When they saw him arriving, the cowmen immediately bowed their heads and nobody mentioned the baby, the cowmen because they didn't know what to say, Pidrèn because he never talked. That day, too, he went to take a look at the trench dug for the vines; and there, where the job hadn't been done perfectly, he simply undid it with the stick that had been the Great Masten's and then, for a short time, Giai's.

The next day was Sunday and that afternoon Luison and Fantina left for Vespers, Gonda went to wash the linen, blood-stained from the birth. Maria remained alone with little Gavriel, who was sleeping in the crib beside her, its gauze curtains rippling in the sun. She looked at the ceiling, at the scrolls painted years ago, and to her they seemed to form, in a corner, the face of an old man with a pointed beard. After all these years she felt profoundly homesick for her house in Moncalvo and that narrow bed seemed to her badly con-structed, *stravis*, as Gonda said. And even though now she liked making love with Pidrèn, he still seemed a stranger and, in sleep, when she accidentally touched him or bumped into his back, she took fright, as if at something improper. When the bells rang for the beginning of the service she was still staring at that old man's head on the ceiling: the eye made by two brown curlicues that stared back at her, giving her some order. But what, she didn't exactly know.

When Luison and Fantina returned from Vespers, Maria was sleeping and, though she was now thirty, she looked like a little girl, her long hair spread out over the pillow. Fantina, to wake her, touched her with the holy water, and Maria opened her eyes: they were beautiful, dark and happy: 'Giai came,' she said, 'he came to see the baby . . .'

Fantina burst out crying, the first time since Giai's death, and her tears seemed to come not only from her eyes but to well up from her whole face, and they ran down over her throat and her hands. 'When?' she asked, in a faint voice.

Maria told how, the moment the bells had stopped ringing, she heard some footsteps on the stairs and thought Pidrèn had come back to look for something; but before those steps paused outside the room, she recognized them. She closed her eyes and her body melted between the sheets as if her milk and her blood had flowed out of it and she were immersed in the warm liquid. And when she opened her eyes again, Giai was bending over the cradle and nodding his head, assenting. Perhaps he was smiling. She would have liked to call him, to call his name: Giai, Giai! There was such silence that you could hear the rustle of the curtains as she looked at his head, covered with curls as in the old days. She hadn't been able to see his hands because he held them clasped behind his back, maybe they were scratched as they had been when Luison saw them. A hawthorn flower peeped from his shirt. But it was all just an instant, she hadn't time for anything, not even to see that smile, if it was really there. The silence in that moment was so great that she moved her fingers over the sheet to make some sound.

For all the time that Maria spoke, Fantina remained at the window, looking out, her weeping became calm, and her eyes were again hidden like molluscs beneath her lids. The moment her sister finished, she ran from the room.

That night Maria heard the violin play and she got up to look out of the window. Fantina was sitting on the edge of the well, and her white shift fell off her shoulders as she followed the music, barely moving her head, her plait falling down her back, her dead-white feet grazing the earth. Maria wanted to tell her to cover herself, but the violin's sound seemed so loud that her sister would never have heard her; so she stood there a long time, watching Fantina, whose shoulders glistened with dew, and her shift slipped down further and further almost as if it were a sheet over the edge of the well as the sound of the violin came closer and circled around her and she became the centre that entwines every space around itself. Fantina bent forward and the shift fell to the ground, baring her rounded hips, even whiter in the darkness. Maria tried to shout but her jealousy, stifled through all those years, had become a crazed horse and it was trampling her under its hoofs. No sound could now express it.

*

29

She remained dumb for three days and during those three days she did nothing but think about what she had seen. The baby didn't exist, Pidrèn didn't exist, or Luison, Gonda; only Fantina existed, on the edge of the well. Lying motionless in her bed Maria witnessed for the first time the spectacle that had gone on for years beneath her eyes, without her seeing it. The curtain had risen and a thousand sounds broke the silence that, like cotton batting, had enfolded Giai's room; and beyond the door she had never dared open, Fantina and Giai enacted their love drama, made up of brief, searing contacts. Of slow actions, full, and complete. Light fell on those shirts that her sister ironed as if she were caressing Giai's shoulders, it illuminated the comb she pulled through the curls of the sick cherub. This is how it had been: Fantina had taken him from her, day by day.

She had begun at once, long before Giai fell ill, from the very beginning, when she came to visit and sat waiting for him under the walnut. And while Maria was lost in a tangle of yearnings, Fantina's mind had kept vigil, lucid, shrewd. Her heart alert, ready to spring. Now Maria sees again the tree and the bench where her sister is sitting (the same one she would take up to Giai's room and set there like a little throne), she sees Giai, his mouth slightly pulled down, half-open in the face pressed against the violin, the fingers vibrating on the strings; and the music seems to be born from the melancholy of his gaze, coming to rest gently on Fantina seated on the stool. Now Maria remembers that even on the day of her marriage Fantina had found the way to sit next to him and as all were drinking toasts, standing, coming back, she had never moved from his side. Unnoticeable, opaque, her hand collecting crumbs, then brushing them aside.

The first thing Maria said once she started talking again was that she wanted no more children. Gavriel would be the first and the last. The fear and the weeping, the musky smell of her blood along with that feeling of being flesh that reproduced more flesh seemed to her, in the shadow the walnut cast in the room, so many wild beasts ready to devour her. Nothing gave her joy, neither the shift always wet with milk nor the baby's fingers gripping her breasts like a mouse's little claws. She would have liked to be an air-bubble and float up high, resting weightless against the scrolls of the ceiling from which that old man continued staring at her.

Pidrèn didn't ask questions; as he had been satisfied with the midwife's explanation of his wife's loss of voice, so he accepted without comment this drastic declaration. The only step he took was the decapitation of the walnut, and when the crown of the tree fell to earth in the racket of the leaves, the room was suddenly full of light. A light that would drive away bad thoughts along with the ghosts. He smiled, he who smiled so rarely, and he kissed his wife on the mouth. During the years he had been away he had known so many different kinds of woman that he had ended up thinking they were all alike, and you could act with one much as you acted with another. Maria attracted him and to him children seemed important for the land and for the house; and when he saw her on her feet again, pale and blooming, her eyes languid with private sighs, he decided to pay no attention to what she had said.

For a little while, in his arms Maria was like a doll, she allowed herself to be undressed and turned in the bed without taking a breath. It was summer and the moon, now free from the walnut boughs, struck the floor, she pricked up her ears in case Giai's violin played. But she hadn't calculated Pidrèn's strength, the strength of someone who has convinced himself and others that what is good for him is good for all. And that sometimes what is good can be what is the least bad. So little by little, forced, dominated by his will, her thoughts once again were guided, like the letters on the lines of a copybook, along the path of family life. Her days recovered their breath and at night her body was again a liquid that took shape in the arms of Pidrèn.

But for the whole course of the year, until the birth of Louis

Charles, soon called Luìs, her jealousy of Fantina never left her; and when she thought she had got over it, it would come back suddenly to wound her. She had only to see one of those mysterious smiles that brightened her sister's face or find her seated, ecstatic, her hands lying among the coloured threads in her lap. And when Maria heard her approaching Gavriel's crib, she would make a leap, to prevent her from touching the baby.

Once when she was left alone in the house she thought she heard Giai's footstep again and she listened, dampening the fire in the stove. She stood motionless for a long time beside the crib, holding the lamp up high so that if Giai were to enter he would be able to admire the baby, sleeping, bound in its swaddling clothes. It was autumn and at the windows there was already darkness, the wagons could be heard returning from the fields, and she shivered at the cold. She would have liked to say many things to Giai, take his hands, and bury her face in them, weeping between his fingers.

But Giai didn't come back that afternoon or afterwards; and one day, when her second pregnancy was already advanced, she went into Fantina's room and, opening the case, took the violin in her hands. She touched the strings lightly: through the window over the yard she could see the sky white with rain, that sky was without breath, flat as the bottom of a pan. The violin slipped from her hands; nothing in here belonged to her and the smell that rose from the shawl dropped on a chair, from the little objects scattered on the dresser, was the same that had lingered in Giai's room. She ran out, as if she had gone in there to steal.

That evening at supper when Fantina, with the pretext of not feeling well, left the table before the others, jealousy clutched Maria's throat and she vomited some food on to her plate. And as Luison tried to help her, slapping her back, Maria saw Fantina slipping through the door to the stairs, her hair already escaping her combs, in her indifference. Maria's hatred was so intense that sweat began to trickle down her brow and if Pidrèn hadn't been there to hold her by her braid, she would have fallen to the floor.

For Pidrèn the year in which his second son was born was a lucky year. In France he had learned new methods of sowing and for the first time he tried them out on his land: the harvest was a third greater than the previous year's and the oats grew so plentifully that Signora Bocca wanted the whole crop for the horses of her daughter, the wife of a marchese in Casale. And, as in the days of the Great Masten, there was again the steady traffic of wagons and the hands had to stay up late, storing the hay under the arches of the loft.

But at times, like a woodworm, the gnawing thought of his brother returns, whom he left in the churchyard as a happy groom, with his bride, and who died without seeing him again. The thought hurts because Giai left behind such faint traces, fragments which it is hard to put in any order, and reassembling them would demand infinite patience. As if Giai had been a light breath of air, a gust in the great storm of life. The mists rise from below, Pidrèn walks among the dark deserted fields, on days when the others all shut themselves in the barn near the warm breath of the cattle. But he doesn't feel the cold, doesn't notice the rain, his boots sink soundlessly into the rotten winter earth, the sparrows rise in brief and rapid flights, they too disappear into the air that freezes the mouth. He doesn't like to lose himself in the labyrinths of the past, or linger now to contemplate one place; he doesn't even have the time, if he wants to restore the neglected land, to be a *particulare* again, with a velvet waistcoat and a gold chain attached to his watch. A *particulare* with his pew in the church, just behind Signora Bocca's. His sons must study and his daughters must have a dowry, every young man must covet them as wives. He has seen so many women while he was roaming about on his horse with the worn saddle, unspeakable sufferings, black pits that have engulfed memory, have annihilated it like an infected organ. There was a time when, as a boy, he chattered and

33

laughed easily, and even sang on certain summer evenings and his voice would stir the Great Masten from his melancholy. His son has just been born and that winter, when he finishes selling all the harvest, he will have enough money to rebuild the roof of the stables, buy more oxen. In the town they are already calling him Sacarlott, the peasants fear him and his wife sometimes looks at him, wondering if he, too, suffers for something that isn't the hail that has spoiled the crop or the lightning that has set fire to a haystack. But he has learned that life must be enclosed in a circle, like those arenas he saw in Spain. To give way to suffering is useless, and it is even more useless to let others see suffering; wounds must be kept hidden, otherwise swarms of flies gather to suck the blood. When Maria chose his brother the pain went on stinging him for a long time. He knew he was the right man for her, he knew their bodies would unite eagerly, and to desire each other and be joined would be the most natural thing in the world. He would bring strength, life. But she hadn't understood and nothing was, or ever could be now, as it should have been.

Pidrèn has big, hairy ears, his legs are short for his body, his mouth appeared greatly to the Margaretha of Einsieden. A mouth that now laughs rarely and its teeth are no longer so white and compact as when he sat in the tallow merchant's house and heard the carriages on the cobbles of the square. Maria is sincerely fond of him, she has many reasons to be grateful to him, not least for the share of the property that he has never mentioned. Food and clothes, the firewood now never lacking for anyone. But her capacity for loving has atrophied in her; prematurely withered, that part of her has been unable to recover its strength. Not even motherhood has given her back the light she once had. She is still young but her flesh becomes more and more spare; her step is measured, without spring. The second child's birth was easy, they named him Louis Charles after the general who was so loved. She has started singing again as she rocks the cradle and she has also stopped expecting Giai because she knows he won't come back again.

She rarely goes to the cemetery and in Gonda's place now Gavriel comes with her, that child bursting with strength who slips away from her and risks being run over by a wagon. In the new cemetery they are building outside the town Pidrèn wants a family chapel, where he will put his brother dead these ten years. But what will be left of Giai at this point? The coffin was cheap, letting in air and water. Pidrèn wants a chapel with the ceiling painted sky blue and stars and the moon drawn on it. She pulls up the grass that has grown around Giai's stone, sticks the dahlias in a vase, one purple, one yellow, one speckled with white. Gavriel falls and skins his knee, looks at her without crying, a strange smile, timid and sly, passes over his face, he wants to prove his courage. The courage that Sacarlott wants. Gavriel's hair, black at birth, has become a beautiful coppery brown, and he amuses himself by running among the graves, then sits on the little mounds of earth, trailing his finger over the names cut in the stone. His mother calls him: 'Gavriel, *andumma!*' He runs along the path. '*Andumma*, let's go!' he cries, waving his arms as if they were wings; she reproaches him, this isn't a place where you can make a racket, she says. The lizards scuttle over the yew hedge, the blue morning glories fall in festoons along the wall.

After Gavriel and Luìs it will be the turn of Bastianina, of Manin, who lived such a short time, and finally of Gioacchino, who died during the terrible summer of '35. But Maria doesn't know any of this yet and she walks slowly in the road of dust, holding the little boy by the hand. Her thoughts go to the eggs to be gathered in the hen coop, the wool to be carded. To Luìs's first dress. In that life that Sacarlott wants to enclose like an arena she has found a shadowy corner, she has drawn a circle even smaller, and from there at times, with no more suffering, she watches her sister become leaf, wind, knowing no circle, great or small, but only the vast spaces of the birds.

*

Fantina has given Signora Bocca the vestments for the church, all the servants of the house have been assembled to admire them, complete with stole and cotta. When an important feast day falls, the priest slips them on cautiously, people come from the neighbouring villages to see them, and sit in the pews, clasping their hands with wonder, the priest chants the *Gloria*, frightened and dazed by the radiance that spreads from his back. And as if he felt on his nape the touch of Fantina's fingers, his voice quavers, turns hoarse. Sacarlott, standing at the back among the men, gazes straight ahead, impassive; soon he'll have the pew behind the one where Signora Bocca is kneeling. Nobody understands what his relationship with God is, whether he feels fear or only respect. Or perhaps nothing.

Fantina sings in the choir and the virgins' white veil covers her hair, where there isn't a strand of grey. The priest holds up the chalice, the peasant women, wearing worn, faded skirts, bow their heads, their eyes ruined by conjunctivitis see almost nothing, only a single, immense glow. Fantina sings on just one note and the music is in her flesh like bread dough as the Baby Jesus' curly head seems to become separate from the priest's back and rise on high between the Archangels Gabriel and Michael, hand in hand, no one will ever see their faces. Maria bows her head, she is pregnant again, and what she bears in her womb seems to her a rabbit, a mouse compared to that Baby Jesus with the silken eyes. Beside her Gavriel stares in terror at the head in the centre of the cope, those curls like golden snakes. He is captivated, lost: has such a beautiful creature ever existed?

'No, never,' Fantina says to him. 'But he could have, yes. He could have.'

Luison is outraged. 'What? The Baby Jesus never existed? What kind of blasphemy is this?'

'*E il Giai, al'era nent bel, il Giai.* And wasn't Giai beautiful then?' Gonda says, who remembers him as a child, the most beautiful of all, and when he went to Mass the old priest used to make him sit on the altar steps, his hair was so long it brushed the stone. The Great Masten, Gonda also says, wanted it cut off, he said the boy was big now and should wear trousers and cut his hair, but the mother wouldn't have it, she was afraid to spoil such beauty. Gonda's eyes fill with tears as she remembers all those dead, her back is so bent that she has to eat with her bowl on a chair, she doesn't have enough breath to sing the *Pursè Soppin* song to the children. She loved Giai, he was kind and when he came upon her carrying the wood basket he would always take it from her arms.

Only Maria seems not to hear their talk, on the cope Fantina embroidered she has been staring for a long time at the drops of blood on the heels of the Archangel Gabriel, red and liquid as if they had just welled up. And now she sees again the brick path of her old house at Moncalvo and Pidrèn and Giai walking one behind the other as she and her sister peek at them through a slit in the curtains. One of them is shorter, stocky, he has the determined look and the bold step of a man who is at ease in life. Both girls immediately liked the other, the one whose head swayed a little, whose smile was barely perceptible. Giai was dressed in corduroy and his scarf was wound around his neck as if it had been forgotten there since winter.

Later, when she went out to collect the branches of the hawthorn just about to blossom, Giai followed her and where she couldn't reach, he tried to break them off, his scarf got caught on the thorns, and to pull it free he scratched himself and drew blood. They had drunk sweet wine that day, that wine was strong, it went to your head; seated on the stone bench under the hazel bushes, she washed his wounded hands and a few drops of blood fell on her lap. Their brows so close they almost touched. So she had chosen him, even though her family would have preferred the other. The one who on entering the house darkened the doorway with his shadow and on the day of the wedding kissed her at the church door: a shudder ran across her back, she felt herself trembling.

*

Already at her birth, Sebastiana, known as Bastianina, had special fingers. And afterwards, as a very little girl, when she held a pencil, those fingers were like spurts of water, they were so quick and moved so lightly over the paper. She drew everywhere, on the walls, on the bricks of the walk, on the ground with her forefinger. She would sit by the hour to watch Fantina embroider, saying from time to time: 'Here I'd do this, here that,' her finger tracing on the material drawings full of imagination.

Fantina loved her and often took her up to her bedroom where, shut away in a trunk, she still had her dowry from her girlhood. Bastianina would plunge her face into those shifts and sheets, never used, and inhale their smell, half-closing her eyes with pleasure. The whole room made her head swim slightly, she touched the wax flowers, she sat on the narrow bed against the wall, and her fingers would shyly graze the gleaming wood of the violin. At times, in a moment of great love, Fantina would allow the girl to run her fingers over the strings, as the two of them looked at each other in silence.

But Maria takes her away, she doesn't want the child to go into that room. Luison, who sleeps nearby, says that at night she hears the violin play, but not as Giai used to play it: this is a mad, shrill sound, it makes her hair stand on end while she lies in bed. 'Come away, come,' she says to Bastianina. But when they are on the steps, the child wriggles free, escapes, runs down the corridor, her dress whips against the walls and she seems about to fall at any moment. 'What are you doing?' Maria cries. From the end of the corridor the child laughs before she disappears again into Fantina's room.

The priest's sister was engaged to give her drawing lessons. For Sacarlott spending money on something so useless was a sacrifice but it could be worthwhile if one day all the youths were to want his daughters for their wives. It was decided that at the beginning Bastianina would practise on ordinary paper and only later would she have at her disposal a big white sheet of drawing paper fixed to a plank in the kitchen of the rectory.

The first thing Bastianina drew on a real sheet of white paper was a well, the well of their house, and on the edge with Corinth black she drew a crow with only one leg. She flew into a tantrum because the priest's sister wanted a turtle dove or a pigeon, she became stubborn and her teacher was forced to give way; and while Bastianina clenched her teeth and stared at her with eyes like pins, the priest's sister felt as if she were facing, after all these years, the Great Masten, in a miniature version.

It was a lovely June evening and Bastianina brought home the paper, rolled up and tied with string; the bats crisscrossed along the road and one, lower than the others, grazed her head; in her fright she let go of the string and the drawing unrolled, flapping, almost bigger than she, who was tiny and obstinate. Then she went into the house, where the whole family was preparing to eat.

For the first time Sacarlott felt ill-at-ease with his daughter. Bastianina had hung the drawing from a nail, and asked why she had drawn a crow, she answered that it was Giai, turned into a bird after he died. As Maria, frightened, covered her face with her hands, Fantina admired the drawing, praising it in a loud voice, and Gonda began to cry; but nowadays she cried over anything and, even in June, sat with the warming-pan under her skirts.

Sacarlott was tired, his eyes stung after the day's sun and that paper with its skilful drawing made his entrails ache. With no thought of the money it had cost him, he tore it into four pieces and flung it into the kitchen fireplace. Bastianina didn't dare say anything; she only stared at the crow, which writhed among the flames until it vanished into nothingness. But at table she wouldn't eat and she fell asleep in her chair, like a little bundle of rags.

That night it was as if the devil had entered the house, Gavriel vomited till daybreak and little Manin was seized with convulsions. Luìs was found sleeping huddled in the soot of the fireplace; and he himself didn't know how he had ended

39

up there. Maria spent the night beside Manin's crib, and when the little girl was calmer, Maria thought she had Giai at her side at night when he kissed her on the mouth and she forgot all her yearnings.

Manin died three days later. She was only eighteen months old and the doctor didn't even come to examine her because his mare had broken a leg. Luison had gone all the way to his house, and he sent her back with instructions to plunge the baby three times, first in hot water, then in cold, but Sacarlott was against it because at Einsieden he had seen a soldier die like that. Manin had been a beautiful baby very like Gavriel and even after she was dead everyone was amazed to see her still rosy-cheeked with her pale eyes half-opened that seemed to look at anyone who bent down to kiss her. The tomb with the ceiling painted blue was not yet ready and she was buried in the ground among the other children, so many grey stones all the same, in a tight row. Scarvé had made the coffin, but as it was little, he had done a hasty job and you could stick a finger between the planks, the sun entered through the cracks and the flies buzzed around. The only one who wept was Gonda, holding Bastianina by the hand; Bastianina made faces and Luìs couldn't help laughing as he followed the procession led by the priest's assistant, wiping sweat from his face.

Before the burial was over, Sacarlott had to leave because a man was waiting for him who wanted to buy a couple of calves. He hurried out of the cemetery and once on the road he realized that he felt great grief, more than he had imagined possible and perhaps even more than if in Manin's place there had been Bastianina or Luìs. He looked for a reason, something to justify the suffering that increased at every step as, behind him, the cemetery and its wall of red brick receded.

Perhaps, he said to himself, it had been Manin's eyes, so limpid they looked like liquid stars, *Stèira d'acquei*, as Gonda said.

Or, on the contrary, perhaps it was her smile, which showed all her baby teeth, and those lips moist and cool when they touched his cheek. Her head, which she rested against his shoulder with such trust. But as he walked on, and now cared nothing about the sale of the calves, he knew that none of these was the right reason, and he would have liked to punch himself in the head to drive away the sorrow. A sorrow like a chain that, one link after another, pulled up all the others he had forgotten. Giai, the Gavriel killed at Wagram, General Desaix.

2

THE COSSACKS

In 1831 Sacarlott had the pew in church right behind Signora Bocca's, with his name inscribed on a brass plate, and
every Wednesday from San Salvatore Signor Capra came
to paint his portrait. And every time Signor Capra thought
he had finished it, Sacarlott told him to come back, for some
adjustment or addition, like the charm on his watch-chain
or the tie-pin that had been given him by the Municipal
Council in recognition of his achievements in agriculture.

Gavriel was seventeen and hadn't the slightest desire to
continue studying, nor did he want to rise with the birds and
follow his father into the fields damp with dew. The dogs were
still shaking off their sleep, and his belly was stirring. For
Sacarlott wants the lively step and the clear head you have only
when you're fasting and he walks on ahead briskly, proud of
hearing his son's footsteps behind him as if son and land
comprised one thing, something squared off in time. A geo-
metric progression where each would be transformed, but not
lost.

Gavriel looks like him, has his short and stocky body, his
round head, the same big, warm hands that caused the girl in
Seville to wriggle so. Sacarlott doesn't even realize that, walking
after him, his son dawdles and, of his father, glimpses only the
heavy, dark bulk because sleep makes his eyelids heavy. Gavriel
wants his warm bed again and the milk that Gonda pours for
him onto the warm slices of polenta; and when his father turns,
proud of all those oats, that barley, that corn, the rows of vines,

the boy crumples, huddles into himself until he disappears and nothing remains before his father, the words pierce air.

As soon as he can, Gavriel goes to stretch out in a field of clover, his back against the earth's dampness and his face and neck warming in the sun while his eyes follow the sway of the elms in the sky, the round face of a little hawk. Thus from that field of clover he first saw her as if she too were a dragonfly or a finch, and the ends of the ribbon that circled her waist were her wings. She spoke to her maid without even turning, and because of the heat she had loosened her bodice, and beneath the bodice, also her shift. The maid was dressed in black and followed her, carrying a basket of fruit, paying scant attention to what she was saying, intent only on filling the gap where a fig had been eaten. She took long strides, lightly, and at the same time shook her mass of hair, so thick it seemed a spun-sugar trophy, and she talked and talked, the maid answered in monosyllables, her cheeks bulging, but she noticed nothing and the hem of her dress was all soiled as if she had been walking through mud or across a dungheap.

Peau d'ange, Fantina had said the day before, referring to the apple blossoms. *Peau d'ange*, Gavriel thought of her face that peeped, finely drawn, from the hive of hair. Her name was Elisabetta and she, too, was seventeen. Unluckily for Gavriel she was the granddaughter of Signora Bocca, daughter of that marchese who, at Casale, kept a carriage and horses.

Signora Bocca's house stood opposite the church and to set itself apart from all the others it had a square garden surrounding it and the trees that grew there produced mostly leaves and flowers like the two immense magnolias flanking the gate. Only Fantina, with her embroidery, had access to that house, and Sacarlott, when he had to sell his oats, and Signora Bocca received them in a room so dark that they had a hard time seeing where they were to sit. That June, when it was time to sell the oats, Gavriel wanted to go, too; he washed himself for a long time in the zinc tub set out to warm in the sun and he begged Luison to iron the only shirt he possessed.

The whole time his father talked about horses and oats, he kept looking at the french window that gave on to the garden. Signora Bocca was old and fat but she never took her eyes off him because she liked good-looking boys and there was much talk of her carryings-on with peasant lads or itinerant pedlars. She stank of a certain whale oil she ordered from France to keep her skin smooth and she didn't bother to remove it for Sacarlott. Now she was sorry and she constantly fanned herself even if in the room, its green draperies drawn, it was cold as winter.

When the visit ended and Sacarlott stood up, Gavriel had a bitter taste of disappointment in his mouth and would have liked to fall on the floor in a faint. But Signora Bocca came to his aid as she heaved a great sigh and said she wanted to show Sacarlott her cherry tree that had come from the Far East, brought to her by the Blessed Nicodemi, a Jesuit in China for more than thirty years. In the garden, in the only patch of sun amid all that shade, Elisabetta was reading a book, her blue sash hanging down from the bench and her hair climbing up, falling, twisting in a great confusion around her face. When they had almost come up to her, Signora Bocca put her hand on Sacarlott's arm: '*Amperchè adveni nent a sena con u so fieu?*' she asked, 'Why don't you come for supper with your son?'

The girl raised her eyes from the book and her round, white neck seemed tensed for flight.

'*Puss nent*, I can't,' Sacarlott answered at once, terrified by the difficulty of such a dinner.

'I can!' Gavriel cried, so loud that the girl couldn't help smiling.

Among the many things nobody had ever taught Gavriel was the art of eating with all the proper cutlery, and drinking when you have more than one glass in front of you, and he did nothing but smile at the maid who moved around him with the dishes, to express his happiness to someone.

But Elisabetta said not a word throughout the entire meal

44

and Signora Bocca's voice droned in a falsetto sing-song until the end of the baked custard. She mixed dialect phrases with French expressions and her hands moved as if they were of butter, so fat that the handle of the silverware vanished inside them. The whole time she talked about churches and priests, about Novenas, about the Shrine of the Madonna of the Snows, which could be reached only on foot and the brambles tore the women's skirts. So far this year she had been unable to go because of the rain, she said, but she meant to visit it with Elisabetta. Every time her name was mentioned the girl went right on eating, slowly and precisely, as if Elisabetta were not she but the maid or a distant sister. Her pointed tongue darted, rapid and pink, over her lips, her blue irises enclosed in a darker circle remained fixed on the wall opposite her as a motionless thought made them as transparent as water. A beauty that shattered the heart.

The visit to the Madonna of the Snows was arranged for the last Sunday in June and it went off so well that not two weeks later they were at the Shrine of Conzano and then immediately at the sanctuary, abandoned for decades, of Castelgrana. Signora Bocca made Gavriel sit beside her in the carriage with the yellow curtains and, for the whole journey, she pressed against him. She was warm, full of perfumes and powder, and Gavriel's head swam. She took his hand to make him feel the mole on the back of her neck, hidden by her hair, she then held that hand for a long time and rubbed it over herself more or less everywhere as Elisabetta, who sat facing them, with her eyes closed, swayed her head, following the movement of the carriage, her bodice and shift undone because of the heat.

In the town everybody gossiped about the strange trio that, from time to time, became a couple, because Elisabetta tired easily and would nap in the shade of some tree, her head resting on her arms, her skirt spread out on the ground, ants wandering on it; and Gavriel and Signora Bocca would continue on their own, still talking of Saints and Miracles. Saints who could make a breast grow back overnight or reattach a leg cut off by a scythe. Signora Bocca wore drawers embroidered by the nuns and always kept within reach a little bottle of wine, very sweet, a topaz colour, blessed by Our Lady of Guadalupe.

In boarding school Gavriel had learned nothing about women, and once he was out of it, from his mother and from Fantina he had learned even less because those who knew kept their knowledge to themselves, so his curiosity was great. The wine Signora Bocca made him drink, warmed by her body and by all that journey in the carriage, pounded at his temples, while the vision of Elisabetta sleeping in the shade gave him long shudders. He closed his eyes and his feverish hands sought, blind and deluded. In the darkness of those empty churches he would furiously clasp Signora Bocca as if he were holding in his arms the girl who had remained sleeping amid patches of sunlight, her head flung back on the ground. He undid that blue ribbon, undid and rumpled that honeyed hair.

Maria couldn't sleep. The idea that Gavriel, her beautiful Gavriel, could even be touched by that old woman with dyed hair who chewed mint to disguise her bad breath, drove her crazy. At night she would enter her son's room, to make sure he was in his bed; if he was sleeping she would wake him, ask him mindless questions. Because she didn't dare, had never dared call anything by its name. Like a fury she would rip the covers off him and send him out to fetch wood at four in the morning, she would force him to drink camomile because she swore she had heard him groaning in his sleep. She would hide his shirt so he couldn't go out. But it was all in vain; the next day Signora Bocca would send the maid with ten silk shirts, five for Gavriel and five for Sacarlott, who would turn them over with his fingers, dumbfounded. And, in addition, a basket of quinces for Maria, to perfume the sheets.

Sacarlott said nothing; faced by his wife's distress, he remained lost in his own thoughts, barely narrowing his eyes as if to discern the shadows better. If he were to say something perhaps Maria would find the courage to name the thing that had always remained sealed behind her lips. But Sacarlott confined himself to sucking in his cheeks, a habit he got into when he began losing his teeth. The years are kind to him, he has bought back all the land that once belonged to the Great Masten plus still more land, he has taught his wife order and economy and if someone important shows up in the town he is always among the first to be invited to pay his respects. Gavriel must find his way, he says, and if Signora Bocca has taken a shine to him, it won't hurt anybody; in fact, it's all to the good, because that silly boy has lost his head over the granddaughter, and he will surely never be able to have her. He sees his wife writhing, her cheeks flushed, her eyes grim and hollow; Maria is even more beautiful with something pained about her face, the lost dreams have bared a structure of great purity. Honed, intense. Their last son, Gioacchino, has just turned seven, there can be no more children now and they will no longer smell about the house the odour of rancid milk, cloths soaked with pee, odours that exist where there are little children, the odours of youth.

'*Laissez-le,*' he says to her, in a sudden outburst. '*Laissez-le,*' in French that comes back to him as in the days when he imagined her happy with his brother and, far away, tortured himself with jealousy.

But he has no idea, either, of what is really going on. The Saints and the Miracles whose images fill Luison's devotional books are not familiar to him and for them he has the respect and the indifference of men profoundly attached to life. Certain contaminations never even cross his mind. In the town very few know the whole truth and those few keep silent because they fear the devil as they fear God. Even the priest, every Thursday evening, when he goes to supper at Signora Bocca's and she asks him endless questions about the liturgy or about devout reading, eats his boiled guinea hen with horseradish sauce serenely. And if Elisabetta seems to take an interest in the conversation he is delighted, hoping secretly that she will be called to the religious life. He drinks avidly the wine that

47

Signora Bocca orders from the Langhe area; and every question uttered by the admirable lips of young Elisabetta makes that wine all the more wondrous. A girl who is pure contemplation, in fact she does not embroider (and how could she, with those fingers, delicate and white as birch twigs?), she doesn't press dried leaves, doesn't draw and doesn't write poems or couplets in the little bound book she carries with her everywhere. Only from time to time she reads some edifying words recommended by her aunt, but nothing seems to remain in her memory. In fact, when she is questioned she gives vague answers, smiling, nodding at once, in a thick cascade of curls.

She speaks so little that Gavriel knows by heart her every sentence: *Today is a lovely day, I've lost my handkerchief, Gran-Maman doesn't like peaches, but they're so good.* Sentences Gavriel repeats to himself countless times as he helps his mother pick fruit. He whispers them softly, and Maria believes he is praying, as penance for the sins committed with Signora Bocca, while Gioacchino watches his older brother's lips, enchanted by this song without notes.

But Gavriel does not see mother or fruit or Gioacchino, so strong in his mind is the image of Elisabetta, and his thoughts follow her every step, the flutter of the blue ribbon that girds her waist, the light down visible, gilded and fine, when a shiver runs through her. If he closes his eyes he can see every blade of grass crushed by her shoes, every pebble on the bed of the stream when she gives him her hand to cross over on the log thrown between the two banks. A hand of cartilage, inert, barely moist, a hand that, once she has reached the other side, she leaves a moment longer as if she had forgotten it.

'Gavriel, the *cavagna!*' Maria's voice is sharp. 'The basket! Where is your head . . . ?'

Where indeed? Gavriel doesn't think of the future, but even the present has gaps of anguish because once the wine's effect has passed, Signora Bocca horrifies him. That blind satisfaction in the dark pathways of the body leaves him in a hollow stupor, like a sleep-walker. Something in him rebels and every time

48

he enters the gate between the two big magnolias, his heart beats with fear, his mouth is dry, while a mad hope makes his hands tremble, and his eyes seek Elisabetta, the white flash of her dress among the trees. But then when Signora Bocca takes his hand, perhaps because of the carriage's jolting, or the heat, he follows her as if he had to wrench a suffering from his soul, she leads him into those abandoned churches where a few old rickety benches have remained and there in the silence she undresses him, pulls up her skirts, bares her big breasts, still ripe, and rubs them against him. Horror has a bitter taste, bottomless, thrilling, he no longer knows if this is being a man or not. Angel, as Signora Bocca calls him, or goat: this is how, as a child, he imagined the devil. Then Signora Bocca slowly recovers herself, her big body blacks out the Madonnas and the Saints, she recites some brief prayers, like a penitent she licks the floor grey with dust, the worm-eaten pews.

How can Sacarlott know this? How can he even imagine it, despite all the things he has seen. But at times as his son accompanies him to the farm he has just bought on Gru hill, it seems to him that the boy's step falters, that a sudden fear, as if he had seen a flash of lightning or heard an explosion, takes his breath away. But the real torture comes on Sunday, when the boy constantly finds excuses not to go to Mass. He lies, he says he went to seven o'clock, though Luison did nothing but crane her neck and didn't see a sign of him. And if his mother forces him, he sits through Mass stiffly, his hat clutched in his hands, his face all bony and livid pale. Without saying one prayer, his gaze lost in the cascade of Elisabetta's hair, thick and billowing over the silk of her dress, as Signora Bocca prostrates herself in the pew, overcome, for her part, by intense concentration, her face hidden in her hands from which folds of fat escape, her black veil falling to the kneeler. And at the moment of Communion, she sticks out her tongue as if she yearned only for that host held in the priest's fingers. Gavriel clenches his jaw, to control the trembling that seizes him.

*

Maria went to speak with the priest; she entered, full of determination, holding little Gioacchino by the hand. Sacarlott had realized what she was going to do when he saw her putting on her black percale dress and washing the child's face. The priest listened to her, aghast; he thinks that Maria, the beautiful Maria, is suffering from some female disorder. Something to give a wide berth. He doesn't invite her to sit down, he keeps her standing because he is still a little frightened of her, those dark and deep eyes, those teeth which she has kept, almost all of them, cruel in those words she is saying. He strokes Gioacchino's head: as for Gavriel's being in love with Elisabetta, that's only natural, he says, who wouldn't be, at the boy's age? But Elisabetta is not the question: Maria's voice becomes agitated and the things never said fall from her lips, like black worms, one after the other.

'*Sta cittu!*' The priest suddenly calls her *tu* as if they were already companions in hell. 'Be silent!' He doesn't want to hear the terrible things Maria is saying; he just might be able to listen to them from behind the grille of the confessional, but not with that face in front of him, flushed with emotion. Signora Bocca is a sainted woman, she has donated to the parish the most beautiful vestments of the whole province. Summer is ending, the days are growing shorter all the time, and soon, after the vintage, Signora Bocca will be going back to Casale, her granddaughter, they say, is to marry a Viceroy of the King, a Count related to the Duke of Genoa. They say, they say, but then who knows how much truth there is in it . . . A country priest is only a poor wretch like other men; he, too, has to struggle to pile up enough wood to keep from freezing to death in winter, when the snow turns to ice on the door of the rectory, and in the morning you have to break the ice formed on the water in the pitcher, and the hens stop laying and the herrings hung up to smoke are hard to the teeth. Let Gavriel start working the land, and stop going to that house all the time to gawp at Elisabetta, the priest sees him from the window, always lurking around; what else can that sainted

Signora Bocca do but try to lead him to religious habits, taking him to visit those shrines that everyone else has forgotten now, for times have changed . . .

Maria has suddenly fallen silent, something she doesn't understand, that escapes her, seems more and more monstrous to her, and she squeezes hard the child's hand clinging to her skirt. If not even God wants to help her then that means the family has been struck by a curse, maybe Sacarlott committed some crime for money, or else the fault lies with Fantina who rebelled against God because He wanted Giai in heaven. A light rain wets the dust in the courtyard and the priest's sister arrives, to cover the corn spread out on the ground, the priest's cassock is threadbare, it flaps, empty, over his belly. On her way home Maria stops at Signora Bocca's gate, the rain has become heavier and it glides off the shiny leaves of the magnolias, the garden is deserted and the dark curtains allow no glimpse into the rooms. She clutches the rough, dripping bars of the gate, not caring that her good dress is getting wet, that Gioacchino whines, covering his head with his smock, she has to look at the gravel path her son follows every day, the short flight of stone steps, the closed door. But she is unable to imagine anything, her helplessness has deprived her body, and her imagination, too, of all strength.

That evening Sacarlott made a frightening scene; and all about nothing. Gioacchino had already been taken up to bed by Luison, and the rest of them were sitting around the lamp, talking about the new farm. Gavriel was in one corner, silent, he had poured himself a second glass of wine and instead of putting the jug back in its place, he had set it beside himself, on the ground. Anyone might have committed such a venial sin. But the second glass in itself had already irritated Sacarlott; and when, with an awkward movement, Gavriel or, more likely, the dog knocked the jug over, it broke and the wine spread out in a black pool on the floor.

Sacarlott's yells woke the child on the floor above, and

Gonda, who was sleeping on a chair in the kitchen. His voice was thunder, a hurricane, and even if they all had learned to fear his rages nobody knew what intensity they could reach. In those cries were concentrated the silences of years, his measured looks, his mute irritations; and the target was his dumbstruck son in a corner. He cursed in dialect, in French, and swore he was ready to kill Gavriel. He kicked at the chair, at the pieces of the jug on the ground, at the dog, now whimpering under the table. Gavriel, hypnotized, looked at the man's neck, swollen as if it were going to burst, and at the hands, big and pale, that trembled with the desire to break his bones.

His mother didn't defend him, motionless in her chair, allowing the wine to wet her shoes, without shifting her feet, without saying a word. Without displaying fear; and Gavriel went out into the damp and dark night with the rain rattling on the leaves. Through the door, which had remained open, he could still hear his father's imprecations, those shouts that made direct hits on his brain, shattering it. One moment he felt he was a victim, the next his shame dried up his saliva. He sat down on the well where once Giai had played the violin, but his father stood in the doorway, peering into the darkness to reach him with his insults. So Gavriel went off, starting down the driveway along the blank wall of the house opposite, while Sacarlott called and then called again, now frightened at the silence broken only by the beating of the rain.

Gavriel's footsteps make no sound on the wet earth, he goes off without hat, without cloak, farewell Sacarlott, nausea fills my mouth, I am filled with shit and yet I feel I am an angel. Elisabetta will soon marry, Signora Bocca has shown him the linen that her granddaughter will wear that day, lace with a thousand ribbons that the King's Viceroy will untie one by one. He held to his lips that fabric, so fine it could be clenched in a fist; he stuffed the lace into his mouth until it stifled him. Now he is walking through the deserted town, no light filters from the houses, these are poor people who pay great heed to their tallow and their wine, lucky is the man who has some, for it helps conquer the fear of the darkness. Gavriel goes off, with his seventeen years of gall, seventeen was his mother's age when she fell in love with Giai and anxiously waited to cross the threshold of the house with the painted ceiling; and instead she entered a maze with a candle in her hand. But he is sturdy, as the young Sacarlott was, and he will be a hired hand, anything, but he never wants to see his father again. In the sky, among the clouds that are separating, a heavy and opaque moon appears, too dim to define shadows, while above, distant, the houses of Lu are a black mound. Lu is where Mandrognin went to live, he is a saddler there, sometimes he comes down to see Maria, who gives him a chicken or a rabbit.

It was past midnight when Gavriel reached the top of the village. Mandrognin had become so poor that he didn't even have any straw for the boy to sleep on, and holding up his trousers he stared at Gavriel, frightened that, with the hunger legible on his face, the boy would take what little bread he kept in the bin.

That night Mandrognin didn't sleep, having Maria's son in his house troubled him, and in the morning, before Gavriel got up, he set out to go to Sacarlott. He found the family gathered around the table and he was invited to sit down with them. Luison, who was deaf and had understood nothing the night before, thought he had come at the urging of her nephew. 'Good, good,' she said, addressing Sacarlott, 'we must never forget those who are worse off than we are.' But Fantina, who always knew everything, for secret reasons no one wanted to probe more deeply, said Signora Bocca had got scabies and spent all her time scratching.

'Scabies,' Gioacchino explained, 'comes to dusty places, where the wood is wormy and full of dust.'

'How do you know that?' his mother asked, amazed.

Gioacchino shrugged, pathetically little and skinny, his legs swinging from the chair.

53

How Signora Bocca could have got scabies nobody knew, or at least nobody said. You get scabies, Gioacchino added, through saliva or hair. Any kind of hair. Even cat fur. But Signora Bocca had no cats. It was at this point that Mandrognin said Gavriel was at his house.

'*A l'à la rogna anca lui?* Does he have mange, too?' Sacarlott asked, then he said nothing further and went back outside to his work, while Gioacchino started crying silently because he realized his brother wasn't coming back.

In fact, Gavriel came back only on the afternoon when he knew Elisabetta would be leaving for Casale to meet the King's Viceroy. The carriage was already prepared with all the cases, and she came out in great haste, running past him, holding her skirt, which revealed her ankles, smooth as a child's, wearing pink stockings; her hat was askew and her cloak had still to be buttoned. Once in the carriage she looked out of the window and as the driver turned the horses, she smiled at Gavriel, a melancholy smile, and full of grace. '*Je vous aime*,' she said to him. The carriage, black with yellow curtains, went through the gate, and Gavriel's vision clouded, as it had that afternoon when he had looked at her for the first time, lying in the clover field. It didn't matter that she was going off to be the bride of the King's Viceroy, it didn't even matter that he would never see her again.

This was autumn, early autumn, of 1831. Many things have changed. Napoleon is dead, and all those freedoms that men enjoyed have rapidly dissolved as if they had never existed, their life has been so brief. But Sacarlott has learned to direct his gaze at a distance closer all the time, not to look around, not to ask himself questions, never allow his desires, his future, to go beyond the fields and the house, the dusty road that rises towards Lu. Not even the events of '21, and yet he was still young then, shook his unswerving conviction that the only way to save your soul is to forget what has happened, good or bad. His old comrades have stopped writing to him, and he has stopped answering anyone who does, like the legendary Anna who, putting on a uniform, had followed her husband to the war. And yet he had also loved her a little in those long evenings in the camp and once, in Amiens, he had danced with her in the square by the light of the torches. Two, three, perhaps four letters that asked for help because King Carlo Felice had erased women like her from his ledgers. Now Carlo Felice is dead and they have buried him at Hautecombe at the edge of the lake's icy waters, and Sacarlott cares nothing that in his place Carlo Alberto has come. He learned this in the barn from an old companion of his youth and he went on poking the straw with a stick to see if it was clean underneath.

Meanwhile the *bacterium choli* enters Europe, coming from the East, and it finds the way easy with the new steam vessels, the new roads opened by progress to trade. It is a known fact that two experts have set out from Milan to verify the phenomenon in the infected provinces of the Hapsburg Empire, but the word *cholera* is not among those that frighten Sacarlott, much more worried about the way his chickens are dying off, hens and capons, who fold over as if they were hollow. And while he watches Gerumin pick up a hen who is dribbling a white liquid from her beak he calls Gioacchino to him because he doesn't want the boy to touch any of those sick animals, afraid of anything that might threaten the health of his last child.

Gioacchino obeys, reluctantly; it has been a summer of great drought and his hair is parched by the sun. Smooth, fine hair, which Luison cuts with great snips of the scissors; and every snip leaves its mark. But what does his hair matter to a little boy, a little boy who amuses himself by chasing the geese and at night is spellbound looking at the stars, he wants to know their names, their movement, their route through the sky. He is a great friend of the son of Tambiss and at dusk they go off together hunting fireflies, to shut them up in a jar.

'An old couple's child,' people say when they look at him, so small, his bones visible beneath his clothes. A little boy full of grace and determination, with precise movements that never make a mistake. Immediately and infallibly, he finds the comic aspect of everything, and from his earliest childhood his laughter has exploded with irresistible force. His broad mouth, beautiful like his mother's, opens wide over his big and even teeth, and, a little ugly, he becomes handsome instantly. Since he first began walking he has always moved quickly, in an unending contest with the adults surrounding him, always ready to trot after Sacarlott, Luison, Gavriel (before, to the child's great sorrow, Gavriel went away). At times he sits beside Gonda and watches her doze, noting the sounds that come from her mouth, like the wind whistling in the chimney. Or else he stops to observe Luison working at her lace-cushion and he tries it himself, his wrinkled little fingers with their dirty nails, the skin ruined by the earth.

Until he was seven Maria kept him in bed with her, and Gioacchino slept in the middle, hugging first his mother then his father, and Sacarlott tolerated from him things that he would not even have imagined possible from his other children. He clasped that frail little body, filled with sleep, and against his mouth he pressed that hair, and kept still for fear of waking him. The father in those moments thought he was happy, happy as he had dreamed of being in those far-off nights of freezing and horror.

Gioacchino likes trees, the frogs that hop in the ditches, the rows of vines where the hares dart among the furrows. But more than anything he likes the stars and when he grows up he will be an astronomer. He says this to the priest, who teaches him Latin, and instead of the *Fables* of Phaedrus, he wants the priest to read him something about the moon and the stars. But the priest says he must learn Latin if he wants to know the stars' names one day and understand their mystery. And go to the city, where there are domes that reproduce the whole firmament.

But meanwhile Sacarlott has begun buying some books, which Gioacchino reads by the window of the living-room, with his finger on the open page. He stays there for hours and hours making an effort to understand things nobody would be capable of explaining to him; and when finally he understands, he sings. So loud that even Gonda, in the barn to get warm, hears him and proudly looks all around, as if Gioacchino were her own son.

Only Fantina is irritated at that voice and purses her lips, disapproving all that freedom, all that joy, all that unrestrained exuberance. She has never allowed Gioacchino to touch Giai's violin and if the child approaches the loom she sends him away with an irked gesture. When he was very little and she heard him trotting after her she would wheel around, freezing him with her colourless stare. As if Gioacchino had arrived in that house at the wrong time to disturb an established order, to upset an archive already veiled with dust. She is troubled by the culpable weakness of Sacarlott, so stern with his other children. She is troubled even by the child's grace and style, by his laughter. When she hears it she abruptly closes the door and her eyes concentrate on what she is doing.

Ever since Bastianina went off to boarding school, Fantina has shut herself up in her room. More often they see her beyond the yard, bent over her work or lost in thought as if she had a book on her lap. What does she – who can barely read – decipher with such attention? And yet in the town, if somebody has an evil presentiment or wants news of a lover, of a son off in the army, they come to ask her.

To tell the truth, what Fantina has ever divined or foreseen, nobody knows. Or what exchange she may have had with these girls, women, crones, who came to her with a bottle of wine from as far as Cuccaro even or Rosignano. She spoke to them in the privacy of the living-room for hours and hours, provided they had brought some light rosé, from the first pressing. For since she began drinking she has always liked this wine, slightly sweet, scented, and she keeps it jealously on a shelf in the cellar along with other wine that she orders from the Langhe. Because she doesn't lack for money now and what she doesn't spend on wine she lays aside for Bastianina, for her dowry when she decides to enter the convent and become an abbess.

She drinks alone and in company, and her face, formerly so uniform and pale, is scattered with purplish patches, her eyes begin to water, but these are not real tears and she whispers softly the tunes Giai once played on the violin. What she embroiders on these occasions has neither head nor tail, fantastic ciphers full of curlicues, but by now she has become so famous that whatever she embroiders is considered the highest perfection. Even if a crown of thorns appears on a sheet or if a tablecloth has twigs of butcher's broom in its centre. This, they say, is by Fantina: and lengths of linen arrive from Turin, from Milan, she no longer has time to do anything for Signora Bocca. The last thing was the sheets for the Signora's grand-daughter Elisabetta and on those sheets, they say, now half of Turin has lain, for the wife of the King's Viceroy has that many lovers.

Sacarlott died in February of 1836, of cholera. The year before, Gioacchino had died, after a fall from the hayloft.

Gioacchino's death was an accident. Something that should not have happened on that June Sunday with the corn already tall in the fields and the vines so laden that they all had to be tied up a second time. For Maria and Sacarlott it was an upheaval, like an earthquake, the searing eruption of a volcano. Or perhaps rather like the beginning of an ice age that imprisoned them in its emptiness.

'*Auanda che ata scapi acmè in selvatic?* Why must you run off like a savage?' Gonda had asked that morning, when Gioacchino passed like a meteor through the house in the sunny noonday light. '*Aspecia in mumenti,* wait a minute.' She would have liked the child to sit down at the table as he had done when he was little and eat a nice bowl of rabbit and potatoes. The Sunday dinner is cooking on the stove, there is a new girl helping in the kitchen, she is called Gramissa because of her emaciated look even though since she has been working in the house she has developed a full, round face like the moon's. Gramissa stops stirring the pot and looks for a moment at that hair pale as straw, escaping from his cap.

But Gioacchino is already outside, running through the fields, biting a piece of bread, he has skipped out of Mass without even waiting for the final Benediction and he is out of breath when he arrives at the lock of the canal, where they fish for eels. Tambiss's son is already there, standing erect in the midst of the shouting men, bare-legged in the water. The eels, by the hundreds, maybe by the thousands, slither, glints of mother-of-pearl, the men grab them, slam them on the stones, or pick up a stone to smash the head of the bigger ones, spattering their hands with the sticky blood, and their bared arms, their legs. From the basket Tambiss's son takes the ones already dead and holds them up by the tail; they are long, limp, a final shudder running through them. The smell of the grass steeped in the water ferments in the sun, the running has made Gioacchino sweat, his dazed eyes stare at the eels, which still writhe, entwine; his hands in his pockets stroke absently the pebbles collected on another Sunday, a different Sunday. He throws them away; and when Tambiss's son turns, Gioacchino is already in the distance, breaking off the top of a reed to make himself a pipe.

His friend calls him, but he doesn't answer. He stops where the water is channelled among the poplars, the pipe between his lips. Tambiss's son joins him and sits down beside him. I don't eat eels, he says, eels are disgusting, it's like putting worms in your mouth . . .

Later, they are hungry, the scant bread has quickly dissolved in Gioacchino's stomach, but he doesn't have any great desire to go home because of that escape from church without waiting even for the *ite missa est*. And his good suit is all rumpled and dusty, so they go off among the vineyards looking for some ripe peaches. They pick the mulberries from the trees, one climbing on the other's shoulders. A sister of Gonda's, bent double to hoe her little patch of land, sees them and calls to them, she offers them some cherries and asks what they're doing here at this hour, when everybody is sitting down to dinner. The old woman has no teeth and you can hardly understand what she says, Tambiss's son laughs but Gioacchino thanks her gravely, enunciating each syllable, and meanwhile he bites into the cherries, the juice stains his lips. How can he go home when he has also lost his cap and now one of the boys down at the lock has thrown away his own cap, old, moth-eaten, and put the new one on his head?

Later Gerumin saw them going past the little chapel of the Madonna, Gioacchino blessed himself hastily (if you don't, Luison always tells him, the devil comes at night and pulls you by the feet) while Tambiss's son offered the Madonna a last cherry, slipping it through an opening in the grille.

That cherry was still there in the days that followed and in time it became black and dry.

Then they came in through the vegetable garden, peering among the tomato plants, already high, to see if Sacarlott was about. But on the lawn there was only Fantina pulling ticks off the dog and Tambiss's son ran to hide in the hayloft while Gioacchino slipped into the kitchen to look for something to eat.

Gonda could hardly believe her luck, being able to fill a pan with the remains of the rabbit for him, Maria had gone to Vespers, and the old woman began rummaging until she also found two eggs and set them beside the pan. 'Don't drop them,' she said to him.

Maybe it was the fault of those two eggs that he had to keep balanced; but what really happened nobody would ever know. If it was because of the ladder that was always propped against the loft on the outside, it was always there, it was there when Tambiss's son climbed up, but afterwards it wasn't there, somebody must have shifted it a moment before. It was known for sure that Gioacchino climbed up from the stable and once up there he heard the voice of Sacarlott. Tambiss's son climbed up still higher, to hide among the bales stored for the winter, and Gioacchino found himself alone with a full dish in his hand, an earthenware plate with a broken handle. Maybe he tried to reach his friend, but the hay gave, he slipped, found nothing to grasp. Or else he had only meant to escape to the yard, down the ladder, sure he would find it there.

He flew down without a cry. Slowly, floating, his fine, smooth hair fluttering in the air, his short brown jacket like wings. This is how Fantina saw him, and Scarvé, who had come to ask for money to mend the roof. It wasn't a body falling, they said, but a feather that flew and flew and seemed never to stop as if that hayloft had been higher than the tower of San Giorgio. He flew without weight, white as wax, and Scarvé and Fantina hadn't the breath to cry out. The strength to run. The dish spun around, scattering pieces of rabbit; and in its fall, it made a hellish clatter, sowing fragments everywhere, making Sacarlott come running out to see what all this racket was.

Gioacchino was on the ground, shuddering in a last spasm. Intact, only a line of blood trickled from his ear.

Who had taken away that ladder, and why? Why at just that moment? Who had done it? Who? Maria screamed and screamed, this question wouldn't give her a moment's peace, it echoed in the corridor, through the rooms, even down in the oil press. She wanted to know why, who it had been. As if the answer would dispel the black cloud that had suddenly imprisoned her and was preventing her from crying or sleeping. 'It was Smangiun, *l'è stà il Nadal, la Gramissa, il Pipen, il Girumin . . .*' Names tangle, clash like bursts of a crazed organ, they are shadows cast by the moon, boughs that strike the panes. She has found the pipe in his trouser pocket, has clenched it in her fist, and she never wants to open that hand again. She cries out in the morning and she cries out in the night, she wants to know who did it. But no one is guilty: how can she understand this?

The priest sits beside her, takes her hand, and holds it tight between his own, soft hands, sweating in the heat; she withdraws hers, with revulsion, if she hadn't gone to Vespers perhaps it wouldn't have happened. The priest, too, is guilty, she looks at him, hostile, the pupils that have invaded all the space cancel her beautiful, velvety irises. This is how, sometimes, the eyes of wild animals are, in the night. She doesn't want to see again the Redeemer in his blue cloak, she doesn't want to see the little flames burning around him, she doesn't want to recite the Requiem Aeternum.

She doesn't even want to go to the cemetery; from behind the muslin curtain she watches the coffin, painted pale blue, carried on the shoulder of Gavriel, who has come down from Lu wearing cowman's clogs. She has set only one condition: the place closest to Gioacchino must be hers, him above and her below, as if she were still holding him on her lap. Her greatest hatred is concentrated on Tambiss's son and as she watches him follow the short cortège along the brick path, his trousers held up by one strap, it seems to her that the boy is laughing. It's not possible, but that's how it seems to her.

She sits and leafs through the astrology books that Sacarlott had ordered from far away. She reads aloud, slowly, because she can read little and understands nothing. But nobody must disturb her because she is 'studying'; the reed pipe is reduced to a wisp of straw in her hand. And the little boots dusty from that last race through the fields, on a June Sunday: nobody must touch them, either, or take them away from her. Quick to peer from the window in case Tambiss's son comes to ask for anything at the kitchen door. She screams then from the window to send him away as if he were a mangy dog and the boy runs off barefoot, terrified by that voice. This is how he appeared at the top of the hayloft, his hair standing up in fright, his arms raised to seek help from God, from the Madonna, from Scarvé, or Fantina, as Maria stared at him, frightening, accusing him: why not you, ignorant, ugly, always filthy with cow dung?

*

62

Gioacchino's flight was long talked about in the town; evening after evening Sacarlott made Fantina tell it to him. How was it possible, for him to fly, he would ask her. And yet that was what happened, Scarvé saw it too, Fantina says, and he's ready to swear to it before the crucifix. He was a feather in the blue sky, nothing like it has ever been seen, maybe Gioacchino had hollow bones, like birds. Sacarlott listens intently, that long glide, floating in the sky, consoles him because Gioacchino's death then is not like the death of others, like that of Manin or Giai. Maybe while he was flying his thoughts and his desires, his great gaiety, went off through the air and were now safe somewhere. Sacarlott's face relaxes, his wrinkles lose their shadows, Fantina begins the story again and Gioacchino flies away from her pudgy hands, he is a breath only slightly sour from rosé.

If only Maria were willing to listen to that story, if she also would try to imagine Gioacchino suspended in the heavens, she would find in her child's life all sorts of evidence, details to confirm his bird's soul. She would forgive Fantina many things, and Bastianina, Gonda. Even Tambiss's son. But she will hear nothing of their fantasies. She has different questions; and Bastianina, home from school on vacation, feels at times her mother's gaze on the back of her neck as she sits drawing beside her aunt. She doesn't need to turn to know that Maria is standing just behind her. A gaze that falls like lead when the girl happens to joke with Gramissa; and then a shudder runs down her back at the thought that her mother would so gladly trade her for her little brother buried near Giai.

The two famous physicians who came from Milan to study the cholera have long gone back and they have concluded little from their extended stay in the eastern provinces of the Hapsburg Empire. If the epidemic seems worse than worm fever or scurvy, it is surely less frightening than the plague carried by the rats that nested in the holds and at night poured out through the cellars, dropping down softly into the grain stores. Or else they scuttled along the walls, slipping furtively between a pair of ill-closed shutters. This time it is a parasite that travels in the bellies of soldiers as in everything that transports barley and millet and it navigates in gutters, in ditches, in canals. It's at the watering-troughs of livestock and in the fountains in the squares. It has no fear of rain or frost or even of heat, the sultriest.

The first to die was Gonda's sister, she was seventy, and nobody paid any attention. Then it was the turn of the priest's sister, the one who had given Bastianina painting lessons. When Tambiss's first cousin and Gerumin's granddaughter died, a little girl of twelve, everyone was gripped by panic. It was already cold and the sound of the Tribundina pierced the air, frozen and white, at the service in church there was hardly anybody, people were afraid to kneel in the pews where the previous Sunday the girl had been, her braids tied with ribbon.

The day Luison took to her bed with diarrhoea and vomiting, Sacarlott held a family council. He couldn't leave the land, he said, but if he was bound to die somebody had to be saved, to go on farming it. Luìs was too young and nobody could count on Gavriel, so there was no other choice: Maria had to go away with Bastianina, whom the sisters had sent home from the school; as for Fantina, she could decide where she preferred to stay. To be separated from his wife, he added, was a bad thing, he felt; but there was nothing else he could do, Maria had run the place once before and she could do it again and better than in the past. The best place, he then said, was Mandrognin's house in Lu. Hardly more than a stable, but Lu was up high and the wind swept the air clean, the rain washed the steep roads and his house, the highest of all, was so hard to climb up to that almost no one ever came to it.

When he finished speaking Sacarlott rested his forehead against the pane; the winter was getting ready to be one of the worst in these past years and the apple trees' branches stretched out already white with ice, the grass was bending under the frost. The dog, his tail standing up stiffly, was numb and trembling and he also seemed to be waiting for some great event in that leaden air where even the sparrows had stopped flying. And as if it had been projected into that silence outside, not even the thought that he could die managed to budge Sacarlott from the colourless calm that had taken possession of him.

Behind him, the whole house had begun to move, doors slammed, voices were channelled along the corridors. Strange sounds that precede an earthquake, flurry of wings, bustle of those preparing to seek safety. He with his brow glued to the glass hears nothing, not Maria's weeping, not Bastianina's protests, not the news that runs from one to the other: it's hit Tajalargh, and Gatagnú, Veronica . . .

Maria's life in Mandrognin's house was the worst imaginable, as far as comfort was concerned. No water, no sign of a well, scant light even during the day with those little windows barely a handspan wide. And such cold. The fireplace smoked and if the door was opened, the house filled with chickens. After two days Bastianina managed to have an attack of black bile and the only solution was to send her back to the school, saying she wanted to become a nun.

And yet for Maria it was a period never to be forgotten, a pause in her life like a picture whose details, even the most insignificant, have their own mysterious power. Mandrognin was her servant and her slave, he went out each morning at dawn to fetch fresh milk for her; at times a flower or a pear, a bunch of raisins he had searched out God knows where.

Maria's arrival had made him crazy, for years he had been in a lethargy, living like an animal, a blind mole in its tunnel.

Without desires, without energy, without willpower, and without dreams. And now Maria was in his house, he could look at her as much as he liked, talk to her, and even touch her when he passed close to her, feel her skirt brush his face as he filled the fireplace with wood, so much wood that the flue was blocked. He had God in his house. And Gavriel existed only to assist him. He commanded the boy, gave him no respite, it'll warm you up anyway, he said to him. He had sent him to sleep in a storage space, and he himself managed to sleep among the hens and the wood, so the whole house was at Maria's disposal and she could go from one room to the other with no fear of having anybody underfoot.

Mandrognin had a head thick with stiff, white hair, and a clear gaze, almost sky-blue, a bird's; at certain moments Maria found herself looking at him, spellbound. She liked his spare body and his hands, big and broad, like a bear's paws. She was amused by his precipitate way of doing things, his clumsy movements, his fanciful clothes dug out of some old trunk. In the morning when he brought her water, and some of it always spilled on the floor, she had to laugh and Mandrognin would laugh, too, happy because God let herself be seen in her shift with only a shawl. And God was so beautiful.

There was a single tree in front of the house, a fig, and under that fig Mandrognin had put his table and his tools, there he mended saddles in the open because he didn't want to bring that stinking leather into the house. Over all these years he had become insensitive to cold and if Maria, when she saw darkness falling and the ice thickening in the tub, called him inside, he would smile at her, and shake his great white head. And in the early winter dusk his head was the moon peeping from the mountains. He knew and remembered many things, Mandrognin, a hundred details of the house at Moncalvo and he would tell about how he used to go and lend a hand at vintage time and she was little more than a child, ready to dance to any music, even the *Veni Creator* that the devout Beata sang in the house opposite. He would see her seated on the bench beneath the hazel bushes listlessly sticking the needle into the frame; and the moment Luison looked away, she would jump up, sending the coloured skeins flying to the ground. He remembers still a cake that she and Matelda made for Easter Monday, and took to their father to taste, and a piece was given also to him. He had never eaten a cake that good, never again had a house existed as marvellous as the house in Moncalvo, such a bench, hazel bushes so thick.

'The cake was surely a *turtun*,' Maria says. 'We didn't know how to make anything else . . .'

Mandrognin looks at her: how gay you were, how beautiful you were, Maria, in all Moncalvo there wasn't another girl who could dance like you. I tried once myself, but I was so excited my feet went in separate directions, and you angrily turned your back on me. Maria laughs now, her hands folded in her lap, of the Mandrognin of that time she remembers only that he came to see her father and sometimes he stopped with them to see how you do Venetian stitch or hemstitch, and she and Matelda made fun of him because embroidery wasn't men's work. She remembers nothing else: oh yes, happiness, that, and now it seems to her that a little of that happiness comes back to her with Mandrognin's tales, it is released from his wild eyes buried beneath the thicket of his brows.

News arrives from Sacarlott that Luison is well again but has been left so weak that they have had to set up a bed for her in the living-room because she can't climb the stairs and she talks with the paintings on the ceiling. When a ray of sun breaks through the clouds they put her in a chair outside the door, she has gone completely bald and on her head she wears a bonnet that Bastianina wore in her cradle, the old woman's head has become that small. Up there, on the contrary, they are full of strength and every day Gavriel goes to clean the stables on the surrounding hills, and at evening he quickly climbs the path to the house, carrying a salami, a live goose in his hand, half a pound of butter.

Since his mother's arrival his enduring, insatiable hunger has ended, in the evening they drink the wine Mandrognin has sought out at the most remote farms, Maria prepares the polenta, the whole house is redolent of sausages and milk. Maria has trouble fastening her dresses, they have become so tight on her, at times she looks at herself in the piece of mirror that Mandrognin has set up in her room, and she smiles at her image as it hasn't occurred to her to do in years. If her feet are too cold she calls her cousin and he takes them in his big hands and rubs them and squeezes them until they are boiling hot. He has sewn for her two little boots made of feathers for when she goes to bed, and to warm her hands he has taken a rabbit's skin and stuffed it with feathers, too.

Winter has filled the valleys with white, up there the snow slides along the branches of the fig tree, is encrusted, frozen, on the steps. The wind has piled it up in mounds many feet high, and Mandrognin uses the pick where the shovel is not enough, so Maria will find the path free every day and her shoes won't get wet if she wants to reach the church.

But Maria forgets to go to church, Mass is rung and she is still drinking milk, opposite Mandrognin, who is telling her about when she was a girl in Moncalvo. She clasps the hot cup between her hands and her eyes shine as they did in the old days, Mandrognin smells of leather and burnt wood, the bells have stopped ringing, by now it is late: she'll go to Mass tomorrow, or later still. Because if a fine day turns up at last, she slips on the clogs Mandrognin has carved for her and together they take a long walk in the fields all levelled by the snow and only he knows how to find the buried paths. They arrive at wells frozen a bluish white, they watch the ravens shake their great black wings, then rise in flight, cawing. Mandrognin wants to build a sled and take Maria on it like a queen. It will be a sleigh with feather cushions and 'Maria' written in silver letters. It will have studs all around, a stool to rest your feet on. It will have a blanket of lamb's fleece and a little basket for bread to be thrown to the ravens. Handles to cling to when the horse pulls fast and it will be all painted red and blue.

When they came to fetch Maria, Mandrognin was out delivering saddles. She didn't wait for him to come back and went off without even saying thank you to him; because at that moment thank you was hard to say. She carried with her the little feather boots and the rabbit skin, beside the fireplace she left the clogs still damp after their last walk. And once again it was impossible for her to weep.

They had already buried Sacarlott; this was how he wanted it, she was to arrive when it was all over, everything disinfected, burned. And as with Giai, another woman had taken her place beside her husband. For days and days Fantina had wiped away Sacarlott's sweat, changed his linen, gone up and down, to and from the kitchen with water, had emptied the bedpans. Because all the others had fled and even Gramissa had abandoned the dirty pots and pans, carrying off the cat, wrapped in her apron; and a total silence, thick, blind, had possessed the house. In that silence Fantina had become mistress once again in the imperceptible swing of her skirts, and even her sleep had become only a closing of her eyes. Her presence beside Sacarlott had not wavered for a second and her face, covered with blotches from age and drinking, had watched over him, popping out like a gnome from the mists of his drowsiness.

Nobody knows what, in those days, passed through the head of Sacarlott and of Fantina, alone, face to face, what images advanced, each on its own route, never encountering one another. Not even Luison knew, left on the floor below, moving her dumb lips under the painted ceiling of the big room, her head no bigger than an orange on its pillow. Fantina had brought out her bench once again and seated beside the bed she was ready to get up at every desire that appeared in Sacarlott's eyes: drink, bath, help in turning over. Nothing else, never. A great silence that lasted for days and days, grown so important that any word would have aroused fear, while their thoughts went on, on, no one could say where, or how. Only, on the last day, when a faint dawn crept over the floor and its glints announced cold and splendid weather, Sacarlott screamed.

It was a single cry, wild, very shrill, that shook the rooms and made the panes tremble. The sparrows flew off the branches and the ice on the sill cracked. Fantina, her eyes still half-closed in that dawn light, crumpled, her hand on her heart: Sacarlott was erect in bed, his hair standing up on his skull as white as wax. 'The Cossacks!' he yelled. 'The Cossacks!' and his now-blind pupils stared at them, terrified, as they galloped over the curtains, motionless in the dawn.

3

GAVRIEL AND LUÌS

It was pouring rain the day Luìs suddenly left boarding school. He had almost completed his studies and his application had earned him more than one 'specials mention'. Once, during a brief summer vacation, Sacarlott took him to Casale to buy eyeglasses, for his sight had been ruined by all the time spent over his books. Those eyeglasses now balanced on his long, thin nose and gave him, in the livid winter dusk, the look of a young Waldensian pastor who had survived shipwreck. Water streamed from his hair, dripped down from his trousers, forming a lake around his long feet, while through his glasses, clouded by the steam of his body, his family appeared to him a shapeless, shouting mass.

There was no one left now to reproach him for his sudden defection, and only Luison managed to protest faintly at that still spreading pool on the floor. Luìs shook himself like a dog, wetting those closest to him, then he turned to Gavriel, who regarded him in silence: it was a long time since they had met, and on that last occasion Luìs had still been in short trousers. And as they all continued asking questions and touching his soaked clothing, he sought his brother's eyes. He sought his assent, and at the same time he gauged his brother's strength.

Gavriel gave Luìs's eyes no reply. Immobile on his short, stocky legs, physically so much the son of Sacarlott but so different from his father in mind and heart, he was impassive even when Luìs passed in front of him, bumping his big sack of books against him. At supper, when nobody yet knew

71

whether they should celebrate a homecoming or punish a desertion, Gavriel concerned himself only with eating, never resting his gaze for more than a second on his brother. And Luìs, for his part, was too hungry to continue the inquiry.

But those threads that started out from the room itself, from Gonda's old songs, from the same odours and sounds, the same tastes, the same childish trembling at Sacarlott's voice, had invisibly continued their route, unnoticed and ignored even by those who had once held them tight in their fingers. Perhaps it was Luìs who was in search of them. Luìs, after so much loneliness, such cold, such imprisonment. Or perhaps it was Gavriel, who had entered life from the darkest side, already advanced in that labyrinth chosen by accident. Attracted by his opposite, fascinated by his solar brother.

Luìs was untidy, noisy. His boots left prints in every room, on the stairs, in the kitchen; his vocal cords knew no low tones and even when he thought he was whispering he could be heard from one end of the house to the other. He was constantly going out and coming in, and in the rare moments when he happened to be seated, he would rock in his chair. His soft, thin mouth ate, laughed, spoke, and if it remained dumb, his grey-blue eyes went on expressing attention, interest, desire. He was a stranger to idleness, the depressing pauses in the day; and everyone wondered what had happened in that school, to make the calm and silent child, his nose always buried in a book, into this lanky boy quick to catch the first gust of air, the first different sound. Who would surprise Gramissa by grabbing her waist and blowing in her ear, and Gramissa would run from one door to the other, shouting in her fear and excitement.

'*Aspò propri nent dì cu seiia bel,*' they said the first Sunday they saw him at Mass, 'You can't really say he's handsome.' But as he entered the church with his long feet, his head piled high with hair, the girls did nothing but adjust their veils and twist their eyes to look at him. He looked at them, too, and it was clear immediately that very few caught his fancy. And while he had no preferences about what clothes he wore and heed-lessly put on an old cut-down suit of Sacarlott's or a jacket that changed colour if it rained, he paid great attention to hats. He liked to choose fanciful ones, and change them, and if he set one on his brown curls, he was quick to doff it at the first encounter. A great sweep of the hat and a smile whose irony concealed his shyness and his desire. An impulse, then quickly he replaced his hat on his head.

After all the years Luìs had spent in school, Maria was expecting her son to take over the accounts-book from her. Instead, Luìs declared at once that book-keeping was some-thing he would never do. Everything else was fine with him, they could send him out to keep an eye on the vineyard or the sowing, to milk the cows or handle the sale of the oats. As long as he could move about and feel the air and the earth around him, the changing of the seasons. He even liked the fog, the mud that weighed down his boots. And he made no difficulties about going to call on Signora Bocca and sitting in her green living-room, where Gavriel's anxieties and dreams had left their mark on every object.

Signora Bocca had heard much talk of him from the girls in her service, and seated on her sofa she tried to draw aside the curtain to get a better look at this lanky youth who talked about oats, drumming his fingers on his knee. But her sight had failed, and old age had finally defeated her. She had let herself go, was deaf, grey; and she who had spent sleepless nights on Gavriel's account could find nothing in Luìs to stir her from her listlessness. She didn't catch the gleam of his eyes, or if she did, it was like a high, distant echo, beyond grasping. Her scabies had long disappeared, but she always felt an itch somewhere and scratched it with a little stick that had an ivory hand at its end. When she asked Luìs to help her, he set to vigorously, the semi-darkness of the room made him ill-at-ease and from Signora Bocca's silk clothes came a clinging odour, sharp, of old age, while she uttered frightened little cries. Nothing more than that. Luìs hastily withdrew his hand.

When he went out, Signora Bocca watched with relief as he passed between the two big magnolias at either side of the gate.

The sun was setting, the smell of stew came from the kitchen. For years Elisabetta had not paid a visit, and the Signora no longer felt any desire to eat with the priest or with anyone else. She took her meals alone; and Gonda, whose niece worked there, said the old woman ate meat even on Friday.

Maria's first step was to send away Gramissa, who, no longer scrawny, now filled out her clothes, and always suffered from the heat. She unfastened buttons, rolled up her sleeves, and fanned herself under her skirts. In her place Marlatteira was hired, who wore the scapular of the Virgin under her clothes, and if she climbed the stairs she had trouble breathing because of her two hearts. Two hearts so tiny they had found no place to grow in the chest cavity, which had an unusual conformation, a bird's, with the breastbone that jutted prominently from beneath the stuff of her dress.

Gramissa was glad to go because she would be rising a degree, moving to the service of the phlebotomist, where she pounded powders in the mortars; and if she encountered Luìs she was no longer the house servant and could reply to him without embarrassment. But Luìs, the first morning he came down to the kitchen and saw Marlatteira blowing on the fire, turned on his heels and went off without breakfast. The next day, however, he was already resigned, and since he had a merry disposition he started joking with her, too, and Marlatteira flushed with pleasure. She sat down opposite him and while he ate some polenta and milk, she told him her dream.

That was the season of milk-fever and through the fogged windows of the kitchen the sound of the Tribundina came, for some dead baby, a festive sound because an angel had gone to heaven. Marlatteira spoke in the thick dialect of the upper Monferrato region where she was born, and, as she became carried away by her own tale, her eyes, deep in their dark

74

sockets, glistened as if she were twenty, and her long face took on an animal beauty, like a horse's. On that face, life and death, gaiety and grief, despair, happiness faded one into the other, and in Luìs's amazement, bits of polenta fell from his lips, into the milk, without his noticing.

For Marlatteira's dreams exceeded all imagining and, far from being confused, incoherent fragments, they were real stories with a beginning and an end. She could remember every detail, every smell, from the stink of sulphur to the aroma of bread fresh from the oven. There were knights in blood-stained cloaks who carried her to meet the poor souls in Purgatory, and as they picked her up in their arms the ends of her hair burned in the flames. She might dream of embraces that she called 'windy' though out of shame or ignorance she said nothing of their overwhelming emotion, while she blew through her nose to imitate the intensity of that 'wind'; then she would inhale slowly as all dissolved in the perfume of tuberoses and lilies. At other times a devil licked her with a tongue of fire, taking away her nose, but then the Blessed Cunegonda would arrive, kneading the Easter cakes, and would make her a new nose, smeared with gold.

And every time, the sudden happy ending came when the situation already seemed hopeless and she was shaking her head, disconsolate. She would look hard at Luìs and remain silent, as if expecting him to moan at such a tragedy. Then, dazzling, joyous, the end of the dream arrived when she had already resumed her bustling about the kitchen.

Yet Marlatteira never cheated. She was convinced that if she were to lie even just once, the Madonna would punish her: no more dreams, and instead, dark nights, empty except for the scuttling of the mice. Marlatteira was a virgin, and some who had seen her in her shift said she was flat as a child, and under her skirts, too, because at the age of four, making a vow, her mother had consecrated her to the Virgin of Crea. But in return the Madonna had given her dreams. And if one night – but this happened rarely – Marlatteira remained awake, the next morning, when Luìs came down to the kitchen, she wouldn't turn from the stove, roughly driving the cat away from the chair. Luìs asked no questions, ate his polenta standing up, and even if the fire was lighted, the cold made him shiver, the desperation that emanated from Marlatteira's clothes, from the milk that boiled over on the fire when she didn't bother to remove it. Then the notes of the Tribundina that came through the grilles suddenly betrayed all their melancholy, tolled, it seemed, by childish hands, reluctant and mournful, at being separated from this world. And Luìs would run out in haste.

He had fallen in love with Fracin's Rosetta, who went to church only at Christmas, Easter, and on Palm Sunday to get the blessed olive twig. She was one of the anarchist smith's five children, the only girl; and in a big room built with planks stolen from the soldiers during the uprisings of '21, she and her brothers raised silkworms. She had red hair, but her white skin was without a single freckle, and when Luìs approached the house down at the Pontisella, she emerged from the rotting stink of the silkworms in the splendour of her pure skin, her cheeks barely tinged with pink, and she would glare at him defiantly: what did one of those churchmice of Sacarlott want of her? But at times she had to look away to keep from laughing, seeing Luìs, standing there by the little bridge like a stick, his trousers tight at his ankles and the sleeves of his jacket barely covering his elbows, Sacarlott's old clothes never fit him.

The two didn't speak, because Luìs didn't know what to say, and after a little while she would go back inside. Luìs could hear her singing. Her contralto voice was the priest's torment, it would have been so marvellous in the *Sanctus* and in the *Alleluia*. Instead, Fracin's Rosetta sang quite different things and, standing on the Pontisella, Luìs felt his love growing beyond measure. It was the voice of an angel and at the same time an earthly summons full of mystery because she invented the words as she went along and often they made no sense.

When summer came, Luìs did something no one in the family had ever dared do before: he went dancing. In Sacarlott's time the word 'dance' had been meaningless, belonging, as it did, to the vocabulary of the rich or the mad, the only ones who, as Sacarlott said, could have any desire to go and break their legs in some clowning show after a day of hard work; and his gaze chilled anyone who, with a desire vague and imagined like the wrinkle of waves, might, however faintly, have mentioned such a thing.

Luìs, on the contrary, rummaged everywhere, searching for the old silk shirts given by Signora Bocca; he picked out the one that had yellowed least. On his head he stuck one of his little hats, of undefined colour; and the last Sunday of June, in the searing, early-afternoon heat, he set off for the Martini farm, leaving his mother, aunt and great-aunt in despair.

The Martini farm was halfway up one of the Lu hills and when Luìs arrived the dancing had already begun; Fracin's Rosetta was already engaged for all the dances. But when she saw him in the distance, his hat pushed back on his curls, she forgot all her promises and stood, motionless, under a quince tree, waiting for him among the broad and dark leaves. And once Luìs was close to her she put her arms around his neck as if she had been waiting only for him before dancing and Luìs went pale, his hands trembled as he held her by the waist and began to spin.

They spun and spun, and the more Luìs clasped her, the more she let him, and there was a moment when they came close to falling to the ground they were locked so tightly. Nobody knew who had taught Luìs to dance, maybe he had learned on his own or maybe, just great desire to hold the girl gave him all that impetus; but his arms truly yearned, and when he wanted to say something and she turned her face close to his mouth he had to swallow, his words died on his lips. But the moment the music ended one of her brothers came and took her away from him.

Luìs danced with Gramissa, but now dancing with other

77

girls meant nothing to him and he gave each of them a whirl, even the old women, spinsters and married. Fracin's sons hoisted their sister onto a lame mare, to take her home, and from her mount she looked at Luìs and you could tell from her big gilded eyes that if he were to come back to the house down by the little bridge it wouldn't be the way it had been in the past. In her gaze, along with her sadness at being torn from his arms, there was also the exultation of that peerless dance. Unique, unforgettable, Luìs.

Their love was happy and full of surprises. A love opposed by all, from old Fracin, who in his youth had been a friend of Sacarlott then still called Pidrèn, but had later stopped speaking to him because of Napoleon who had made himself Emperor. Opposed by Rosetta's brothers, who felt that this tall, slim boy who waved greetings left and right was not to be counted on. Opposed by Maria, who considered the daughter of a smith many, many degrees below them and didn't believe that the cultivation of silkworms would ever bring in enough to bridge that gap. And besides she's an unbeliever, Luison said; and this destroyed any remaining chance for Fracin's daughter. Even Gonda and Marlatteira shook their heads, because of that red hair.

Only Gavriel liked this love because he felt it was harmless, without tears and reproaches, without anguish; and when he went about the fields with his brother and listened to him talk about the girl, it seemed that his long nose, the focal point of his expression, was outlining a story in which happiness was possible, within reach. It was born on its own, like a natural event, like rain and wind.

So it was for Luìs, his love had no need of any future or even of plans. He went with Fracin's Rosetta to collect the mulberry leaves that fattened the silkworms, he went with her to cut grass for the rabbits; and they forgot the leaves, forgot the grass, for the territory into which they were venturing was so vast and unexplored, and so intense was their desire to know it together.

Never aware of the tragedy that could be just behind them: in the forgotten leaves, in the grass withering at the edge of the meadow. They had no fear either of Rosetta's brothers or of storms and not even of the dead, who can be encountered at dusk near cemeteries. A boundless confidence in themselves turned everything that did not concern them into an indistinct, flat horizon, dispelled in an instant anything that might disturb them or block their love. But this same confidence, one day, would kill their story, would circumscribe its duration in time and then destroy every trace as if, turning back, they were no longer able to recognize anything, only some vague shapes of which some trivial details remained vivid: the flow of a canal, the soaring of a kite. Or the rhymes of the anthem in honour of Ferdinand of Austria, crowned that year in Milan.

Because the only daughter of the anarchist smith has a weakness for Kings and Emperors. 'Hail, sublime son of Austria, Ferdinand Imperator . . .' she declaims, holding her arms wide. Difficult words for her, accustomed to the dialect, and her eyes shine as if she could already see, among the ermines and the carriages, the sparkle of the two-headed eagles of the Hapsburgs. Luìs laughs but she goes on, unperturbed, stubborn, determined to know and to see; Luìs will not stop her, no one will stop her, and now she doesn't want him to interrupt her, she breathes the words in his face, bites the hand that would arrest that river of words. A canal flows between the two banks of trees, she bends to drink, exhausted, and Luìs seizes her wet fingers, sucks them between his lips until he feels them docile and warm, the silence fills their lungs, and only the sound of the water amid the grassy banks resembles the shudder that grips them. Once she lost a clog and they had to look for it after dark, groping in the grass.

Who knows if they ever made love in the full sense, that love that leaves the lovers exhausted and sated? Fracin's Rosetta had a great need to dream and to wait. Surely they must have come very close. Afterwards, when Luìs injured his knee and had to remain immobile for months, he thought at length of

79

those moments, when everything had been possible. He thought of how it would have taken place, of what would have happened to them, afterwards. He thought, mostly, about her disconcerting, fearless gaiety. He imagined her melancholy, in the abandonment in her burnished golden gaze.

Afterwards, when it was too late. When, at the first frosts, he slipped on the now-treacherous bricks of the path and his knee struck the ground with the full weight of his body and a sac of water formed inside, and for months, the more that water was drained, the more it came back. Confined in a chair he peered through the windows to see if by chance Fracin's only daughter might arrive. He peered among the last leaves stubbornly clinging to the apple trees, among the dry stalks of the late asters, planted that year for the first time. A sign, a message. And in the morning, when the sun dispelled the fog and blue patches of sky appeared, he said to himself: today she'll come. She came only once and stopped under the arbour to talk with Fantina, nobody asked her to come in and Luìs struck his fingers in vain against the panes sealed by the frost. She didn't once raise her head, didn't even raise her eyes to look up there, beyond the tangle of the bare vines of the arbour. He saw her red hair escaping from her woollen bonnet, her swollen hands, ruined by her work with the silkworms. And when he saw her going off again along the path he broke the pane with his fist. But she was already gone and didn't hear him shouting.

One afternoon, before Luìs slipped and hurt his knee, they went up on Gru hill to fly a kite. The peasants in the fields stopped their work to look at that strange bird shaken by the wind, always staying in the same spot. A bird that rustled in the sky grey with clouds while the triangular flights of the migrating geese passed above it. On that bird's wings the name of Fracin's daughter was written; but this the peasants could not see, as they could not see the string that kept it moored to the ground as night came down and the smith's sons struck the bell, searching for their sister. If they were to find him, that Luìs, they would smash his bones. It was autumn and Rosetta had stuck her frozen fingers inside Luìs's jacket, over their heads that paper bird whirled and flapped until they forgot about it. Afterwards it was too late, the string became tangled among the brambles, and they ran until they were breathless, because the moon was rising beyond the hills and nobody could have explained to the old smith how important it was to fly a kite. Who could explain it to her brothers? How marvellous it was.

That year, when she went to Confession before Christmas, Fracin's Rosetta stayed in the confessional for ever and afterwards she remained alone, saying her penance, and as the sacristan was putting out the last candles, she still hadn't finished. And at midnight Mass, when the moment of the *Alleluia* came, her voice rose, so limpid and loud that the girls' choir fell silent. The priest stood there, his hands held out, unmoving, over the chalice, and the altar boys turned their heads, dazed. But the voice of Fracin's Rosetta was beautiful in too earthly a way and her *Alleluia* celebrated the light of Christmas, its warmth, the food. The people who filled the church were poor, and they looked at her, frightened.

In spring Maria took Luìs to a famous doctor in Vercelli. The journey was long and arduous and when they arrived, the leg was so swollen that the doctor couldn't even drain it. Luìs had a raging fever, he was delirious. The doctor made an incision the whole length of the knee, and after two leechings he told Maria she was to keep her son awake until the knee had drained, this was the only way he could be saved. All night Maria talked to Luìs, wept, told him her life. Luìs stayed awake to listen to her and the water dripped from his knee, soaking right through the mattress, wetting the floor. In the morning, through the open wound, the bone could be seen.

That journey to Vercelli was decisive. If Luìs had ever had the possibility of walking normally again, that exertion deprived him of it for ever. The water didn't return, because the knee was already worn out, but he was left with one leg thinner, less warm than the other.

It was April when he tried walking again, in the fields still damp from the last snow the grain was beginning to sprout, some cherry trees, more sheltered, had blossomed, and you could smell the elders. Leaning on Gavriel, Luìs got as far as the gate. On the way back he tried to walk alone, he thought of Fracin's Rosetta and of the Gru hill, the kites to come. The dog frisked at his side; Luìs hesitated a moment, then stiffened, staggered, and finally resumed walking. Gavriel looked at him, smiled. Maria, too, who smiled so rarely, seemed to be once again the Maria of the old days.

Anyone who thought that Luìs would accept being handicapped, didn't know him very well. Even with one leg uneven he held himself erect as before, and when summer came he was seen again at dances, wearing his little hat pushed back on his curls, and the jacket that changed colour with the rain.

But Fracin's Rosetta is no longer there, there is no point in seeking her fiery fox hair. The blue linen dress that she made by herself. She is engaged and will marry after the grape harvest, in a white dress that already everybody is talking about. A dress given her by her brothers, who went to Casale to pick out the material. For Rosetta is a good girl and deserves to be rewarded, the pock-marked Camurà has fallen in love with her and he is unwilling to wait even till spring, he is readying the house, a proper house with a garden all around it and an oak at the gate. Camurà is rich, he has made his money at the markets and fairs, where he began going around as a boy, dragging his cart up the hilly roads.

The only one not pleased is the old smith, who goes on hammering like a fury amid swarms of sparks, grim in his grim forge, with a long white moustache that droops onto his chin. He does not like Camurà any more than he liked Luìs, Luìs seems to him a nonentity, but Camurà has glue on his fingers, and whatever he touches remains stuck there. He cheats on the length of cloth and on everything else, he robs rich and poor, the government, the French.

But Luìs is a light-hearted boy, the years in boarding school set in motion something that never ends. A desire to give and take. To stroll at dusk and drink wine, which dispels melancholy. Everyone is born with a path, as if he bore it carved in the palm of his hand. No use trying to alter it: and Luìs feels his fate strongly only at the moment when he abets it. Great pauses are not for him, no expectant pondering of his image in the mirror; the blood that feeds his thoughts, his viscera and his heart, is the kind that heals wounds quickly. Life wins every time; and his mother and Fantina observe with wonder how quickly he has stopped thinking about the girl. He has already stopped mentioning her name, has already stopped whistling her songs, replaced by others he has heard God only knows where.

He has bought some agronomy treatises and at night he stays up late, studying them. He wants the land to be fruitful again as in Sacarlott's days, just as Sacarlott had wanted the land that had been the Great Masten's, and afterwards more land. He has put a chair and a table in one of the rooms where the hemp is stored. The hemp, he says, can be put in the attic, and that room will be his study. He has gone up and bought a bookcase from the Cavaliera, who is selling off piecemeal the last furniture remaining in Braida castle, and he spends many evenings in the house with the summer moon striking the panes. And when he accompanies Gavriel into the fields he waves his arms, describing what he wants to do, he waxes enthusiastic, here he wants to plant acacias and over there sow clover again, next year flax; his long legs leap over the ditches where the summer before he held Fracin's Rosetta in his arms. Gavriel listens to him, glad that Luìs is the way he is.

And often they laugh together, at this reckless, impulsive Luìs. They laugh at Gavriel, always inclined towards the 'no' of life, *Monsieur Catastropho*, Luìs calls him.

Without this capacity for laughter, their life in common

would be perhaps impossible, their affection would not save it. True union, the deep union that goes beyond Maria and Sacarlott, the two of them feel in this mysterious possibility of irreverence towards the same things. At the same moment, with a simultaneity unknown to the others, sometimes amazing even for themselves. And at evening the one who comes home first awaits the other's return, alert to the creak of the front door, the familiar sound of footsteps, just to be able to breathe again that light air, so familiar between them.

For a long time, that summer, the object of their jokes was Bastianina. Tall, built like Sacarlott, Bastianina seemed born to be an abbess. And she felt she was an abbess, even though she was a mere novice and the nuns constantly sent her back to the family, to 'test her vocation'.

As the cart with the young novice turned, swaying, into the driveway, everyone was impelled by a sudden need to do some job and only Gonda remained on her chair in the sun as Bastianina's voice was raised, loud, to call everyone to come for her numerous and cumbersome cases. And her face, framed by the veil, pretty perhaps, was turned solemnly, like that of an heir to the throne.

Bastianina, impassive at the announcement of a hailstorm or a lightning bolt that sets a haystack afire. Not even seeing a rabbit's throat slit causes her the slightest shudder; but the moment she hears the sound of an organ or breathes the smell of incense, she flings back her veil with a burst of pride, radiant, freeing her round girlish cheeks. She doesn't like the *Messa Prima*, the opalescence of dawn and the cold church; she is for the *Messa Granda*, the pomp of the bells, the glittering copes, the altar boys dressed in red. The throb of the organ pipes.

She gives orders, checks, organizes, from her broad mouth, always moist with saliva, comes a delicate and hoarse voice where the purest Italian vibrates like the metallic strings of some toy guitars. No one understands, but they are forced to understand. The inflexible, piercing eyes, a speckled grey, set brains in motion, forcing them to decipher what seems impossible. So she is obeyed. Not infrequently with the most sensational errors.

No one knows if she ever grasped, even once, her brothers' irony. No one ever noticed any sign, not even a darkening of her gaze when they would make her repeat certain expressions over and over. She submitted to their jokes and their feigned stupidity, not deigning to give them a moment's attention. *Fratelli, porcelli,* she used to say: brothers, piglets; and in the evening they heard her reciting the *Officio* in a falsetto voice. From her room the notes crept out, arrogant, implacable in their monotony: they reminded that penance must be done for sins, that God's punishment is prompt to strike the wicked, and where his justice arrives, there weeping and gnashing of teeth will be heard. The closer she came to the final part, the more feverish and shrill her voice grew. Until, in the darkness of the looming night, it became something like the howl of an animal.

She was rich, nobody in the family had the ready money she had. Everything that Fantina had earned and still earned was earmarked for Bastianina's dowry, her trousseau, the habits of the novice who would one day be abbess. And instead of helping her mother in the house she sat in the living-room, painting at a monumental easel, which required half a day just to set up, plus strong arms to raise and lower the wooden pieces, turn them in the right position for the sun as the clogs of the farmhands echoed shyly over the waxed floor.

She painted aquatic birds for the most part, cranes, geese, herons standing on one leg in the water. She loved to copy tropical fauna from the illustrations of a book that had belonged to Gioacchino, and against the great leaves of the banana palms and the tangle of lianas she set her swans in profile, the eye outlined in black. Once finished, the pictures were wrapped in great lengths of white canvas and no one was to touch them, as they were ready to travel with her, to be dispersed later among various convents of the Realm. Some would perhaps

85

navigate, with billowing sails, towards the islands; and one, the most beautiful, with a life-size swan, would perhaps reach Rome, not far from the Pope.

The brothers were rarely granted access to the room, their shadow was irksome on the canvas, and their voices disturbed the serenity of the mind. At times they appeared beyond the window among the pear-trees and apples of the garden, and Luìs would doff his hat. Gavriel would deferentially bow his head to the young novice seated at the easel. With her palette supported by her thumb, an ample smock over her habit, Bastianina looked at them without seeing them, her lips pursed into a pink cherry, to ask for silence. At times, lost in awed contemplation, Fantina would sit beside her. And she, who had embroidered copes now legendary, allowed sighs of admiration to escape her, contemplating those canvases painted with broad layers of colour, strong hues without nuance, few shadows.

Bastianina cannot recall a summer this hot, and, motionless, she waits for a cool bit of shade, a shiver of wind on her face and neck. She yawns, and is so sleepy she cannot even hold the brush in her hand. Then she stands up and asks Fantina to accompany her to the sulphur spring that cures intestinal ailments, hot flushes. And once there, she takes off her shoes and stockings, rolls up her skirt and steps into the pool of clear water enclosed in a circle of trees and from there she calls to her aunt: 'Come in, *Magna!*' she says to her, 'Aunt! you come in, too!'

Fantina shakes her head; she has sat down on the bank in the shade of a locust and she tells how, when she was a girl, a water snake once seized her ankle, coiled around it, slapping its tail against her legs, and Maria had to pull it away with her bare hands, and afterwards they ran off, forgetting their clothes. Ever since then neither of them has gone bathing, and to this day she is afraid even to drink that water where it flows from the spring.

Bastianina shrugs, in the shade of the acacia Fantina's broad face is scattered with spots, some are the leaves' shadows but others are on her skin and it seems impossible to the girl that Fantina can have been young, have had legs white and strong like hers, silvered by the flowing water that disappears into the ground. Bastianina looks at her, seated on the grass in her patched dress, her neck bloated from drinking, and an inexplicable irritation vexes her. Fantina has become stingy, for herself she would not buy so much as a button, even pennies must serve, to make Bastianina rich, the richest of all the novices. For a moment Bastianina closes her eyes, she would like to forget, she doesn't herself know what. Forget. She trickles water down her bosom, and in the silence, now that Fantina is dozing off, she thinks of Fracin's Rosetta, who will soon be married, and of Luìs, when he used to come back with his jacket all rumpled. Once he lost that jacket, he didn't know where, then Gerumin found it, and Gerumin laughed . . . 'Enough,' she says, in a hoarse voice, 'I want to go home.' She wakes Fantina, she is rude, she slips her shoes on again and grumbles because now they have to walk under the sun, her dress is uncomfortable.

Fantina has risen obediently and they walk along past the parched blackberry bushes. The peasant girls have climbed onto the wagons, wearing great hats with holes in them, the oxen struggle, chasing away the flies with their tails, the children's hands and faces are seared with erysipelas. Fantina has opened an umbrella to protect herself from the sun. '*Ven chí sutta,*' she says, 'Come under here,' to Bastianina, who stubbornly walks on, her throat tight. The peasants doff their hats, the children look at her, intimidated. Already they call her *la Munja,* which means the Nun. Fantina responds to the greetings with a slight nod in the black shade of the umbrella, she replies for herself and for Bastianina, unperturbed in the dust raised by her long strides. In this way they cross the town and, under her veil, Bastianina's hair, soaked with sweat, sticks to her head; it itches, but she doesn't move a muscle of her face, doesn't raise a hand to scratch herself. In the square the mayor is about to get into Signora Bocca's carriage to go to Casale and wait upon King Carlo Alberto, who is breaking his journey at the Hotel Mogol. Signora Bocca peers curiously through the yellow curtains at this novice so like Gavriel in the strength of her body. Bastianina goes past, head high, without so much as a glance, her anxiety makes her breathless at the memory of the evening when Gavriel left home amid the cries of Sacarlott. She has never learned what it was that made her father yell like that, what dark conscience drove Gavriel into the night, but she remembers that name shouted by her father like some obscenity. And in a flash she understands, she understands without understanding, in the torture of that day. Further on, she stops; Fantina is still beside the carriage, bowing to Signora Bocca, almost prostrating herself as if she were before the Blessed Sacrament. '*Magna!*' Bastianina calls. '*Magna!*' She has forgotten all her manners and her voice re-echoes in the square, from beneath the umbrella Fantina looks at her aghast, Signora Bocca leans forward between the yellow curtains. '*Magna, andumma!*' she cries, 'Come on!' Only the dialect can express her desperation and her blushes blind her, she wants to cry in shame, sweating down to her thighs.

'Why don't you come dancing, at least once?' Luìs asks her. 'You could give it a try, before it's too late.'

'Dance? Me?' Bastianina puts her hand to her bosom to stay her heart.

'Yes, dance. Dance . . . wouldn't you like to, at least once?'

A flash in Bastianina's eyes, the memory of the smell when, as a girl, holding her mother's hand, she crossed the square on fair days. The music and the dust. One afternoon she stood spellbound by all that swirling and her mother couldn't drag her away. She looks at him: a novice dancing, with a veil on her head?

As if he understood the unspoken question in that gaze Luìs

gently touches her veil. 'Take it off,' he says to her. Instead of flushing, she turns pale: if now, with a sudden movement, she were to slip the veil from her hair, her life could be different. Who knows how, who knows to what extent? Her legs are straight and sturdy, they seem made for dancing, the passion she puts into her painting is a force in her blood, the same as in Sacarlott's. As in the Great Masten's.

Luìs insists. 'Just this once . . .' As children they played together, he was the knight wearing his father's cape, she was Saint Geneviève, besieged by wild animals, and he always came to save her, knelt beside her, stroking her long hair spread out on the floor.

'. . . No, no, what *tabalori*! How stupid!' The little feminine grace left her is lost in the sharp turn she makes, she will not fall into the trap, she will not end up like her mother, like Luison; she will not end up like Fantina.

That afternoon, late, Bastianina was seen walking through the fields with her long stride, her white habit standing out against the dark of the hedges, her veil, which she constantly threw back. Fantina, who had come into the living-room to bring her a slice of watermelon, found a barely begun picture on the easel and the chair empty. Bastianina walked for a long time, almost submerged by the stalks of corn beginning to turn yellow, she passed through the clover wilting in that August heat and through the rye that brushed, pale, against her skirt, far from the barnyards where the peasant women were tending the silkworms. She went as far as the high road to Giarole. From Braida, where they were dancing, some people saw her, with her white veil and dress, and thought she was lost. She stopped in the shade of a mulberry: all that walking, dressed as she was, must have tired her, sweat made everything on her smell, skirt and petticoats, bodice, wimple. She was not yet twenty and she rested her back against the mulberry's trunk and stayed there a long time, looking at the dancing couples. Their distant voices reached her, and their laughter. The music of the instrument played by Zanzìa.

From Braida Luìs recognized her, too, and suddenly felt remorse for all the times he and Gavriel had made fun of her. A deep sorrow made him almost blind for a moment; he didn't want her to stay there, he wanted her to go away; but at a certain point Bastianina took off her veil because of the heat, and her head, down there in the distance, was a wooden puppet's, her hair had been cut so short. Then, as a mazurka began, Luìs forgot her. When he looked down again, the distant shadow of that mulberry was already blended with the countryside, the moon was rising to light the empty high road to Giarole.

Luìs dances again, the moon is high over the Braida tower and his shirt cools the sweat on him. All the wine he has drunk has gone straight to his legs and it seems to him that if he stops he will collapse on the ground like an empty sack. The Cavaliera's youngest daughter, a child still, looks at him, pale and in pain; she looks at him so much that at a certain point Luìs grasps her by the waist and gives her a whirl, too. She is the last of ten children, some married, some dead, some still serving in the King's army; nobody pays any attention to her and she has run out in the dress she wears even in bed, her nails are black with dirt. And now that dress swells, her plaits slap her face, she would like to cry out in wonder but her joy is so great she is breathless, and she clings to Luìs's arm, her feet kick him, as she spins and spins in the odour of the last sausages burning on the embers. The trees spin, the moon, Braida tower, she looks up at Luìs and sees the sweat trickling from his forehead white as a dead man's. I am Antonia, she would like to say to him, the last child of the Cavaliera. But Luìs has already set her on the ground and has gone off to stick his head under the tap.

A castle, Braida, where the turkeys and chickens strut undisturbed through the rooms and the geese spatter the steps. A breed of dumb geese, so they will not disturb the Cavaliera, always ill on a divan, after all those children and the misfortunes that have gradually taken away her furniture, jewels, whole estates. Antonia slips away from the old maidservant who wants to carry her off to bed and she follows Luìs at a few yards' distance, she follows him still as he goes swaying here and there with his little hat askew as the musicians pick up their instruments, grumbling because the pay was scant and the wine bad, the Cavaliera, as everyone knows, is more tight-fisted than the French. The child looks at Luìs at the end of the road, a slim shadow under the moon; one of the players pulls him up into the cart, and only then does Antonia go up to her mother, asleep on the divan with a vinegar-soaked handkerchief on her brow; and she wraps herself in a blanket at her mother's feet, her head in her mother's lap. The Cavaliera in sleep senses her presence and extends a hand to stroke her hair. Slowly, as if the hand were arriving from an unplumbed, painful distance.

But now it rains and rains, Bastianina has gone back to the convent, where next spring she will take her vows. All the dust of that long summer of drought has become mud and when you walk along the roads you are mired up to the knee. The millet crop is poor, many grapes have simply been left on the vine, and no plough can get through the fields, the oxen sink in and then have to be pulled out with ropes, the men's cries can be heard in the distance, under the dark lid of clouds. Maria sits for hours and hours alone playing cards and every now and then she raises her head to look at Luìs, always at the window, studying the sky. And when he goes outside his boots, afterwards, muddy the whole house, including the beds, where he stretches out, not even taking them off.

But nobody dares say anything to him, nobody has the courage after all his work, his devotion, those books read late into the night. All the labour that is now floating away in streams of water, in the smell of mildew that clings to clothes, it is in the beds, the walls, and there is no fire that can dry it out.

'Luìs.' Maria looks at him and meanwhile she replaces a card, she has long been cheating but it seems to her that in the

darkness of the day even cheating is no longer enough, the
noise of the unrelenting rain carries the darkness into her
mind. 'Luìs . . .'

Luìs turns but no sound comes from his lips, his remote
gaze behind his glasses has lost even the last glint of merriment.
Even that merriment which is hardest dying, most stubborn
in its hopes, and on his long, spare face the school years have
returned, dead, grey years.

When the bell began ringing the alarm it was still day but it
was as if night had come down already, the day was so dark,
without beginning or end in the monotony of the rain. A
deep, grim roar rose from the earth and covered the ceaseless
sound of the bell, an indecipherable roar that resembled none
ever heard, and as Luison and Fantina, terrified, fell to
reciting prayers, Gavriel and Luìs ran down the driveway in
the blinding rain. But they didn't get far, the bridge over what
in summer was barely a trickle had been washed away and the
water swirled and slammed against the walls of the houses.
Those who had gone out that morning to look at the high
road to Giarole, on coming back, had barred their doors; but
bars and bolts were of no use now because the water poured
on in one endless torrent. Dark, dense, it dragged along tree-
trunks, animals, wagons with the shafts torn off, and it flung
them against the doors until the planks came loose. There was
no knowing for whom that bell was still being rung, the noise
was so much louder, louder, too, were the screams of those
who called one another from house to house or cried for help
above the lowing of the cattle borne off in that torrent of mud.

The October night of 1839 remained memorable because
of the loss of livestock and possessions but especially because of
the wondrous events that took place. Oxen were lost, chickens,
turkeys, pigs and horses, and many houses were gutted, others
had their doors and windows ripped off, the flood dragged
away walnuts and seeds, sacks of flour, tables, chairs, bins filled
with bread and vats that were still fermenting. It soaked and

scattered the wood piled neatly for fires in the winter and even Fracin's forge was picked up and carried off along with his trays of silkworms and looms for silk. Fracin and family managed to save themselves by climbing to the top of the chimney and from there, with a system of ropes and pulleys, they were carried from roof to roof until they found a refuge.

It was never known what mysterious hand had begun tolling the alarm before the water came pouring down from the high road. When the sacristan heard it ringing he ran to the steeple to see who had pulled the rope but the cloister was empty and the cord hung limp while, up above, the deafening bell continued. He climbed then to the top and from up there saw the water spreading out over the countryside, a leaden lake, engulfing mulberry trees, poplars, vines, and flowing on, on, faster and faster, towards the first houses. But already people were hurrying to safety, warned by that bell, and to make sure it would go on ringing, the sacristan hugged the rope, crazed by the bronze din.

That alarm bell saved all those who lived down at the Pontisella where, a moment later, the flood wave plunged down and rose up in a column of water that burst doors and windows and emptied into the rooms of the lower floors, filling them to the ceiling. But not even the old people were there any more, having galloped off on the shoulders of the young, and one mother saw a cradle floating by, from which a moment before she had snatched her baby.

Gramissa also had a great adventure that night, when she found herself again in Luìs's arms. It was so dark that to recognize each other they had to touch, she had got lost along with the phlebotomist's mare and the mare had slipped and been carried off by the water, Gramissa wept soundlessly because fear had paralysed her voice. Luìs picked her up and she was so light that he could run as if he were carrying a chicken or a rabbit. When they reached Uslun's house, which was the highest in the whole village, Gramissa's weight was breaking his back and Luìs dropped her on a bench. She smiled and, her eyes still closed, she went on clinging to his neck so hard that Luìs was no longer able to straighten up.

That night, in Uslun's house, in the big kitchen with the blackened fireplace, the Cavaliera's youngest daughter mingled with the others and, as usual, nobody paid any attention to her. She wiped her nose with her dress, scratched her lice, and sat on the ground in a corner to look at Gramissa embracing Luìs, who was red with shame: Gramissa sucked the hot milk they had given her to drink without opening her eyes, her round, white arms seemed sealed, by some supernatural force, around Luìs's neck.

But the real protagonist of that night was Gavriel. He organized the rescue parties, had fires lighted, collected the livestock roaming around the fields, and pulled out the animals trapped in the mud, planting his feet firmly, his hands bleeding from the ropes. With the water up to his waist, he went to carry the old people and the children to safety, the women weeping at the windows. He had a rope tied around him and, groping, banging his legs, he rescued Fracin's Rosetta though she didn't want to let go of the chimney even when the water was lapping at the first roof-tiles. He took her on his back and she clung to him as he had ordered and together they started across the stream, which was carrying logs, beams, and brush, dead animals that in the lightning flashes assumed the most indecent shapes. Everybody, on all sides, was shouting and it seemed that at any moment Gavriel would vanish into those waves of mud, but he always reappeared with Rosetta clinging to his hair, her body slumped on top of his.

That night they saw Gavriel everywhere. He was up by the high road, pulling out animals, and down at the lock, taking the boat to go to Braida, where the water had reached the second floor and the Cavaliera refused to budge from her divan, and he stood up in the boat to persuade her from the window, as the water was slamming the few remaining pieces of furniture here and there, on the floor below. And when the Cavaliera was safe somebody remembered that there was still old Nadal in the house, the centenarian who had been the Cavaliera's chief groom when she was rich and a countess and Braida was a real castle. So Gavriel set off again to look for him and meanwhile the rain had let up and the night appeared even blacker, the goats went by, bleating, at either side of the boat and disappeared, swallowed up by the stream. When Gavriel was floating in the courtyard of Braida the water was almost still and it barely gurgled, flowing off into the rooms and the long corridors of the ground floor. Not an animal could be heard now, or a voice, there was no longer one candle alight, and climbing over the sill, Gavriel walked through the empty rooms, groping for the doors, which opened one after the other. Old Nadal was lying supine on the floor and didn't stir even when Gavriel stepped over him. He let himself be loaded into the boat like a bundle of rags, without saying a word, and when Gavriel picked up the oars again he saw a long and narrow boat passing, outside the courtyard. A woman and a child were seated in that boat while the man was standing, and proceeded, slow and solemn, with a long pole. It was the Great Masten, still dressed as in 1793 with pigtail and three-cornered hat, but Gavriel didn't recognize him and when he himself was outside the courtyard the boat couldn't be seen, as the water swirled frighteningly.

That was when he heard the voice, very near. '*Angirmà*,' it said, '*angirmà*,' which means a boy who is spellbound by enchanted words. And when a bit of moon appeared among the clouds he saw the boat very far off with that man standing like a foremast. Immediately after that old Nadal woke from that kind of catalepsy into which he seemed to have fallen and he began to talk, he had a faint and very soft voice and in the rumbling of that flood that threatened to upset the boat he explained about the stars and their course. He talked, old and ignorant as he was, of Cassiopeia and of Berenice, of the constellation Orion, while Gavriel was sweating to keep the boat afloat. His hands were lacerated and he could no longer grasp the oars and he was afraid of dying in the blackness of the water along with that old man. To end in darkness and mud seemed terrible to him, terrible to die because his life had not yet received anything. It was like the life of Gioacchino, who had flown down from the hayloft on a June Sunday or, worse, like the life of Manin, who had died at just eighteen months.

It was that word, repeated very close to his ear, that saved him. '*Angirmà*,' it said, '*angirmà, curàgi . . .*' And tears choked Gavriel because that was the name Gonda had called him as a baby. And suddenly he understood that the now distant boatman was the Great Masten as Gonda had always described him. The Great Masten, come because he, Gavriel, was not to die. He had to hold out until he tore the flesh from his hands and bathed the oars with blood, until he felt two blades in his back from the pain of keeping the boat straight.

The winter was endless, cold, silent. For a long time the fields could not be broached and to fight his melancholy Luìs joined the men and boys who were preparing the play for Carnival. The rehearsals went on for several months and he learned the part of King Herod.

He was the first member of the family to appear on a stage and Maria criticized him for everything, for the waste of time and his way of acting, for King Herod's costume with the tin crown; but, chiefly, for the part itself. An insignificant part that lasted barely a minute.

To see him, they all went and sat in the front row, on the chairs with cushions. Fracin's Rosetta, only a few months married, came too, and she was the first to applaud. Her husband, little, pock-marked, had a reputation as a great lover; she was invisible beneath a broad hat decorated with ribbons; at a certain point she took it off, drawing out a long pin, and her white neck, her round chin, her cheeks, shone in the darkness of the hall. With a single act she showed the dazed audience what a magic touch the dark little man seated beside her possessed, that Camurà who knew about women and money. The actors lost their place on the stage and Luìs came close to falling, the tin crown rolled over the boards.

After the performance cakes and wine were served, but it was a lean year, and the cakes were dry, the flour was mostly corn meal and the wine left an empty, sweetish taste in the mouth. The children ran outside in the cold to hide their slices of cake in their shirts so they could ask for more, Fracin's Rosetta sat stiffly on a chair, in her matronly dress, intimidated by her own radiance. She also seemed to be acting a part, halfway between an angel and Uriah's Bathsheba. Luìs had gone outside and was watching the children, as they stuffed their hollow cheeks with cake. For months he had devoted himself to playing a king who had died two thousand years ago, swallowing his disappointments and being like the others his age. Now all he wanted was to throw himself into the canal and meet the same end as the oxen and the horses on that terrible night. The children irritated him, the stink of the clothes he was wearing irritated him, and the time when he used to go out into the fields with Fracin's Rosetta seemed far away, as if it had never existed. He had wanted to become a better *particulare* than the others, ahead of his time; and he had ended up putting a tin crown on his head to entertain these children brawling around him.

Luìs, on that Carnival day of 1840, was twenty-three years old.

That was also the last time Luison left the house. After the cholera her hair had not grown back and nobody ever saw her head, which she washed with rosewater every morning before she put her bonnet on. It was her dream to have a wig but nobody wanted to buy her one because she was too old and it was a waste of money. The only one who had taken pity on her was Bastianina, who, before entering her novitiate, had given her own thick dark plait to Luison. With that plait she

97

created infinite arrangements, she pinned it to her bonnet, curled it into ringlets, smoothed it into two bands on either side of her face. But on the afternoon of the Carnival perform- ance, as she was running the iron over the hair, she burned it. The stink filled the house. Luison was a woman of principle and she went to the performance all the same, with curls like tufts of cornsilk; and the children laughed behind her back.

On returning home she took off the bonnet and to the whole family, aghast, she showed her bald head, shiny, polished like a bone. Then, saying nothing, she went up to her room and that night they heard her lamenting in a loud voice. She cried out against Maria, Fantina, Gavriel and Luìs, even against Gonda and Marlatteira because of the wig that nobody had ever been willing to buy her. She screamed and screamed. Wakened in their beds by that voice, they remained motionless, no one dared venture along the corridor to calm her, but the next morning Gavriel set off on horseback to go and buy her a wig with real hair. He spent a sum which for that year of poverty meant a sacrifice for them all: light brown, the wig had belonged to a famous actress and its locks with copper glints could be knotted in seven different ways.

It was a day of cold, dry sunshine; and, sitting on her bed, Luison gazed at the wig for a long time, not daring to touch it. Afterwards, when she was left alone, she put it on the chest of drawers, supported by the blue glass jar that held her rosewater, and she sat there looking at it until darkness fell. After all these years she had reverted to her Veneto dialect and nobody could understand what she was saying, her hands clasped in wonder. But from that day on she refused to get up, except to comb and stroke the wig, change its position as the sun moved, the better to see the reddish-brown glints. She was deaf and so she could remain impassive to all pleas to leave her bed, while her gaze, grown glaucous and watery with the years, was raised to her interlocutor and was more absent than her ears.

Sometimes she pinned ribbons to that wig, old cloth flowers from her girlhood. One morning, when Marlatteira brought her the milk, she ordered her to set it on the chest of drawers and give it to the *Prinsèissa*. Meaning, by *Prinsèissa*, the wig. It was the last thing she said, with a smile of her gums, a long smile, full of wrinkles.

Now without Luison, Maria and Fantina felt orphaned, for the first time. Luison had lived with them always, in the house up at Moncalvo and then, again, when Giai died. She had taught them everything, from embroidery to cooking, from the pleasure in washing themselves to the joy of a sunny day. Luison had known the mushrooms and herbs, she would call the girls at dusk to see the moon over the fields or to hear the nightingale sing on June evenings. Her virginity, unquestioned, rooted, obvious, had allowed her liberties otherwise inconceivable; and when, as they grew, they began asking her questions about love, her answers resembled the replies of the Sybil. They could mean one thing and also its opposite, as if the difference between man and woman, the realm and the adventures of love were things belonging to a future so remote that, like dreams, they were part of a life unpredictable in its eccentricity.

Such had been their life with her up at Moncalvo, when Luison would look out at the window to observe their childish games, and later, when she checked to make sure they were sitting quietly at their embroidery, already young ladies in long dresses. She would call them, scold them. She would look at them proudly. Or in the morning, standing erect and still, she saw to it that they washed behind their ears, inside their nostrils, under their arms, with the cold of certain winter dawns when you couldn't see your outstretched hand. But afterwards it was lovely to go to church, Luison in the middle, the two of them flanking her, she walking in great strides, with those nieces who seemed to her so beautiful and sturdy, so clean. And they, proud of how Luison greeted everyone, left and right, as if she were the Queen of Sheba going to visit King Solomon.

Now Luison had gone, beside Sacarlott and Giai, and everybody was thinking about the wig that had come too late. About her cries in the night when the humiliation suffered that Carnival afternoon had been so strong it severed every last wish to live. Even though she was old and toothless by then, and to speak with her you had to yell into her ear. Now Maria and Fantina remember the years of hunger when there were the French and Moncalvo was called Montchauve and there was no news of Pidrèn off in the war, Luison had grown haggard and her jawbones stuck out under her skin. But if anyone asked her if she was hungry she would shrug as if the question were rude.

Maria remembers something else. She doesn't speak of it with Fantina; and she cannot mention it to her children, who would never understand. It is the Luison of a summer day, her plaits undone, her dress rumpled, the back stained with sweat. Luison dancing, spinning by herself, her skirt flying out and coiling around her feet on the lawn. The two of them are little and they watch, Maria weeps because she cannot recognize her aunt in that woman who dances like a girl.

She is still young then, Luison, and as she spins she holds out her arms, her dark hair invades her brow. She is not alone; on the grass with her there is a girl, a man with a white beard and a broad linen hat, another man, younger, who laughs, thrusting out his belly. They are relatives who have come from up north, from that village at the Austrian border where she was born and grew up. A village that must have seen her very different since she now displays herself so shameless and carefree. Even the language they speak has unknown, light cadences, it is a language full of sounds and trills. The girl grasps her by the waist and they dance together, Luison stumbles, falls, her skirt on the grass bares her legs, she laughs. Oh how terrible is that gaiety, it clutches the heart as it so distorts Luison's features, her body sprawled on the grass. The girl laughs, too, the man laughs under his linen hat and his white beard sways on his chin. Suddenly Luison sees them, her and Matelda, and for a moment her eyes express rejection, almost hostility at that everyday sight. A gaze that would like to be blind, and is closed, does not see, while the laughter continues, at length, it seems never to end.

'Mama,' Maria cried then, 'Mama!' Luison got up, slowly her body was recomposed, piece by piece, as her happiness dulled, a mist evaporated as she restored order to her dress. The combs that put her hair back in place.

4

RUST APPLES

The only portrait of Gavriel, a daguerreotype made from a copperplate engraving, bears the date 1842. Gavriel is now twenty-eight and is seated at a table, his hand supporting his chin. He is dressed simply and on his vest there is no sign of the gold chain so proudly displayed by Sacarlott. His face, though serious, retains a boyish quality, you could call him a joyous dreamer. The background is vague; behind the portrait, the date is written, in India ink: 22 July 1842. The day of the full eclipse of the sun that plunged the village for some instants into blackest night. A day surely happy for Gavriel.

And important, so important that he wrote it on his portrait. The eclipse, too, was talked about at length, and for a long time it was a reference point, separating the before from the after. Many went up to see it from the Gru hill and Luìs, who knew the exact hour, set off when it was still dark followed by the hands, who carried the little children in their arms, their heads swaying with sleep. The birds were just beginning to stir among the leaves and Luìs spoke of what they would see in a little while. When they reached the top of the hill they scattered, each a short distance from the others, on the slope overlooking the vineyard. The last stars had vanished, and the sun that was beginning to peer out from the hills struck the red-brick farmhouse. From the stable the peasant brought fresh milk and Luìs pulled out his spyglass, which he kept in a case. Gavriel sat off by himself, and on the road, white with dust, he saw other people climbing up, some on foot, some in carts. Word had spread that Luìs, who had read so many books, would show things never seen before, and Fracin's Rosetta, who had returned to her town for a few days, also came up with her brothers. She was a few months pregnant, but that baby could already be sensed in her empty, languid gaze, in the laziness of her movements and in the special whiteness of her skin. The climb left her breathless.

Her past love for Luìs was no secret for anyone, many had come upon them at least once, hand in hand, and some had caught them kissing; and now everybody looked at Luìs to see what he would do. But Luìs barely greeted her, his spyglass aimed at the sky, where the last colours of dawn were fading. Fracin's Rosetta sat on the ground, stretching her long legs out on the clods, exhausted, and Gavriel offered her his jacket so she could be more comfortable. The ground, he told her, was still damp. Fracin's Rosetta thanked him and made room so he could sit down, too. Then they remained silent, listening to Luìs, who was counting the minutes, holding in his hand the watch that had been Sacarlott's.

And before Luìs had finished counting, the sun began to disappear. In a moment, a darkness without shadows, blind, a darkness like the end of the world swallowed them up, along with the fields and the houses scattered over the hills, the birds suddenly dumb. In her fright Fracin's Rosetta seized Gavriel's hand, he felt her plump, soft palm, and entwined his fingers with hers. Gavriel's hand was cold and rough and it pressed hard, harder all the time, as he felt Rosetta's fingers cling to his, her nails digging into his flesh.

Someone, in that darkness, let out a cry, lasting as long as the eclipse. When the sun glided out from behind the moon and the colours reappeared and the shadows of the trees, they all looked in the direction from which that cry had come: under the porch of the farmhouse Chirassun was lying flat on the ground, his head bashed in. Whether he had fallen or whether someone had hit him, it was impossible to say,

Chirassun had been dumb since birth and his brain had never developed, instead of talking, he whined like an animal.

Chirassun was believed to be a natural son of the smith, and seeing him like that, bathed in his own blood, Fracin's Rosetta fainted, while her brothers ran down to his aid. In the general confusion nobody noticed her, stretched out with her eyes closed, and Gavriel picked her up in his arms and carried her to the farmhouse where he parted her lips to revive her with a bit of cool water. Later he took her home on a cart, walking beside her, his jacket on his shoulder, at the oxen's pace.

Fracin's Rosetta's baby was born without effort and with a flat head. He was a long baby with empty pupils that seemed painted on his face, and Camurà, when the midwife put the baby in his arms, wept for the first time in his life. It was November and since summer Rosetta had been Gavriel's mistress.

Camurà's house was in the plain towards Alessandria and to reach it Gavriel had to ride for over an hour. It was a one-storey house, white, with a garden all around it and a great oak that gave more shade to the road than to the lawn. Camurà was often away selling his bolts of cloth in the markets and among the low-ceilinged rooms, each with its stove, Fracin's Rosetta spent her time looking out of the windows to see if Gavriel's horse had come into view.

But after the birth of that baby, which Gavriel considered God's punishment, to overcome temptation he sent the horse away, up to the Gru farm where his affair with Fracin's Rosetta had begun. She shut herself up in the house and in her grief would see no one, the presents Camurà brought her from the fairs she shut away in a cupboard, not even unwrapping them.

The baby was good and never cried, she stroked its flat head covered with black down, thick and shiny, and she sang him the songs that she had sung as a girl in Fracin's house.

They heard her voice from the road and people stopped to listen. When summer came and the window was left open, some approached the sill and looked at her, so beautiful beside the cradle. It was on one of these days, in late July, that, between an old man and a woman who was passing by selling salt, she saw Gavriel, sitting on his horse, immobile, in the shade of the oak. Forgetting all prudence, and Camurà, who might come back at any moment, as well as her grief and shame for the child, she ran out as she was, her slippers on her feet. They looked at each other, trembling, and that day it began all over again.

Just as Gavriel couldn't give her up, Fracin's Rosetta equally couldn't live without him. Camurà, the new town where she had come to live, even the garden and those stoves in every room had become unbearable to her without Gavriel. And life was a blind road.

To meet her Gavriel sometimes set off before dawn, when the hands were still sleeping in the stables; and his mother, hearing him, turned her head away so as not to know. Even though these moments were rare, because meetings were rare between Gavriel and Camurà's wife.

It all began on the day of the eclipse. That morning, once Chirassun had been tended to, everybody went home as if each had experienced for a moment the death of all things. Even Luìs started down the hill in silence, unprepared for the anguish that had gripped them. Only that couple had felt their blood flow faster and once she was placed in the cart, when the oxen began to move, Fracin's Rosetta couldn't take her eyes off Gavriel's hand resting on the side. She could feel it, that hand, strong and intense as it had been when it gripped hers and his eyes continued staring at her for all the time that the oxen proceeded. That hand, at that hour, in that light, was something she would never forget.

The next day her husband came to fetch her and with the buggy he passed the house where Gavriel was standing at the gate. Camurà stopped the horse to thank Gavriel for the assistance given his wife the day before: in the sunlight the gold circle glistened that he wore in his ear as was once the custom in the country, and to Gavriel it seemed to contain the secret of his good luck: women, money, his young wife. Camurà cracked his whip and the wheels spun off, the buggy disappeared in the dust of the road. Gavriel and Rosetta hadn't even looked at each other, but it was as if everything had already happened; and it mattered nothing that she was Camurà's wife, it didn't even matter that she was pregnant.

They would meet in a hut near the river and already from the distance Fracin's Rosetta could see the horse grazing: desire made her wipe her mouth. Gavriel waited for her outside and again they looked and looked at each other without making a movement so as not to give themselves away if anyone were to pass by. They stared into each other's eyes as they fixed every detail of each other in their minds, clothes, hair, a ribbon.

On some days, as they made love, Gavriel would talk to her, almost raving. Recollections of Signora Bocca's time, and she would hold him tighter in her arms, her lips seeking his to blot out the memory. But on other times she would laugh, instead; her laughter was cruel towards Signora Bocca and the boy Gavriel in love with Elisabetta. That radiant laughter was like a shock for Gavriel. It left him sweating, exhausted.

When she went home Fracin's Rosetta would sit by the cradle and go back in her mind to what had happened in the hut. The baby breathed softly, his skin was pale and his eyes like hers, only the baby's were empty, and that emptiness was a barred road. She cut out some shapes in coloured paper and hung them in festoons over the cradle, he seemed to understand and waved his little hands as if he were trying to pull himself up. But he never had the strength. And then she would burst into tears.

He died one morning, as Fracin's Rosetta was holding him in her arms. He had not suckled for two days and his hands were cold, nothing could warm them. The milk she dripped into his mouth trickled down his chin as if his throat would allow access only to the thread of air that kept him alive. It was winter and because of the fog at the window even the big dark oak was invisible, the dishevelled sparrows sought refuge on the sill. She took the baby, washed him, put on his embroidered baptismal dress and sat beside the cradle until night came and then until morning. Not even Camurà could budge her from there or make her eat. Finally, when they came to put the baby in the coffin she stood up to help, and in the coffin with the baby she put also her bridal veil. She wanted no more children, now or ever. But she couldn't give up Gavriel.

Giving up Fracin's Rosetta was impossible for Gavriel, too, and when his mother proposed this or that girl for a wife he made no answer. One or two of them Maria invited to the house; and as they sat in a circle in the living-room Gavriel seemed so serious and keen on the conversation that each time Maria thought he was on the verge of making up his mind. She looked at him: his ruddy face, his thick and curly hair, his broad shoulders. No girl, she thought, would say no to him. Marlatteira moved around pouring the muscatel from the Gru farm and the girl who put the glass to her lips would turn red just from raising her eyes to Gavriel: surely she would say yes to him. The conversation went on, at times it would falter in a pause filled with hope and the girl's face, already a bit affected by the muscatel, expressed the emotion in her heart.

But Gavriel didn't say that extra word, didn't make that gesture that would have decided his life. His gaze fixed on the apple trees out on the lawn, he let the expectation collapse and the surges of the heart, like pebbles rattling down the well, grew fainter and fainter until they died in the void. The girl at last would stand up and Maria would say something about the apple trees outside, Marlatteira would take away the tray with the glasses.

And before dawn the stable door would be heard creaking, and the sound of the horse's hoofs as he was saddled mixed with Gerumin's voice, choked with phlegm. If the fog was still low, stagnant, the lantern could be seen swaying, attached to the saddle, then it disappeared down the road. In the darkness that the horse crossed at a walk the image of Fracin's Rosetta faded in the monotony of the journey, other memories returned to Gavriel's mind: Signora Bocca, Elisabetta when she sat in the garden wearing her white dress. And it seemed to him that his youth had been cursed, from the beginning.

Luìs's first wife was the Maturlins' Teresina. She was, as everyone would have expected, plump just where plumpness was necessary and she had fiery hair. Not tawny like the smith's daughter's but a barley blonde, intense and thick. She was only seventeen when Luìs went to fetch her in Ivrea from an aunt who had adopted her, the last of six sisters, each more beautiful than the next.

They had met in the summer, when Teresina, with the other Maturlin girls, had come to look at their farm burdened with debts; and the moment Luìs saw her in the shed cluttered with old carts and rotting poles, radiant and fearless in her city dress, he decided she would be his wife.

He left her side only long enough to eat and sleep; he forgot the oats to be harvested, the corn, the acacias, the vines. He thought only about how to reach Ivrea and take the girl for himself, never to leave her again.

The Maturlins' Teresina played the spinet and she used her table-napkin with such grace that it was a pleasure to watch her eat. Her Ivrea aunt had prepared her a trousseau entirely of linen and a muskrat fur complete with high cap and muff such as the town had never seen. She wore little kid boots that came halfway up her calf and silk mitts that protected her plump hands even in the house. She had a warm, harmonious voice and anyone passing the garden at evening could hear it as she accompanied herself on the spinet. The more curious might approach the window overlooking the lawn and be enchanted by the sight of a pale nape illuminated by the candles, by the full, rounded shoulders that vibrated at the high notes as, seated on a stool, she sang the works of Handel and Frescobaldi.

Her great passion was the *rusnent*, the rust apples, which she gathered by herself and ate at all hours, biting deep into them with her strong, little teeth, neatly aligned. She also loved the blossoms of those apples and during the spring she spent in the house she would put them in her hair and at dusk, wilted, they would fall to the ground, a sign of her luminous passage.

Of the six Maturlin sisters, famous for their beauty, she was perhaps the least beautiful, but this had given her, in addition to the ease of being one of a group, also a kind of shyness that made her blush violently and inspired an immediate tenderness. A desire to protect her, to take her hand and lead her along the corridors of the house, the rooms that opened one into the next. And her smile, never affected or imposed, radiantly displayed her gratitude for any attention. All agreed in believing that Luìs couldn't have made a better choice.

They were married in the winter and Maria and Fantina undertook a journey such as they would never have imagined, through snow and ice, a storm that blinded the horses. A wolf followed the stage coach to the gates of Ivrea and from the window they watched it, in terror, howling, grey, as the coach sped and sped until it seemed it should shatter at any moment. Not even the wedding in the Ivrea cathedral could repay them for such suffering. Hundreds and hundreds of candles glinted in the silver branches at either side of the altar, while the sun appeared through the windows, colouring the bride as she advanced along the nave.

After everyone had eaten and drunk to the sound of six violins and a bagpipe, the Maturlins' Teresina danced with each of the guests and even Gavriel let himself be tempted by his adolescent sister-in-law, her cheeks afire from her emotion and her ringlets already in disorder, dazed herself by the perfume her sisters had sprinkled on her neck and her arms. Five beautiful sisters, who had not missed one dance, tall, elegant, with silk ribbons and flowers entwined in their hair. Ready to drink glass after glass, they were so able to hold both wine and grappa. Some already married and some not, but all equally desirable.

A great wedding and a great feast. Even in late afternoon, when it grew dark, dozens of torches lighted the courtyard where the horses waited, their withers steaming, and the drunken postillions snored in the cold. Luìs climbed into a sledge with his new wife wrapped in her muskrat fur and the violins began to play, all were clapping their hands as Luìs cracked the whip and the Maturlins' Teresina clung to the side of the sledge: her eyes, her fur cap, her round chin, everything exulted in her smile. Her aunt, moved, let her head drop against Maria's shoulder. She was crying.

The two sisters from Moncalvo, dazed and confused, awkward in their dark cloaks, the dark taffeta hats rumpled from all the coming and going, weakly waved their hands, Maria's shoulder stiff under the emotional weeping of the Maturlins' aunt, her own eyes smarting in the torches' smoke. And a worm inside her, a worm gnawing: the dowry.

For the Maturlins' Teresina was bringing nothing beyond the spinet and two trunks of sheets, ten damasked tablecloths when there was not a table in the house that could hold them without their dragging on the floor. Not so much as an acre of land, not even two rooms somewhere, no furniture or gold that could come in handy when times were hard. Nothing at all. And Luìs, who paid such attention to the land, to earnings and expenditures, hadn't said a word. No protest: for him it was all right like this. It would have been all right even if he had had to pay for the party, the musicians and the muskrat fur.

He had wanted the Maturlins' Teresina the moment he first saw her; and that night, when for the first time, in the light of the lamp on the chest of drawers, he felt her plump freshness in his hands, he realized he had not been wrong. With her at his side he would become a giant. Goliath.

'Goliath, Goliath? . . . Why, who is he?' Teresina looks at him, her face immediately red. They didn't want the room over the walnut tree so in the one where Luison had slept they put up wallpaper with wisteria vines. Amid the wisteria some overblown roses; and the room now seems a garden, with the bed painted white and the embroidered pillows she brought from Ivrea. On one, a house; on another, a boat; and on still another, a cat playing with a ball of yarn, all done in cross-stitch, the only stitch the Maturlins' Teresina knows. They didn't want to change the bed, either; it is the same that had harboured Luison's virginal dreams, but it is big enough for them because they sleep in each other's arms and their plan to go and buy a new one is postponed day after day.

Goliath, Luìs explains to her, was a giant, killed by David with a stone. A giant able to uproot a tree with one hand. Killed by David? Why does Luìs compare himself with a killed giant? The Maturlins' Teresina frowns, knitting her blonde eyebrows; her breath tastes of honey, her eyes that want to garner everything in their fullness stare at him, curious and a bit frightened. How to explain to her that sometimes happiness can be compared to death? Luìs slips his fingers into her hair, pulling it until it hurts her: let's look into each other's eyes, Teresina, you and I, now. Always. We will never stop, and I will not die.

In the morning she goes down to the kitchen to help Marlatteira, she dries Gonda's teary eyes that through the veil of cataracts see her like a flower, a butterfly in the rustling of her skirts. 'Csì bela . . .' the old woman says to her, 'so beautiful . . .' and wants to kiss her hand. She warms the milk if Marlatteira is outside fetching more wood, she dribbles the polenta into the boiling water and – something to which no one is accustomed in that heavy hour of silence, of melancholy at the day's beginning – she sings. The songs are French, of

ladies and knights, of kings and mistresses killed out of jealousy
with a poisoned rose; but she herself doesn't know the meaning
of the words. She has sung them always, since the time when,
as a little girl, she watched her older and beautiful sisters seated
to receive visitors. Before her aunt took her to live in Ivrea.
And even Fantina smiles when she hears her, the voice is so
well placed, without any shrill tones. Maria forgets the non-
existent dowry and asks her how she managed to embroider
those pillows so well. But everybody knows: cross-stitch is the
simplest stitch there is.

The day Bastianina arrived on vacation from the convent, the
Maturlins' Teresina was sitting under the walnut in the garden
and as she sewed, her feet shifted the gravel on the ground.
Bastianina, now named Sister Geltrude Rosalia after a saint
who had had her breasts torn off with a white-hot iron, was
disappointed. They had told her so much about Luìs's wife
that she was almost angry to see before her that round face
whose pallor made it seem swollen and the much-praised
barley-blonde hair that now hung, dull and lank, over her ears.
The Maturlins' Teresina was pregnant; and as she stirred from
that torpor that had overcome her with her needle in her
fingers, she smiled at her sister-in-law and kissed her on both
cheeks.

To please her brother, but perhaps even more because her
curiosity was piqued by that face which anxiety and joy made
so volatile, Sister Geltrude Rosalia decided to do her portrait.
She would paint it outdoors, under the walnut, where she had
seen the Maturlins' Teresina the first time.

Sister Geltrude Rosalia was tall and heavy, already majestic,
and she painted standing at her easel with a long striped apron
over her habit. The Maturlins' Teresina, seated on the wicker
chair, looked even smaller and rounder by comparison, barely
emerging from adolescence but already marked by that belly
that seemed awkward among the little flowers of her muslin
dress. To while away the posing time Teresina knitted, with

some effort because she had only recently learned how, and as she kept dropping stitches, she pursed her lips, concentrating. Sister Geltrude Rosalia saw that intent, sad face, she could catch no spark in it. Marlatteira, who had a long tongue, had told her about the five sisters, some married and some not. Sisters who apparently had the gift of ubiquity, as they were seen everywhere. It was said even that the oldest had reached America, Baltimore.

Baltimore? The Maturlins' Teresina raises her eyes, amazed, her knitting falls into her lap, Sister Geltrude Rosalia shrugs as if to say that she cares little where the Maturlin sisters go and with great care she dabs the brush in the paint. Teresina is distracted, her gaze is lost among the leaves of the pear tree opposite her.

Sister Geltrude Rosalia is the only one to see a flaw in such perfection, the point that obscures the centre. The cat comes by, rubs against Teresina's legs, Sister Geltrude Rosalia paints that cat as well and the walnut and the abandoned knitting. 'Do you like it here?' she asks. Teresina wakes from her absence and says yes many times, staring almost frightened because she can read doubt in her sister-in-law's enquiring eyes. 'And you?' she asks. 'Do you like it, in the convent?' Sister Geltrude Rosalia waits an instant before answering: the lawn, the heat, the long pears among the leaves, Luìs's wife: everything testifies to a pleasure in life so different, where even melancholy is tempered in Teresina's extreme youth. 'Of course,' she says, 'I chose it.' But this is not what interests her now, she adds, Teresina must sit a little more still, looking straight ahead as she had before.

'I feel so good here, with all of you, I'm so happy here . . .' The little dot has retreated into the background, the eyes, halfway between brown and green, smile at the sun, at the shadow of the leaves. She tells now about her life before, at her aunt's in Ivrea, she tells about the walks along the Dora when the snow is melting, the tumblers performing in the square, the concerts. The only thing lacking, she says, is music.

She took lessons and she and her teacher often played four hands, or he would play alone and she would sing, and her aunt would come in to listen and would be amazed by how well they made music together. An excellent teacher even though he was young, she says. 'How young?' asks Sister Geltrude Rosalia, pausing, brush in hand. 'Young . . . twenty, twenty-one. I don't know.' 'Twenty?' In the face framed by the veil, the eyes look at her, stern, amazed, round.

The Maturlins' Teresina has turned red, a young teacher costs much less, she explains. And what was this teacher like? Oh, very good, so good that when the Prince of Carignano paid an official visit, this young man was chosen to play Mozart. But Sister Geltrude Rosalia doesn't even know who Mozart is and she looks at Teresina suspiciously. The blush has faded from Teresina's face, she is staring absently ahead and sighs because now, she says, the teacher will have no one to play four hands with, if she had studied a little longer they might have been able to go to court and give a concert before the King. A cloud covers the sun, Teresina feels cold and her mouth loses colour, in the shadow that makes everything uniform it is pointless to go on painting and Sister Geltrude Rosalia shakes off the little summer insects that have settled on her apron. The Maturlins' Teresina stands up with some effort and smiles as she collects the cat, pressing him in the hollow between her face and neck. For Sister Geltrude Rosalia this is a revolting sight; if for her beauty must be in the perfume of incense and in shirts worn one over the other to erase all the body's shape, how can she accept this sister-in-law, in a dress so light that at every moment it displays the offended suppleness and instead of concealing her pregnancy it allows every sign of it to appear? And she has already forgotten, in the pleasure of the soft stroking of the cat, her melancholy over a music master foolish enough to have fallen in love with his young pupil.

But, in spite of everything, Sister Geltrude Rosalia wishes she would never finish the portrait and when Teresina is busy and cannot pose the painter becomes nervous and, at her easel, touches and retouches, alters, a brushstroke on the hair, another on the forefinger, on the ball of yarn. At times she rises from the table and leaves her meal half-eaten because she has thought of lightening a shadow or adding a colour to a fold; and the dish grows cold or, worse, the cat jumps on it and then everything has to be thrown out because Sister Geltrude Rosalia is repelled by animals and in cats she sees the devil.

She eats alone in the room adjoining the kitchen because the rule of her order requires silence during meals, and seated at the table by the window she hears only the clucking of the hens in the yard outside as Marlatteira sets the dishes before her and then quickly vanishes as though that solitary meal seems to her something against nature. But now that the Maturlins' Teresina is there those meals have changed, Teresina sits opposite her with her knitting in her hand and smiles when their eyes meet; that nun, tall and cumbersome, her black shoes peeping from beneath her skirt, does not frighten her. She is likeable. Sister Geltrude Rosalia shows no gratitude for this: on the contrary, she seems not to see her, the Maturlins' Teresina, at all, and she sucks her soup from the spoon; but if Teresina gets up or someone calls her, she follows the girl with her eyes until she comes and sits down again, her back to the window; the mass of her hair luminous against the barred rectangle.

At times they go out together on the road that climbs up to Lu, they walk slowly and their gaze is fixed on the outline of the Alps in the sky gripped by the sunset colours. The Maturlins' Teresina has a belly that must be burdensome to carry and her face is coming more and more to resemble an adolescent Magdalene's. Her body and its desires, the sudden shifts of her dreams appear and mar her grace. But their talk, step after step along the road, has nothing to do with bodies or with desires. They talk of God because Sister Geltrude Rosalia has got it into her head to convert her sister-in-law, so lukewarm in the practice of her religion, and as Teresina listens with widened eyes, the nun illustrates the delights of Paradise. Delights that Sister Geltrude Rosalia sees alive with fountains and spurting water, cranes, herons, flamingos with pink wings. Where there will be music also by that Mozart and other music Teresina loves, like the *Ode for Queen Anne* that she sings so well at the spinet. And the radiance of God, his mercy and his justice, are identified for Teresina with the mild radiance of the house, with the elms whose leaves have a golden shimmer, with those pinkish swords that rise high behind the Alps already in shadow. To please her Sister Geltrude Rosalia goes so far as to put the music master in Paradise too and the king before whom Teresina wanted to play four hands. As she speaks, Sister Geltrude Rosalia becomes impassioned, her cheeks are afire, and she feels as if she were already entering Paradise, leading the Maturlins' Teresina by the hand and the child in her womb, too. From time to time that baby stirs and Teresina stops, to press her hands against her belly, Sister Geltrude Rosalia has to catch her breath.

Luìs is jealous of that concord between the sisters-in-law, he distrusts his sister and warns his wife, telling her his sister is capable of spitefulness, arrogance. That she is hard, heartless. After everything Fantina did for her, now that Fantina is old, she has cast her aside like some useless object. The Maturlins' Teresina shakes her head, Luìs is mistaken, no one has ever understood Bastianina, not even her mother, who gave so much love to Gioacchino, and not even Fantina, who now moves in the impalpable world of shadows with the skill of an old watchman.

If, indeed, Fantina once talked with the seeds and the ants, now she speaks with the lights that filter through the darkness, she interrogates the black shadows that thicken in the corners and at night she never sleeps, they hear her come and go, tapping the panes with her fingers. She revolts Sister Geltrude Rosalia; seeing the old woman before her while a fly crawls over her brow or grazes the corner of her mouth and she does not trouble to brush it away, the nun is frightened. As if

Fantina's long communion with shadows prefigures a beyond quite different from the Paradise the nun describes to the Maturlins' Teresina as they walk along the road that climbs up to Lu. And when she hears the old woman coming up behind her as she is painting, she stiffens, stands immobile, without turning her head, to avoid meeting the gaze in Fantina's yellowish face, still without a wrinkle, its texture like the body of a plucked chicken. The gaze is a fissure, you have to seek it out and, once encountered, it casts a spell like the gaze of certain snakes.

Luìs is jealous of his sister, but Sister Geltrude Rosalia feels herself flush fiercely, when her brother takes his wife by the waist and kisses her in public. A scandal. Something unheard of, never before seen in this house. She furiously looks away, and her tread on the stairs makes the railing shake. Then, once upstairs, she cannot resist, and through the parted shutters she looks down and wrings her hands, hearing their voices, picturing their smiles and their expressions of complicity.

And at evening when the Maturlins' Teresina sits at the spinet in her pretty dress of white muslin and the earrings Luìs ordered for her, two gold daisies with a little ruby in the centre, the nun quickly sits down on the stool beside her, before her brother can come, her habit falling over the seat, her veil askew, her big black shoes planted, possessively, beside Teresina's feet, on the pedals of the spinet. She has a great passion for the music created by the plump fingers of the youngest Maturlin, by her well-placed voice. For Handel, for Frescobaldi, and for that Mozart whose name Teresina pronounces with such respect. She questions, she seeks information between pieces and Teresina explains the notes on the page, bending the blonde head close to hers, she feels her light breath, that perfume of apples that always accompanies the young sister-in-law as if her two breasts, which the muslin is no longer able to repress, were apples, too. Teresina's finger follows the lines while, in the light of the candles on either side of the spinet, her lips, full and pale, reveal her teeth like a wolf cub's.

Through the open window the night air enters mixed with petunias and roses, vanilla flowers, and a distant, warm odour of stable. Sister Geltrude Rosalia has never known such evenings, and before going to bed, kneeling on the floor, she folds her hands to thank God.

The Maturlins' Teresina died in childbirth on February 18th, 1844. Two nights earlier there was a heavy snowfall, which then continued the next morning, and in the afternoon, with Luìs, she took a brief turn about the garden now plunged into silence. The snow weighed down the branches, bending them, and at the slightest sway, or at a louder tone of voice, it fell in pure white clumps. And when Gavriel came back with the horse, which had to struggle up the drive, they sat, all three, on the little wall, which they had cleared as best they could. It was a bright afternoon, warm as always after a snow, and the sun appeared for a moment to outline shadows on the white, still intact. Gavriel was in a good mood and as he recounted Zanzìa's love affairs, she sat and watched the two brothers laugh, her shoulders wrapped in her shawl.

At dawn the first pains began, by evening the Maturlins' Teresina was already cold, her flesh taking on the damp, hard consistency of death as Marlatteira, weeping, wiped up the blood that had dripped on the floor through the mattress. Outside the snow had been swept from the path and was piled up at the edges, the glow of the lamps lighted in the front hall fell on the whiteness crystallized by frost. In the house there was an uninterrupted to-and-fro, footsteps, iron basins being replaced and drawers that creaked and scraped in the search for some object or other, some article of clothing. Bodiless voices as if the words had been distorted joined a grim bass sound, insane, prolonged, as a new smell, horrible because it resembled no other, filtered from the room where Teresina had been laid out, among the walls covered with paper with wisteria vines and, at intervals, overblown roses.

*

Sister Geltrude Rosalia had already returned to the convent in October and all this time had done nothing but think of her sister-in-law and their strolls at dusk when they talked about God and the Maturlins' Teresina listened to her with such attention. In chapel, during morning Mass or when she said her Office in the early darkness of the evening, her thoughts sped to their footsteps on the road marked by wagons, to the dusty hedges, to Teresina's voice filled with amazement and wonder, the questions she was so proud to answer. A Maturlin girl to whom they had taught so little of Paradise and so much of earth and who thought she could reconcile earth and Paradise, if only her mind were alert enough. Between verses of the psalm, in the darkness of the pews barely illuminated by the candles, her gaze reconstructed the image of Teresina with her back to the window and her knitting in her plump hands, her silent smile in the sound of the cutlery against the plate. She felt again the subtle anguish when she saw her stand and the skirt brushed against the table. The dark spot in her gaze that only the nun had seen and had tried to repeat on the canvas, she had grown angry with her paints, had maltreated her brushes. For the first time, that summer she had felt incapable, clumsy in the face of that little device like the delicate heart of a watch that she could not recapture in its oscillations; and the Maturlin she had painted had portrayed the one all of them saw. Gavriel, Fantina, Maria, Luìs. Blind Luìs, who had not noticed the dark spot, the cleft that opened in the green-brown surface of Teresina's gaze. The sudden faltering of the foot.

When the news of her death reached the convent, Sister Geltrude Rosalia was in bed with fever and the Mother Superior, fearing that sorrow would bring about a worsening of her condition, said nothing. When she made up her mind later, the Maturlins' Teresina had been in the ground for a month and the baby to whom they had given the name Pietro Giuseppe was amazing everyone with his vigour, as he kicked in his swaddling-clothes.

Sister Geltrude Rosalia came out of the Mother Superior's parlour as if in a dream; and as in one of those nightmares, endless, that paralyze the legs, she tried to combat the unreality. The door closed behind her and she was alone in the long corridor where, at the end, a window opened onto the uniform sky, grey as dirty fleece. She had difficulty remaining on her feet, so overwhelming was the desire to fling herself on the ground and cry, outstretched there, with the dust of the floor in her mouth. Her hands had turned to ice and all her blood had flowed to her face, which was scorching her, or perhaps the blood crashed this way and that in her breast shaken by sobs that emitted no sound. I want to die, she thought, I want to die, and what seemed to her the most terrible thing was not having known it when it happened, to have gone on nourishing herself with broths and purées, calm and blissful between her sheets, even polite with the lay-sisters who emptied her chamber pot, she was so pleased to lie there thinking of next summer, of all the things that she and Teresina had to say to each other about God and about Mozart. And with the falling snow she had been glad, all that snow covered the roads, she imagined the Maturlins' Teresina with the baby tight in her arms looking at the swirling flakes. A plump, big baby like the angels supporting the holy-water font in the cathedral.

Now she wishes never to see that baby. In her mind he is ugly and hairy, a stray dog, a cat. She clasps her hands in the chapel but what comes from her mouth is not prayers, and as her sisters chant the Angelus or the responses to the Confiteor, from her lips fall infected words, ulcerated with grief. She is still weak and the perfume of the incense makes her faint, she staggers, her hands are unable to clutch the pew, her knees strike the ground hard.

Trying to distract her, the Mother Superior asks her to paint the Presentation of the Virgin Mary in the Temple for the coming May novena. She sits at her easel, her empty gaze fixed on the flat countryside where the farms surface amid broad puddles of water. She looks at the row of poppies, slender and fragile, stirred only by the heavy flight of the crows; and on the canvas appear emerald fields at sunset, the edge of the Alps, and the road pale with dust, the corn ripe for harvesting. The brush moves tirelessly and the maiden who climbs the long staircase of the Temple is the Maturlins' Teresina, barefoot, to enter Paradise; and as she works, Sister Geltrude Rosalia weeps, the tears trickle down into the paints, are kneaded into the colours on the canvas. But neither God nor those paints can bring the Maturlins' Teresina back to life or make Time retrace its steps now that it has seized her hair and dragged her far away. Give back even just one of those footsteps along the road towards Lu.

The picture is so ugly that the Mother Superior doesn't want it for the chapel, she wants a proper Madonna with veil and blue dress, a crown of stars; and she orders Sister Geltrude Rosalia to paint on the other side of the canvas some lovely bird, a crane or heron like those she painted in the past that so pleased the Bishop. She will forgo the Presentation in the Temple. Sister Geltrude Rosalia must obey if she wants ever to become Abbess. But Sister Geltrude Rosalia wants only to die and she is the first to come down with typhoid, which till then had spared the Novi Convent.

The higher the fever rises, the more pleased she is, in her delirium she talks with the Maturlins' Teresina and they say the most foolish things to each other, it seems the two of them are going to pick the *rusnent* apples from the tree at the end of the garden, Teresina climbs up among the branches despite all her skirts, and the first things to fall are her handsome kid boots, then the apples also roll down. She calls up to her, but Teresina is no longer in the tree, there is Gioacchino, and it is not true that Gioacchino flies, he comes down like lead and makes a deafening noise, the noise of an avalanche, of a torrent that has burst through its embankments.

Poor Sister Geltrude Rosalia, who screams in the middle of the night and no longer has a hair on her head, all left on her pillow because of the typhoid, while the new growth is a baby chick's down on her round skull. From home they send her wine and salami, eggs and a whole turkey that she doesn't even touch, thinking of the Maturlins' Teresina dead in childbirth at eighteen. And when the organist Sister comes to visit she asks her about Mozart and if by chance she knows his *Turkish March*. He was a German, the organist Sister tells her, and wrote some shameful works.

The muskrat fur was given to the oldest Maturlin sister, who asked for it, it would not have fit anyone, cut as it was to the measure of a slim, round body. Since she was taking the fur, Teresina's sister asked also for the cap and the muff, which completed the *parure*, and she tried them all on in front of the bedroom mirror among the wisteria vines interrupted by overblown roses. She didn't see Pietro Giuseppe because he was with his wet-nurse in the hills but she was assured he was well and Luìs went up every week to see him. The oldest Maturlin sister would also gladly have taken the spinet, she let her fingers run over it, and said that there, in that living-room, the damp would ruin it. 'Does anyone in the house play it?' she asked, looking at Luìs, her upper lip barely raised to show her teeth, because if not, she added, sooner or later it would be ruined completely: the lip relaxed in a sad, sweet smile.

Luìs, who had looked at her in silence, as she turned before the mirror in the fur, breathtakingly beautiful with her immense blue eyes peering from the thick fur, refused to give it to her. He refused her the dresses, the cashmere shawl bought on their wedding trip, and even one of the cushions embroidered in cross-stitch that she wanted as a memento. Nobody invited her to stay and drink a glass of muscatel and taste the cake that Marlatteira had just taken from the oven. Nobody offered her a chair or asked for news of her aunt and her sisters. The house seemed uninhabited and Luìs, his mother, and Fantina all on the verge of leaving it, too; in the end the oldest Maturlin went off along the path among the bare trees, soiling her boots in the mire left by the snow, taking little steps like a great lady, enfolded in the muskrat fur, the cap engulfing her little, frozen ears. She was followed by the boy who had come along to carry the 'weight', a big bundle in which she had folded her old cloak; from it hung the creased ribbons of a bonnet.

Gavriel, who encountered her as he came along the drive, turned red with shame because they were allowing a woman to go off alone, not even accompanying her. But his heart leapt when he recognized the fur and the cap and he also said nothing to her, merely doffing his hat for a moment. Followed by the boy, she took no notice of the curtness of that greeting and gave Gavriel the same sad, sweet smile she had addressed to Luìs: the Maturlins forgave everything, slights, crudeness, bigotry. They were women of the world.

As soon as Luìs saw her vanish with the light sound of her heels, he went to the spinet and replaced the strip of felt on the keys. Standing at the kitchen door, Marlatteira looked at him. '*Al'è bela acmè ina Madona*,' she said, 'Beautiful as a Madonna.' She was holding the cake on a plate and clearly she would gladly have asked him some questions about that visitor; but the sharp report of the lid being closed arrested them on her lips.

The day word came of new cases of cholera in the province, Gavriel set off with the cart to bring Pietro Giuseppe home. It had always been Gavriel, when Luìs could no longer find the time, who went up every week to the farm where the baby stayed with his nurse, and he had enjoyed bouncing the boy on his knees, watching him take his first steps.

They reached home towards evening. Pietro Giuseppe was sleeping in a basket and Limasa sat beside him, her legs hanging from the cart; without waiting for the mare to stop, she jumped down and looked around with curiosity: this was the first time she crossed the threshold of a *particulare*'s house. She was barefoot, wearing her only dress, and when she saw underthings spread out on the grass she burst out laughing because she didn't know what they were. She scratched her head and then ate what was caught under her fingernails.

This habit was the hardest to rid her of. The peasants who had adopted her had given her the nickname *Limasa*, which means snail, because she did everything at an invincibly slow, stubborn pace. Neither yells nor blows would stir her, and yet Gavriel sensed the possibilities hidden behind her slow movement, her sluggish steps. He admired the promptness with which she avoided the hand raised to hit her and the flash of intelligence that flared up in her crossed eyes as soon as she realized that Gavriel was on her side. And she had not lost sight of him for a moment, as in thick dialect, almost incomprehensible, she repeated obsessively: take me with you, take me with you.

She was thirteen and, at first, she spoke to no one. Her task was to care for Pietro Giuseppe and at dawn she was already in the barn waiting for them to give her the baby's milk. She bathed him in a zinc tub, testing the water's temperature with her tongue, and she changed him several times a day, revealing a great love for perfection; and when she put him to sleep, rocking him, with little prayers, her hand brushed away the flies as if, instead of Luìs's son, the cradle held the Dauphin of France. Every time she lifted him in her arms it looked as if she would collapse under his weight but instead she went on and on tirelessly, her feet thrust into an old pair of slippers. At times she set him astride her shoulders and trotted up and down the drive, Pietro Giuseppe laughing and she laughing with him. The truth of the matter was that she had liked the baby from the first moment whereas the house and the *particulari* had disappointed her. They were, after all, the same as everybody else, they ate, they cleaned their teeth with their fingernails, they snored, and their shit was emptied into the compost heap along with the others'. And the house, when the wind blew from the direction of the stable, stank like the farmhouse where Gavriel had found her.

In the space of a few years the thin and silent child of that July afternoon developed into a big girl with flesh solid as if they had moulded her in plaster and a broad face where the smallpox scars had dilated like little craters. Her loud and resonant voice was never still and her prayers had been replaced by a repertory that ranged from *Cavalier Franseis* to Carnival songs.

When Luìs went off as a volunteer, in March of '48, she learned the alphabet along with Pietro Giuseppe, the grammar book open on the table in the room where once Sister Geltrude Rosalia had eaten, looking at the Maturlins' Teresina.

Pietro Giuseppe is a precocious child and even though he is only four he follows with attention the letters that accompany the illustrations. Into the room, as in the past, comes the clucking of hens from the yard, but the two of them never raise their heads, stubbornly determined to understand. Pietro Giuseppe's head is round, like his uncle Gavriel's, and like Sacarlott's before him. Shaven because of lice, somewhere between brown and blond. He has inherited almost nothing from his mother and resembles her only in his voice, the ease with which he picks up any tune. He has only to hear a song once and he can hum it through while he sits on the floor playing.

The morning his father left for the war he was asleep with Limasa and Luìs went off without saying goodbye to him. It was dawn and in the square Zanzìa's cart was waiting, for he had offered to carry the volunteers as far as Alessandria. To see Luìs off only Gavriel had come, he was hatless and the gusts of March wind ruffled his hair as the cocks cried from one chicken run to another. Zanzìa, who was offering transport out of love for the fatherland, expected something from Luìs and looked at his hands, his pockets. But Luìs had other things on his mind, he stared at his brother, shivering in the middle of the square, and his eyes still narrow with sleep, he asked

Gavriel to look after his son and the land. Absolution for this choice that was his alone. And as from the end of the square other young men began to appear with bundles under their arms, with mothers and sisters accompanying them, Gavriel made a sign with his hand: he promised. Then, before the other volunteers arrived, he turned on his heel and retraced the climb towards home.

Maria was in the study, betrayed by Luìs's departure: he had abandoned everything to go off and get himself shot by the Austrians, the guardians of order. Before the two brothers had even reached the square, she was already rummaging among her son's papers to find a culprit, who and what had driven him to the subversive decision that left the house and a baby in the care of two women alone. Because there was never any relying on Gavriel, always off night and day on his horse.

But the books are no help either; they all deal with agronomy and have clear and familiar illustrations: grain, animals, plants. Where had Luìs found that desire to kill and to get himself killed, surely enemies come from elsewhere like that *franseis* who had once lured Pidrèn away, only to leave him worse off than a peasant. And when Limasa looks in at the door, holding Pietro Giuseppe by the hand, Maria yells at her to cover the child, what is he doing here barefoot. Limasa is frightened. He's gone, he's gone, Maria shouts; she can already see poverty, the livestock all scrawny, the dark, cold evenings.

Limasa runs into the kitchen, pulling the child after her, she slips on his stockings, two wool undershirts, one over the other, and then together they eat milk and polenta as the first sun glides, golden, over the copper pans hanging from their hooks. Her tears dry quickly, they laugh and kick under the table. '*Smettla!*' Limasa says, pulling her chair back, 'Stop it!' Now they play the looking-into-the-eyes game, the loser is the one who blinks first, she thinks that she has never seen eyes so grey and she would like to call Pietro Giuseppe *Grisòn*. But Luìs will not have it, he insists on the whole name, like a king's. And now Luìs has gone off, maybe he will die and never come back. '*Bel Grisòn*,' she says to him, giving the child a loud kiss on his mouth smeared with polenta.

Maria and Fantina are still picking up Luìs's papers, which have dropped on the floor, Luìs who believes an Italy exists and must be put back together, piece by piece. Maria's hands tremble as they move, piling up books and notebooks together; Fantina collects a page, replaces a pencil, stoppers an ink bottle. She feels no sorrow for her sister, but rather perhaps a keen and subtle pleasure as her narrowed gaze perceives the dishevelled hair, the wrinkles around the mouth, the trembling hands. What does she want, what is Maria still looking for, as in the days when she proceeded with confidence in her beauty and no one could resist her? Fantina has other treasures and she preserves them with the violin in the case lined with red plush which the moths have consumed until it is impalpable; and beneath her pale, full brow, a fat brow if a brow can be fat, her thoughts teem like a hive of bees, accumulating and working in a continuous bustle.

Luìs is already far away, beyond the cemetery where his young wife was buried wearing the dress she had worn that day in Ivrea when she passed through the coloured lights of the nave and the candlelight flickered on her mouth. The dress that was rumpled as all those hands clasped her by the waist, sweating, and the hem was torn; someone in the enthusiasm of the dance had trampled on it. Luìs has not shaved and he will never shave again; when he comes home, Pietro Giuseppe will have a hard time recognizing him; and as the climb at San Salvatore makes the horses slow down, the sharp cold of the dawn gives way to a warmth of sun, the white pigeons fly off from the roofs to go and peck in the fields. More volunteers scramble aboard at San Salvatore, at Castelletto, Val Madonna, and instead of going to the war they seem to be going to a fair, the boys sing *Dona lumbarda/ Spuséme mì, spuséme mì* . . . Marry me, Lombard woman, and at every stop the women offer wine, eggs, apples and there is no understanding why, but Luìs is the first one they offer their gifts to. The sun is high and far off you can see the land just emerged from the snow and here and there the first wheat can be glimpsed like a fuzz. The spire with the onion dome is lost behind the hills, but you can still see, with its tall, twisted elm, the Maturlin farmhouse that a man from Alessandria has bought, to make bricks from its clayey soil.

The Maturlins' Teresina had her back to him the first time Luìs climbed up there. Word had spread that the six sisters needed money and would sell everything cheap, he had ridden up behind Gavriel and while his brother went down towards the vineyards, he headed for the shed. She had her back turned, an image against the light, in the glow from the sun outside, like an omen, her progress towards the darkness and the unknown. Nothing had yet begun and the farewell was already there, in that shed cluttered with wagon shafts, wheels with broken spokes, rusted harrows; such for years had been the Maturlins' neglect (six beautiful girls who thought only of dancing, dressing up, curling their hair with the iron, and not one ever found an hour to sit at the table and do the accounts. Not even the youngest, the one that an aunt in Ivrea had taken to live with her to save her at least from ruin). But then Teresina turned and Luìs saw her face in her blonde hair, she spoke to him, calling him Sir, determined to do her part in the best possible way, to sell the land and pay those who were owed money. 'Sir . . .' She showed him the fields, she who understood nothing of the country, and the withered vines, the elm, and everything reflected in her gaze became beautiful; such had been the love of life in the youngest Maturlin when she studied music and played four hands. With her he had felt a giant. Their life could be long and full, a rock where each event marks a different time, the house could be full of voices, of the red *salvia splendens* and of running footsteps. 'Sir . . .' To go back to that point, to start again from there. Once more; even just for one instant. One.

What kind of love can be borne towards a son who has cost a separation so abrupt and complete? Who has divided the happiness of the *before* from the unhappiness of the *after*?

5

BRAIDA

The '48 war was a blessing for Fracin's Rosetta. If it wasn't Lamarmora's sharpshooters, it was Ramorino's infantry, or, still more, the Royal Cavalry; Camurà hardly had time to go and buy his bolts of cloth before he needed the same amount again, the wear and tear on uniforms was so great, the burns from grazing bullets or simply the rubbing of saddles. But, above all, the increasing numbers of sharpshooters, infantrymen, light cavalry.

Camurà couldn't stay home two days in a row, and when he did arrive there were accounts to check and visits to receive, of people who had already decided to absolve him of his sins. Corpulent gentlemen come to talk with him about silk spinning, others want to interest him in cattle or ask for his contribution to the restoration of a chapel; and all admire the tile stoves, the warmth of the rooms, the oak, the lovely wife. Camurà is flattered by their interest, and even if he occasionally taps his foot impatiently on the floor, he has little time left for his wife and he cannot pay much attention to her. He tries to divine her thoughts, to learn where her hopes are directed when she gazes absently out the window or stares, spellbound, into the void.

And then there is a constant passage of troops and of Royal Highnesses with their suites, mounted messengers raising so much dust that the road is obscured. Wagons of provender, soldiers asking for something to drink; who can notice Gavriel's horse, the sound of his footsteps on the gravel at night? What Fracin's Rosetta has desired for such a long time, what had seemed impossible, can, on the contrary, now happen. She can say tomorrow, Wednesday, Saturday. She and Gavriel together for a whole night, to make love and sleep, to wake and make love and then sleep again and turn in sleep to kiss a hand, an arm, a mouth. In Camurà's big walnut bed the night has a different pace, very long and brief, so brief it hardly exists and at the first light of dawn she gets up to open the shutters and looks at Gavriel's curly head on the pillow, his body relaxed in sleep. That body starts if she touches it, the fright of an animal surprised in its den, and she laughs, her mouth is light, a little cold from the dawn.

What Maria says is true, nobody can rely on Gavriel because for one of those nights he is willing to sell his soul. He forgets Pietro Giuseppe, the land, his mother; and Maria's heart pounds when she hears him at dusk, his boots impatient on the bricks of the path, his voice giving some hasty order to Gerumin, who will never carry it out for it is clear to all that nothing matters to Gavriel any more and his thoughts are already racing ahead of the horse on the high road. He is already there in the night, in Camurà's bed. Maria bows her head over her solitaire to deceive her anxiety with superstition: there, if the Ace of Coins now turns up, Gavriel will return at daybreak, but if the card that comes out is a Knight then he will be later. And if the Queen of Swords appears then something will happen to him and her hands cannot repress their trembling, she prays God to make that card disappear from the deck, she blasphemes a little, such had always been and still was the nature of the two sisters from Moncalvo. God and the cards must now have pity on her son, less prudent every day as if the war allowed everything, and licit and illicit could be confused.

Sometimes, in Camurà's bed, Gavriel wakes with his fingers still entwined in those of Fracin's Rosetta and he remembers the night of the flood when he carried her to safety on his back and through the soaked clothing he felt her body for the first time. He speaks to her softly, his mouth against her ear, he speaks to her of that current that wanted to drag her off, the cold that made it still harder to hold out, everyone was afraid of seeing them vanish at any moment and they, on the contrary, felt so alive, it began then . . . She turns and her eyes open in the face buried in her hair, they look at him, full of sleep, in the light of the *veilleuse*. But words do not exist to tell of the tree that has put down its roots in Gavriel's heart and tears trickle down his cheeks because for him everything is Fracin's Rosetta.

Their story is a noose, it was born with no hope and no future and soon, in the bed that Gavriel has just left, Camurà will return, tireless in making money and love. Jealousy is lying in wait for Gavriel the moment he mounts his horse and it dogs him, perverse, at every step. Through the rooms of the house, in the fields, and then at evening it is still there to torment him when he sits with Fantina, her eyes glistening from wine, and Maria lays out the cards on the table, talking to herself. Gavriel could drink like his aunt, who on certain evenings staggers out of the room and sings softly as if she still had to tuck in Giai's blankets, comb his fine curls. But Gavriel is spare with food and wine, the years spent with Mandrognin have taught him to nourish himself on little, to be satisfied with half a glass. He doesn't want to forget; and even if he is jealous of Camurà he still doesn't want to forget because the feeling born and grown for Fracin's Rosetta is his very breath. Can a man live without breathing, without feeling the air in his lungs even if it stings like the air of glaciers?

Meanwhile there is Goito, and Peschiera, Pastrengo, Camurà hasn't a moment's respite and he goes from Biella to Cremona, where he buys his wife a moiré dress and a tortoiseshell comb. He is in Milan, Pavia, and from each journey he brings back presents, grander and grander, cockades and tricolour ribbons. One night's sleep, a glance at his wife as she tries on the dress and gathers her heavy, tawny hair in the little tortoiseshell comb. The war will end soon, soon and badly because the army is poor and with a great confusion of people, Tuscans, Neapolitans, languages they don't understand even among themselves while the Austrians who come down from Verona have gleaming uniforms, weapons that fire at the first try and Feldmarschalls marked by glorious scars. Piedmont and her King are insects that stain the lapel of the jacket, to be brushed aside with a well-aimed, precise blow. But meanwhile he is making more and more money and his wife will have time to enjoy it later, as soon as the Austrians have put order in this new Babel. Then, too, new uniforms will be needed and the fashion will change, he is already prepared, in contact with the importers of English wools, cashmeres so light that you don't even feel them on your body. Rosetta is a lucky woman, where can you find a husband who comes home each time with so many presents, dresses that reflect the colour of the sky, silk shawls as wide as sheets? And one day he will take her to live in Alessandria in a palace with a balcony overlooking the gardens, the daughter of that anarchist blacksmith who wouldn't accept money from royalists or even from priests, and in the end had no money from anybody.

But now we must not think of what will be, who can know destiny, who knows how and where events will be superimposed on preconceived images; life fades and allows what was hidden to appear. Fracin's Rosetta strokes the horse down at the river, it is a hot summer, and the corn grows tall, they go down where the herons nest and the water opens out in a hundred rills among the stones, the sultriness makes her head swim. They go into the water and Fracin's Rosetta has feet that are broad and pink while Gavriel's have nails as thick as his horse's hoofs. Feet that are embarrassing, but the intimacy of their bodies is deep, knows no modesty, and their feet touch, follow one another, caress as the stream breaks transparently at their ankles. Fracin's Rosetta is light-hearted and Gavriel follows her obediently, she wets her legs, her face, her neck.

She undresses, her clothes make a little pile on the stones. Yes, they have what many have never had, not Fantina or Giai, not even Pidrèn. Nor Sister Geltrude Rosalia, who, exhausted by the heat, took off her veil and from the distance watched her brother dancing at Braida.

Luìs earned a medal in the war for having killed two Uhlans and putting a third to flight. This happened at Valeggio when he found himself facing three Austrians and he ran two of them through with his bayonet, the third dashed off towards the Mincio. He gave chase but his thinner leg made him stumble and the Uhlan disappeared into the brush along the shore.

These were the first men Luìs killed and he did it as he would have hit some sparrows with his slingshot, but when he stood up again, full of anger because the third had escaped him and he saw the two on the ground, suddenly they seemed unreal to him. The day was unreal and so was the sun high among the trees. His first impulse was to run away and not see them; but the corporal and his soldiers were awaiting an order. And Luìs sent them off to hunt for the third Uhlan; then he leaned against a wall and wept at his fear that was past. His horror at those disembowelled bodies.

General D'Arvillars, who was passing by those parts with his aides and had seen everything from afar, reined in his horse at the farm where Luìs, leaning against a wall, was weeping. The general asked his full name, regiment and birthplace; he did not see the tears, or pretended not to see them, and promised him the medal. At that moment the soldiers came back from the embankment empty-handed, there was no trace of the third Uhlan, perhaps he was already on the other side of the river. And Luìs's joy was so great that he embraced one of the soldiers. From the height of his saddle, General D'Arvillars smiled benevolently, convinced that this joy was because of the promised medal.

All this and more Luìs wrote in a long letter to his brother. Gavriel held Pietro Giuseppe on his knees and read it to him slowly, word by word. Fantina wanted to hear it, too, and also Maria sat and listened, one hand covering her face. When Gavriel had finished reading he carried his nephew to the great map spread out on the table in the living-room and Pietro Giuseppe stuck a little tricolour flag on Valeggio and another on Goito.

After that letter for many weeks there was no word from Luìs; the news that did arrive, confused and contradictory, spoke of Austrian troops descending in ever greater numbers and the little flags that had advanced so boldly began to prick the map farther and farther back. And when Sister Geltrude Rosalia arrived on her vacation that map disappeared because she would hear no talk of the war. All Freemasons, Carbonari and bandits, Luìs included.

Pietro Giuseppe calls her the *Magna Munja*, which means the aunt nun, and he doesn't want her even to touch him. Still, for her nephew Sister Geltrude Rosalia has a love similar to a dog's for its master, a servile and blind love. But if Pietro Giuseppe remains seated in his highchair, which she has set beside her easel, it is only out of fear; and he, always so talkative, is dumb, his broad grey eyes filled with alarm. The more Sister Geltrude Rosalia tries to pet him, the more he makes himself tiny, cold, insignificant. He doesn't even look at what she is painting and the colours that she puts in his hand, carmine, blue, green, golden yellow, also remain inert in his fingers, the white pages forgotten in his lap. Poor *ninin*, Sister Geltrude Rosalia says to him, taking his silence for an orphan's sadness. Poor *ninin*, and she clasps him to her bosom.

It is her smell that he cannot bear, the smell of flesh that never receives the light and follows its cycle in darkness. A smell connected with that of the flowers rotting in the vases in front of the Maturlin girl's tomb, where Sister Geltrude Rosalia takes him to pray and, kneeling on the ground, chants the *De Profundis*. The metal wreath propped against the tomb is dull with dust, and as the wasps that have nested in a corner of the grille light on Sister Geltrude Rosalia's veil, he raises his eyes to the stars Sacarlott had painted against the blue of the ceiling. He looks and looks at them to prevent that lump in his throat from turning into tears. But sometimes they flow anyway, desolate, down his cheeks, and then the Magna Munja interrupts her prayers and bends down to console him, stifling him with her veil. Her smell blinds him with anger, he clenches his fists and pushes her away with concentrated strength, filled with rage.

Lightning bolts dart through the barred windows, doors slam, and water pours down in torrents from the drainpipes that cannot manage to contain it. By now the war is coming to an end, the King of Sardinia's army is routed, and the soldiers are coming home under a storm that sends roof-tiles flying, one of those August storms that find the ditches dry and fill them, making the river dangerous. In Milan the crowd has insulted Carlo Alberto and some stones have been flung at the palace where he has shut himself up. The King left at night in the silence of the stars, only the trampling of the horses along the empty streets and the hollow rotation of the wheels of the carriages. Fear is now a flood-wave and it strikes those who stay and those who leave, fear of the death that has just passed and of that which is still to come. And like so many years before, at the time of the Revolution that sent sovereigns and priests to their death, Maria wants to hide the seeds, the sacks of wheat. Wall up the wine-cellar.

General Salasco has signed the armistice and Radetzky's Austrians have come back to Milan, they are in Modena, in Reggio Emilia. Garibaldi has withdrawn beyond the Ticino, and once the great storm has passed the August heat has returned; but there is still no news of Luìs. Some say they saw him in Milan, some that he has gone with Garibaldi beyond the river. Some San Salvatore infantrymen, passing Zanzìa's house one night, say Luìs has crossed the border, he is in France. In Paris perhaps, Sister Geltrude Rosalia says, looking Pietro Giuseppe in the eyes, do you know, sweet *ninin*, where Paris is? And her hand dismisses Luìs, dispels him beyond the Alps blurred by the day's haze. But that evening, when Limasa puts him to bed, Pietro Giuseppe asks how many more days the Magna Munja will stay on her vacation, how many days before she goes back to the convent. '*Spussa*,' he says to Limasa, who scolds him, 'She smells . . .'

August is not yet over when, one afternoon, Limasa comes running in, to shout that Luìs is arriving, they've seen him on the Occimiano road, maybe he's already in the town. She washes Pietro Giuseppe's face while Maria takes an umbrella against the sun and rushes towards the square; and as she passes, she says to the women, left and right, who look at her, so unused to seeing her: 'Luìs is back! He's back . . .' then she flushes with embarrassment but also with joy. And fear, of seeing him return with a leg missing, his head wounded.

But Luìs has come home all in one piece and he sits beneath the walnut, unshaven, his face baked by the sun, his body lean as if he had kept it in salt, his uniform tattered. As a present for his son he has brought two Cossacks carved from wood and painted with the colours of the Tsar Alexander. They have tunics with fur and shakos, but Pietro Giuseppe hardly dares to touch them. He has never received such a beautiful present, the Cossacks can raise and lower their arms, they move one foot forward, then the other.

Luìs tells the assembled family about the three days at Sommacampagna without water and without food as the soldiers fell to the ground exhausted, their mouths twisted in thirst. Others, he tells, went crazy when the sun set, and ran straight towards the enemy, the Austrian cannons swept them away amid the dust and smoke. Nobody came to collect the wounded, who called and called, while their companions wept at their side. He sucked the grass he managed to pull from the ground, he dug with his nails to find some dampness. Now he supports his temples with his fingers; the sun, he says, the sun . . . Gavriel, Fantina look at him. Maria is red with the happiness of seeing him there safe, she thinks of nothing else.

A sun that in the morning began to rise again and hammered dully in the veins, the wounded who had not died during the night moaned more and more faintly, the others covered their faces with handkerchiefs to keep the flies from tormenting them. Poor army, the wagons of provisions lost along the way, ending up God knows where, to fill the bellies of shirkers and thieves.

Sister Geltrude Rosalia has stood up, her broad white back and her veil sway under the pergola beneath the tender green of the vine shoots, then disappear into the darkness of the apple trees. She doesn't want to stay and hear Luìs, her convent was sacked by the 'rebels' and among them were also soldiers of the King; who knows? perhaps her brother was also off robbing somewhere, who can say where those two handsome wooden soldiers came from, those Cossacks, toys suited to a little prince? Who knows where? And now she doesn't feel safe even at home.

But she is mistaken, the war has made Luìs forget many things and has made him recall others again. He is still young and if he glances at himself in the mirror he sees a man who does not look thirty, tall, slim, with a sparse beard from which a thin mouth emerges, restless and prompt. No one could explain just what makes Luìs so interesting, even to married women, what provokes such expectation at the dances where he has begun to appear again with his fanciful hats pushed back on his curls.

Once again Luìs has a girl here and one there, the names are never uttered in the house as is only proper with girls who follow the dancing from village to village and are not shy about talking to a newcomer. So much the better, Maria says, better than those great loves that bring only turmoil and sorrow. But

Sister Geltrude Rosalia, who is now known to all as the Magna Munja, a title that enthrones her like a Carolingian king, feels her heart contract when she sees Pietro Giuseppe learning to count with the tutor, poor country priest in his long black habit, spattered with stains. She is hurt by that voice assuming a stentorian tone to teach that child seated facing the abacus. All of them learned to count from their father, this is shameful. Luìs's betrayal of his son seems to her a double betrayal, which erases every mark, every shadow and sign of that young wife. Every ribbon gathering dust on the bottom of a drawer. And a blow straight to the heart when the tutor opens the spinet and with his thick fingers presses on the C, the G, the F sharp, presuming, that son of poor farmhands, to teach the wondrous thing that was the music that came from the fingers of the youngest Maturlin. Then her voice becomes even more shrill and, with the authority of the habit she wears, she issues orders left and right. Also to the tutor, who because of the little benefice he enjoys and could quite possibly not enjoy tomorrow is easily terrified by the cries of the landowners.

Because the Magna Munja is climbing, one by one, the steps of power; not yet thirty, she is the favourite of the Mother Superior, and when the priest welcomes her at the rectory, he puts on the cassock reserved for special occasions. Her exercise of power has even managed to change the subject of the pictures she paints in her hours of leisure. No cranes now, or herons with pink wings, or swans with eyes circled in black, but grapes, peaches, pomegranates with fiery seeds, and in the roundness of that fruit, her soul, a secret and intense place, bursts out like a churning river. But that soul is also innocent and, unaware, she paints voluptuously, breathing through her nostrils, moaning, as the colours are revealed, heavy and bright. And if she is interrupted, she raises her eyes, a gaze lost, limp, beneath her lashes.

Pictures destined to disturb cardinals and bishops of un-known identity because no one yet knows which lucky prelates are to untie the great canvas bundles, wrapping after wrapping, to arrive at those fruits that seem to exude their bitter juice. Not even Fantina knows their names, perhaps the Magna Munja whispers them into Pietro Giuseppe's ear: this one is for the Archbishop Romilli, this for Cardinal di Bianzè. This one will be seen by the Pope, and her voice quivers with pleasure.

The winter that followed was very cold, the rivers froze and the snow made the roof of the stable cave in, a cow and two calves were crushed and their moans were heard for a long time in the night.

That day, too, Fracin's last son died, Camurà's brother-in-law. They found him the next morning on his horse with the snow up to his belly, and they had to break his legs to get him into the coffin he had become so hard. Camurà sent word that his wife could not come to the burial, the roads are too dangerous he told Tambiss to say, the old pedlar who still made his rounds selling underwear. And Tambiss told everybody about the drawers with lace, the silken *intimes* that Camurà ordered every time for his wife.

Few went to the burial, the cold had frozen the hinges of the gate fast and the coffin was unloaded outside the cemetery, to wait for better weather. The tutor, because by now the priest rarely attended burials, ran off in haste on the pretext of a lesson with Pietro Giuseppe and the moment he entered the house he glued himself to the stove, his cassock steaming. Only Mandrognin stayed with the casket to make sure no wolves came at sunset. He had been Fracin's friend in his youth and had held the dead man on his lap as a boy and as the sun began to withdraw in a livid stripe on the horizon, he began to sing softly as in the days when he had bounced the baby on his knees. And Tambiss, going home on his cart, took fright and from the distance threatened him with his whip. Mandrognin didn't budge; and when he was sure that the wolves would no longer come he slipped on the snowshoes he had made with rope and wood and began to climb up towards Lu.

Mandrognin has no difficulty walking on the snow, and where others sink in, he floats, from the houses they can see him at the most unlikely hours navigating with his black cloak over the white sea of the fields. He doesn't repair saddles any more and he keeps himself alive mending earthenware pots; when the women see him going by they call him and he sits in the farmyard working, his heavy head bent, still bristling with hair. In that hair lice come and go like crickets along corn-ears. He leaves them alone, never scratches himself, and as he restores the earthenware with wires, the women and children look spellbound at his big silvery head that shines like King Herod's tin crown. Never have such big lice been seen and maybe they have some traffic with the devil, the women say, some devil that lives in Mandrognin's house at the top of the hill where the fig tree stands more erect after each freeze. The same devil that has allowed him to keep all his teeth so no matter what he is offered to eat he polishes it off in an instant, not even the crumbs remain on his beard. Mandrognin, the women sometimes ask, what do you do all alone up in that devil's house? I dance and sing and make merry, he answers, raising his eyes, which are still as blue as the eyes in paintings. But the children are afraid and keep their distance. Fear of Mandrognin and of his lice, of his mad love for Maria whose house he no longer goes near, each time he goes well out of his way to avoid it. And if he absolutely has to pass in front of it, he covers his face with his hands so as not to see, not to remember. Not remember when he wanted to build a sledge and take Maria out on the snow like a queen.

But that winter Maria never went beyond the threshold of the house, even at Mass she was never seen. If the priest wants me, she said, he can come and say Mass here. God could come to her house, God's house was too cold and chilled her bones. Her brow resting against the window, she watched the others go, Limasa last, holding Pietro Giuseppe's hand. Her eyes followed them until she saw the boy's long coloured scarf flap finally in the drive: her breath clouding the pane, alone in the big empty house, where the doors creaked and came open at every gust of wind, she waited for their return.

So it was that one Sunday she saw Sacarlott among the skeletal boughs, holding Gioacchino by the hand. Sacarlott was wearing his best suit with the gold chain across his waistcoat and he waved to her to come outside. She opened the window, her hands trembling with joy, and she heard Gioacchino's voice. '*Mama,*' he said to her, 'Bring me my shoes . . .' Then she realized that the boy was barefoot. '*Speta lì,*' she answered him, 'Wait there . . . I'll find your shoes' but, in her emotion, her voice made no sound, the words stopped her mouth like cotton. She ran upstairs and rummaged in the drawers until she found the little shoes hidden at the bottom of a wardrobe, but as she ran down, clutching them to her breast, she felt them so dry and hard, there would be no putting them on. And she went to the kitchen to get some lard to grease them with but when she came back to the window Sacarlott and Gioacchino had gone. Then she began looking for them, following their prints in the snow, she went among the apple trees, sinking in up to her knees, her face burning with anguish at having lost them.

Returning from Mass, they found her with her clothes all soaked and the little shoes in her lap, greased and shiny. The disorder upstairs had made the room unrecognizable. Nobody would then believe her story and Fantina, with a veiled smile of sympathy, had to pull her almost bodily from the window where she went on waiting.

But Luìs took pity on his mother and went outside, moving among the bare apple trees, under the arbour now like a spiderweb stretched among the columns greenish with copper-sulphate. He crossed the drive and got as far as the barn, where Gerumin was carrying out the dung, and he stopped at the hayloft. If Gioacchino had come back, he had to be up there, where he had flown down on a far-off June Sunday, up there in that hay that swelled, yellow, under the roof thick with snow. And suddenly Luìs remembered how he had been jealous of his younger brother, jealous of his father's attentions and love, jealous because everybody loved Gioacchino and, instead of walking, Gioacchino always hopped and skipped, he was so pursued by happiness. Then he called him softly, once, twice, and Gerumin, going by with the steaming barrow of dung, stopped. '*Al'ò vist anche mi*,' he said, '*al'era acmè so pari*, I saw him, too; he was with his father,' and he made a gesture, as if to say the two of them had gone off. Far away, off down the road.

When March came and the snow was still a hard crust on the land, King Carlo Alberto passed through Alessandria with his troops. The war was beginning again; but Luìs did not have time to set off once more. An intestinal fever (suspicious and dangerous, Bigiot said, pressing his belly) kept him in bed, exhausted. Cholera had reappeared in the towns along the Scrivia, and the soldiers were spreading it by the streams. The phlebotomist turned his eyes, desolate, to Maria and to Gavriel, then assuming a tone of command he sent away Pietro Giuseppe, seated on the floor playing with his two Cossacks. When the boy had gone, he asked for some water to wash his hands. They would have to send for a professor from Casale, he said, and for the present no one should go out, so as not to infect the village.

The King was defeated at Borgo San Siro, at Gambolò, at La Sforzesca, at Mortara. But Luìs was cured, a few leechings were enough to bring his fever down and put his intestines in order. Pietro Giuseppe and Limasa started going out again and were seen in the shops, Maria sent Marlatteira to the priest to have him ring the bells to celebrate the danger overcome.

The priest refused: the King had abdicated and General Passalacqua had died with hundreds of soldiers. The flag, the tricolour, had ended up in the Austrians' hands. The priest is crying and the tutor looks at him aghast, he would never have imagined that the old priest was a friend of Carbonari and Freemasons. Marlatteira runs out and stops at every door to say the priest is crying because the war is lost. And when she finally reaches home and tells everything, Luìs, sitting up in bed to eat a bowl of rice, his hair stuck to his head after his long sweating, listens in silence. He doesn't say whether he knew that general, he asks no questions. Nor does he protest when Marlatteira tells how the fleeing soldiers steal and do even worse things. Maria repeats Sacarlott's story about the death of General Desaix, but as she tells it, that story now seems to her a fairy tale, as the existence of a Sacarlott known as Pidrèn is also a fairy tale, and how this Pidrèn wept, sitting on a bench, at the death of his general. That death had crowned a victory, it had been full of blood but also of glory and sunlight; and sorrow, instead of sapping strength, had instilled courage. In the pallor of this late-winter day, Luìs sitting up in bed, his belly empty as if he had a hole in its place, refuses death, sorrow. He detests glory.

The Austrians came as far as Casale and fear was great. On windy days echoes of rifle-shots could be heard, and the old men started telling stories again about when Napoleon came and you could no longer tell who owned what. The seeds were buried and Fantina hid her embroidery along with the twelve silver spoons used on special occasions. Also the snuffbox given her by Monsieur La Ville was placed between two sheets and the trunk was walled up under the stairs for fear of seeing Radetzky's soldiers appear at any moment, in their red and white uniforms.

Gavriel set out to see Fracin's Rosetta. Camurà had crossed the lines and was in Milan, already discussing with the Austrians the new red *drap*, smooth as velvet. For three days Gavriel remained secretly in the house shut off by the hawthorn bushes that were putting out their first shoots, and every morning Fracin's Rosetta went down to the river to give his horse some oats. With the shutters closed, among the hundred pieces of bric-à-brac that Camurà had brought as souvenirs of his journeys, among the stoves constantly burning and glowing even at night, Gavriel, dazed, exhausted, held Fracin's Rosetta close, kissed her in sleep, more beautiful and dear than ever: and after having made love shamelessly, there among the pillows she seemed an innocent girl.

At the dawn of the fourth day she accompanied him to the river, it was clear and after so much fog you could see the distant hills again and the houses, one by one. The water sparkled among the stones and the birds woke in the poplars with long cries.

Gavriel would have liked to make love one more time, not because he felt any desire but because it seemed to him that would make her forget him less, and only by repeating it again and again could he smother the jealousy that sickened his soul. But Fracin's Rosetta slips away from him, she is cold, and in the morning air she feels only a great wish to go. Sighing, she strokes the horse's withers: and her eyes, which manage to communicate so much gaiety to Gavriel, can also create an unbridgeable distance, made up of impatience and cruelty. There is nothing for Gavriel to do but climb into the saddle and go off on his horse as, across the river, some disbanded soldiers wave their arms to ask for help. They are hungry, they want bread.

Luìs, still convalescent, has gone to Braida, where some soldiers have camped, after being routed at Vignale. He has taken Pietro Giuseppe with him and he walks with great strides, forgetting about his son's short legs, and about the rain, which has begun to fall again. In the courtyard of the Castle there is a great confusion, children are playing barefoot in the puddles, their fingers covered with chilblain sores. It has been a long time since Luìs last came here and decay has consumed the walls and the stables. Learning of his arrival, the Cavaliera sends for him and he leaves Pietro Giuseppe aghast among the other children, a round ripe apple among a pile of little, worm-eaten windfalls.

The Cavaliera is resting, stretched out on the *dormeuse*, with the marten cloak on the floor; her near-sighted eyes stare at him blindly, the smell of her vinegar-soaked cloths spreads through the great bare salon and the cold is so intense that indoors and out seem the same to Luìs. When he enters she immediately waves him closer and before he can even mention the reason for his visit the Cavaliera begins to talk, and she talks so fast that no word of his can be inserted between one sentence and the next. She tells about the Austrians and the French when they went by here, and she tells about the Russians who fought Napoleon. She tells of misfortunes and splendours and she asks Luìs about the young Emperor of Austria who has just ascended the throne and his soldiers: what are they doing now? But before Luìs can answer, she has already gone on, she has given herself the answer and her little, genteel mouth makes the broad folds of fat on her cheeks move. In all this excessive abundance her hands have remained tiny and pale; they smooth the threadbare, moth-eaten fur of the cloak and her lilting voice is almost like music.

When Luìs managed to free himself he went to the stables, where five soldiers were eating bread and sausage around a fire built with the wood of the old mangers. The roof had partly collapsed and rain dripped on their backs but they went on roasting the sausages, their eyes watering from the smoke. They ate in silence, and around them the peasants looked at their every morsel. When they saw Luìs they made room for him, but the soldiers did not even look up and, at his questions, they replied with a shrug: there was no army any more, there was no king. The Austrians? Maybe they were in Turin already, in Asti, Vercelli ... In their dialects, some Ligurian, some from Cuneo, they cursed the generals, the rain, their hunger. Erect among the peasants, Antonia listened intently, so slender that for a moment, in the darkness of the stable, Luìs took her for a child. She looked at the soldiers, then looked at Luìs, waiting for him to say something. But Luìs disappointed her; the soldiers ate every last sausage of the house and Antonia slipped away in the silence of her black dress.

When he was outside again Luìs had to search for Pietro Giuseppe, whom one of the Cavaliera's girls had taken around the castle. It was nearly dark when he set off with the boy along the planks thrown over the mud. It seemed he and Antonia were not to meet then or ever, but, on the contrary, she appeared suddenly opposite him on the other side of the plank footway and they were so close that Antonia smelled on her face the odour of the wine Luìs had just drunk. His hands grasped her to keep her from falling: Antonia was thin, and she could hardly have been otherwise in a house where they ate little and badly, but though thin she had a soft, round fullness. Luìs's arms instinctively locked to hold her and she let herself be embraced, smiling without a hint of shyness. Then the arms let her go and Luìs stepped down in the mud, holding the boy up high to let her pass.

Before disappearing into the courtyard, Antonia turned as if she wanted to say something, but then the only word that emerged from her lips was *Merci*. Luìs would gladly have answered her in French but he didn't know any and so, holding the boy by the hand, he took the road that ran alongside the stream. It had stopped raining and he wanted to show his son the weir, where the water churned and made white spray.

Antonia had had different dreams. The tales her mother had told about her girlhood had cast images like those of a magic lantern. On the faded plaster, which still bore marks of the flood of '39, her imagination had animated the Cavaliera's stories and love had glowed in the flame of a thousand candles, her body had floated dancing in salons with marble columns, her heart had throbbed along staircases where the gowns dragged from step to step their glittering trains.

Dreams doomed to remain dreams, because nobody would take her, so dark-skinned, in that courtyard where a lone egg would be hunted down, and at every moment you risked breaking your neck on the shattered steps. That evening, after Luìs had gone, she went up to her mother and, resting her head on the marten cloak, told about the meeting just now on the footway. The Cavaliera stroked her hair and, as her hand moved down to the girl's eyes, she felt them bathed in tears. Antonia was weeping.

Luìs, too, would never have thought of taking another wife, or of taking one so poor and without any land, without even new sheets to put on the bed because the Cavaliera had put together her last daughter's trousseau with the remains of her own. Linens with embroidered coronets but full of patches and damasked towels that you could see through, they were so worn. A scandal, Maria said. Not even Limasa would have dared present herself in a family in that state. Even Marlatteira's sheets were hemstitched and made of a cotton so strong that they were hard to fold. For once Fantina was in agreement with her sister and said that when she saw Antonia it was like seeing the Virgin of Crea, darkened by the elements.

Why Luìs was in such a hurry to ask for her nobody could understand, he went on with his everyday life and only twice a week, in the evening, he went to Braida, where the Cavaliera received him on the *dormeuse* and told him about her girlhood in Moncalieri and Turin, she told him about Rome, where her husband had gone as Ambassador Extraordinary and the Pope had blessed him three times before naming him a Knight of the Holy Sepulchre. She told about the receptions, the ceremonies, the journey in the King's entourage to Paris and she told him about her fifty rings, each with a different stone. Opal from Japan, zircon from Peru, cornelian from Siberia, sapphire from Ceylon; and a holy-water stoup that had belonged to the wife of Peter the Great, a deep pale blue like the colour of her eyes then. And in the semi-darkness of the great hall the Cavaliera's pupils stared at Luìs as if they still had the flame of a candle within.

Antonia, seated on a stool, was freezing, her dark skin turned grey with the cold. From her parted lips came a white breath, and she listened, spellbound, her hands entwined against her thin knees. When Luìs went away she accompanied him down the dark steps, keeping at a distance; and if Luìs tried to touch her hand, he felt it was frozen. And yet those slender fingers, fine as dark twigs, spoke their own rare language. They promised much, and they vowed fidelity and love.

Antonia was ignorant. The Cavaliera had never chosen to send her children to school but when it was the turn of the last daughter not even the poor tutor would have been satisfied with what she was prepared to pay. So Antonia had learned to read with the books saved from the flood, French *mémoires* of the seventeenth and eighteenth centuries, that narrated the loves of Madame de Maintenon and du Barry, Mazarin's intrigues, and Henrietta of England's, and the Duc de Guise. But she knew nothing else and when Luìs spoke she listened, knitting her brows, making an effort to understand whether it was about legislation on the leasing of land or the battles of Napoleon. With the same attention she followed a poem published by the *Gazzettino Letterario* and De Candolle's treatise on botany. Her eyes, glued to Luìs's mouth, were prompt to catch every detail. And at times she laughed if something seemed comical to her. With her hand she then covered her mouth, which she thought was too wide; and that movement, without her knowledge, was full of charm.

Luìs was impatient to marry her, impelled by the curiosity and the desire that her every gesture wakened in him. Even the way that, now summer had come, she went around barefoot, as she had done ever since childhood, was a freedom so natural that instead of making her vulnerable, it became a source of strength. And there was no one, man or boy, who dared show her any lack of respect even if at times, at a sudden movement, her smooth, dark calves would flash. A skin that with the sun had lost the winter's grey pallor, and the odour of her sweat made Luìs quiver.

Many stories were told about Antonia, it was said she was the result of a mature love of the Cavaliera for a soldier from Santo Domingo who had come down into Italy following Napoleon and had stayed on after the Emperor's fall, to treat the nobility for every sort of ailment. A mestizo who had smeared unguents on the rheumatic, contracted back of the Ambassador Extraordinary whom the Pope had blessed three times. And the touch of his fingers had been so marvellous that the Cavaliera wanted to test it, too; from that day on, the former soldier from Santo Domingo had become a second master. And when the Ambassador died, the Cavaliera, already on in years, was three months pregnant and the French mestizo drove around Moncalieri in a four-in-hand. But in the space of a few months debts had consumed the palace, the carriages and the horses, the fifty rings each with a different stone, and Antonia was born in that general disorder that follows all great changes, a move of house or the arrival of the bailiffs, amid tears, doors loudly slammed. Because the former soldier of Napoleon had disappeared with the last jewels, including that aquamarine that had belonged to the Tsarina Eudoxia, and the only souvenir of him was the zinc tub where he had taken his bath every day and where now the wet-nurse laid the baby to sleep. Big, resonant, bordered with copper friezes, the very sight of it gave the Cavaliera terrible pains in the temples. Those pains that some time later confined her to the *dormeuse* with vinegar-soaked cloths on her forehead.

Now the Cavaliera would like to hasten the wedding but at Braida there is not one penny to put together even the most modest of ceremonies. The money, as always happens now, has gone out even before it came in, and every day the Cavaliera sends to ask if the promised sum has arrived from the oldest of her sons, captain in the King's army. The only one not in a hurry is Antonia. Desperately in love with Luìs, she is afraid. Every time she looks at herself in the mirror she trembles at the thought of showing herself to him, so dark, a body that in its most secret places becomes as black as a forest. And with her hand before her face she looks at her reflection through her fingers, terrified by that image, which seems to her to reveal something animal.

*

That summer, in July, Carlo Alberto died. The German troops had long withdrawn after having restored order, taxes, and a considerable series of prohibitions that the new king had pledged himself to respect. The brief parenthesis of the Roman Republic had also ended and the scandal of the priest's weeping was forgiven. Asti, Turin, Casale had been spared and everything seemed to be as it had been before. Pietro Giuseppe caught chicken pox but, after great anxiety over his health, one morning he had started playing with the cat again; and a few days later the tutor had reappeared, wearing his familiar black cassock and the shoes that so irked Maria when they went back and forth in the room. And Limasa suddenly realized she was no longer able to ride the child around on her back, he had grown so tall and lanky.

One August afternoon, late in the day, the cart bringing the Magna Munja turned again into the drive. Pietro Giuseppe stopped eating and watched her get out along with her canvases, still blank. The Magna Munja had become, if that were possible, even bigger, the face enclosed in the wimple was bigger, the flesh more substantial; and when she bent to kiss him, Pietro Giuseppe felt all her weight, like tons and tons that stifled his breath. But he no longer closed his eyes and he stared at her, not moving, as the ancient Jews had stared at Golems to tame them. Only in the evening, when the Magna Munja assembles the family to say the rosary, he is seized with a fever and lies on his bed as if lifeless, clenching his fists, as Limasa bathes his brow.

The meeting between the Magna Munja and Antonia took place on an afternoon so hot that the leaves hung limply and the grass crackled under the soles of their shoes. When the Magna Munja saw the girl coming up the drive, alone and hatless, she pretended to take her for a gypsy and made the sign of the cross. Antonia stopped under the apple trees and Pietro Giuseppe ran to meet her, he loved Antonia, he liked her laugh, fresh if infrequent, he liked her silence and her great calm. Her kisses, also infrequent, which did not bring bad breath like Fantina's or the

Magna Munja's. That afternoon he took her by the hand and led her towards his aunt, who was painting under the walnut. Only then did the Magna Munja let on that she had understood who this was and she dropped her brush as a sign of surprise. A sudden, total hatred blanched her lips.

Yes, here she was: she would sit on the stool at the spinet, would take the cool at evening in the garden in the little wicker chair as if it had always been hers, she would give orders to Limasa and Marlatteira. It was *this* whom Luìs, in his folly and his ghastly forgetting, in his stupid infidelity, would impose on them all.

She would touch, use, throw away everything that remained, erasing with her dark presence the labile, solar traces of the Maturlins' Teresina. With crude and infallible intuition, the nun understood what had attracted Luìs. In a moment she saw the round forms, the skin, she sensed the animal inside the faded cotton dress. She bent to pick up her brush from the ground; and she had already devised a strategy.

Standing straight again, she raised her distracted gaze and lowered her eyelids slightly as a greeting, then she went back with her brush to the canvas while Antonia, quick and impulsive, remained with her hands outstretched, her mouth already pursed for a kiss. The silence spread out between the young woman standing and the nun seated at her easel. One dipped the brush into the paint and tried it on the palette as if nothing else in the world mattered, the other stood in the shade of the walnut and attempted to say something about the fruit painted on the canvas and her words dropped into the void. Inert, inaudible to the ears of the nun, they sank beneath the buzzing of a wasp, among the limp petunias, the dwarf carnations.

Pietro Giuseppe stared at a lizard motionless on the gravel: whoosh! and its tongue captured an imperceptible insect. Pietro Giuseppe started: '*Mama*,' he said, tugging at Antonia's hand. '*Mama* . . .' The Magna Munja's hatred struck him, too, like a rifle-shot. Antonia, trembling at the insult, felt tears choke her but she would have nailed herself to the gravel before she would give way, the effort to produce her voice had begun to make her sweat. 'Are those *portugali*?' she asked, pointing her finger at the canvas, where some oranges were painted. Her eyes were burning and the Magna Munja could feel their intensity without even looking at her; but she didn't answer: Antonia did not exist, was not there. 'Look, *portugali*,' Antonia said then, turning to the boy, annihilated by his aunt's look; and before Pietro Giuseppe could answer her, she started calling in a loud voice: 'Luìs,' she cried, 'Luìs, *viens voir* . . . *portugali* . . .' and her voice cracked, weeping.

She was to be married, married at once. Without a lira, without even a new dress, not even a white one. She was married even poorer than Maria had been all those years ago when Pidrèn came back from the war. Her sister in Vigevano sent her own wedding dress, long and tight across the bosom, but she would make it do if it suffocated her. Immediately, Luìs, immediately. Hurry, Luìs, hurry: the slender hands, sweating, entwine with Luìs's, it is like diving headlong, the mouth can no longer smile. The Magna Munja's insult has stung her at her most sensitive spot, where all the threads of her existence come together, and now her pride is a scaring iron. Luìs no longer dares clasp her in his arms and his hands rise to the hair pulled tight at the temples, loosen a few pins, the hair falls down, dark and heavy, she remains motionless: now Luìs will run away, will be ashamed of her. But Luìs's hands have remained on her head as if caught, his eyes look at her, what he expects from her is far more than she thinks and fears she cannot give, he wants the strength he senses in her body, the stubbornness and the intelligence, the calm of her footsteps and her infrequent smile. All the rest counts for nothing, not the Magna Munja and not even the land lost through foreclosures or the story of the soldier from Santo Domingo.

The word love has never been uttered between them and Luìs doesn't say it even now, she presses her eyes shut so as not to desire it. Now or ever.

*

People talked for a long time about the marriage of Luìs and Antonia. They spoke of it even as far away as Moncalvo, Lu, Giarole, because such a marriage had never been seen before. In the courtyard, when Antonia came down in the white dress, the peasants had gathered along with some villagers curious to find out how it would end. The oldest of the Cavaliera's grandsons had come to lead her to the altar, a tall blond boy so amazed to find himself there that he seemed to have turned to wood.

The Cavaliera did not come down, not even on that day would she abandon the *dormeuse*, because she no longer possessed shoes into which she could slip her feet, and she blessed her daughter in the salon with her little hand that the years had made as weak as a leaf. She held Antonia tight against her womb and Antonia plunged her face into the silk of the dress that preserved unchanged the smells she had known since her infancy. In her mother slumped on the *dormeuse* she worshipped the sharp odour as of a great whale cast up adrift on the last beach, and she remained dumb, her mouth pressed against the cloth. It had never happened before, the Cavaliera holding her so long, and her heart, squeezed by the white dress, began to pound erratically.

Of her family, except for the young nephew who was now playing the violin in a corner of the chapel, nobody had come, whereas the family of Luìs, complete, was crammed into the two rickety benches to the left of the altar. Compact, dressed in festive clothes, with a great abundance of taffeta and ribbons, which if they had cut a fine figure at the Ivrea wedding now underlined the different time and season; the wedding guests were sweating; and the pigeons that had nested in the niche over the altar went in and out of the unglazed windows. In the empty pews, prepared in vain for the Cavaliera's family, little by little, shyly, the peasants had taken places and they ecstatically watched the young blond ephebe make his bow vibrate, his cheeks purple with discomfort. The priest had some difficulty finding the things he needed for saying Mass and the altar boys, infected by the atmosphere of the day, chased the geese that peered in at the door from the yard. Pietro Giuseppe followed them with his eyes, trembling with the desire to join them, but Limasa held him firmly by the hand, ready to be moved if only the opportunity arose.

But the opportunity never did. The priest's speech was brief, dry, a few sentences exhorting them to fidelity and fear of God, who sees all, even *ina na furmìja nera*, a black ant, in a black night, upon a black stone. And for those present, who thought that the bride, squeezed into the white dress, looked darker than ever, the reference to the *furmìja nera* was a source of some uneasiness. The priest's eyes had rested on Luìs: what could be read in his face did not seem very reassuring. And besides, this was a second wife. All well and good: but if Luìs were ever to enter Paradise, at whose side would he stand?

The one great victor of the day, majestic in her immaculate habit, was the Magna Munja, who without batting an eyelid tolerated that heat, the geese, the romping of the altar boys. That ceremony was God's just punishment and a contemptuous smile set her apart from the rest of the family, shielding her from that shameless comedy. And yet her heart became small and bitter, that chapel emanated an irrepressible sadness, the frescoes made unrecognizable by mildew, the altar crumbling with some sickness of the stone. The thought of death dominated that stratification of events, making unrecognizable all that has been vital and shining. Even Pietro Giuseppe she seemed to see with different eyes: elusive, transitory. And as she watched him wriggle impatiently from Limasa's grasp, she could not dismiss the thought that in a little while that child would no longer be. She saw the boy, then the man. Pietro Giuseppe was ephemeral, as the young nun had been ephemeral, who had strolled at sunset talking of God and of Mozart, ephemeral Luìs, who had clasped the waist of his pregnant wife while the still-unborn child stirred in her womb. Beside her, Maria wept softly. From emotion, or shame? Or something else? It was almost a whimper, and if the Magna Munja had been a good nun, concerned with Christian compassion, she should have taken into her hands that hand, weary and misshapen by arthritis, that pressed on the pew. But the Magna Munja could not forgive; and besides that violinist was drawing his bow over the last notes of some music that horribly resembled what she had listened to on summer evenings now far away.

There was no wedding trip for Luìs and Antonia, the corn had to be harvested and threshed, and vintage time was near. They went away for just three days – no one ever learned where Luìs had taken his new wife – and Maria took to her bed, ill, so as to speak to no one about the wedding at Braida, and the Magna Munja prolonged the evening rosary with a recitation of all three of the mysteries.

When Luìs and Antonia came back it seemed a day like all other days, hot and plagued by flies. Everything followed its normal course and Antonia took her seat at the table beside Maria as if she had always sat there, facing the window with the shutters half-closed and the apple trees visible between them. Nobody realized how on that day something was changing profoundly just as for so many years nobody had realized the house was proceeding on its own, like a boat carried by the current. For a long time Maria had taken no interest in anything, and Fantina, if she wasn't talking with the shadows, remained silent; and when she drank, her talk went far beyond the walls of the house, like her desires.

Antonia's authority arrived unexpectedly. Indisputable, all the more so for being discreet. Her unruffled tone knew no hesitation, never wavered even in the most difficult moments. She spoke a dialect punctuated with phrases in a clear, lofty French. *Furmìja nera adrenta ina nocc nera.* In the black night, besides God, Luìs, too, had seen her.

For the two of them he had chosen the big room overlooking the walnut tree and for the first time she found herself among freshly painted walls, in a bed so big and comfortable she could sink into it with her arms wide; and never in her dreams of handsome Lancers of the King had there been moments so intense. Luìs put his hand on her mouth to stifle her cries because at the faintest creak of the bed the Magna Munja, in a loud voice, would recite prayers imploring the Archangel Michael to put to flight the devil that was nesting in the house.

6

THE DRAGOON JUNOT

Antonia and Luìs had five children, and if it had not been for Luìs, she would have wanted more. Pregnancy did not disturb the cadence of her life, her hunger, her quickness. Her slim and strong body became concentrated, compact, around her womb and she carried that weight as, in her girlhood, she had carried buckets of water to her mother, and until the last day she went up and down the stairs tirelessly, tidying, helping Luìs with the accounts. The babies were all born with hair on their heads, some black, some brown, some still with that frail blond that had distinguished the lords of Braida. Some had pale skin and some dark with eyes as sweet as chestnuts. None was ever sent to wet-nurse: like a savage she is, the Magna Munja said, she held them to her breast and kept them there until they could climb the stairs on their own. All equally squalling from their first moment of life; and in the barn, when they heard the first cry of the baby that had just come into the world, they knew Madama had given birth once again.

For in a short time the dark and often barefoot girl who, in summer, wore her hair gathered beneath a kerchief like a peasant, had become *La Madama*. A title that had never been given Maria but on Antonia had been conferred soon, like an investiture. It was her voice, her gestures, her walk. Her gaze, in which intelligence was combined with a remote gentility, connected with her family's heyday. The lords of Braida had been crusaders, governors of Milan under the Spanish, some had frequented the Gonzaga court, others the Valois. In Antonia's way of handing an egg to Marlatteira or running the comb through Pietro Giuseppe's tangled hair, something distinguished her movements from those of the others. Even her patience had an ancient imprint, composed of expectation and confidence as the patience of sovereigns must once have been. And when she gave an order she was obeyed with enthusiasm as if she had a greater right than the others, her voice decreed to command by some supreme power. But, above all, Madama never asked for anything useless or foolish.

Those children growing up around her, physically so different from one another, like kittens, white, black, striped, all had her grace in common. Poverty, the hardships of her life as a child had stripped from the allure of her birth all arrogance, leaving intact only that gleaming strand that seemed to run through her like gold.

She should have been happy, perhaps at times she was. But at other moments, when fatigue created a sudden emptiness in her, she would make a mechanical gesture that gave her away. With the nail of her forefinger she would scratch whatever object was within her reach, even the most delicate. Irresistibly, she scraped away the paint, arrived at the wood, the plaster, until her finger bled. If she was caught at it, she would suddenly become animated, to make them overlook her misdeed. But it cost her a terrible effort, her lips turned white, her eyes seemed sucked into the grey pallor of her face. Often she would stare, spellbound, out of the little window at the end of the corridor at the spire, the onion dome sheathed in copper. What she was thinking nobody could imagine, as that pose was in such contrast to her usual, practical calm. Far from dreams. She seemed to be waiting for the hours to strike, the only thing that could tear her from the closed circle of her suffering as her nail scratched away the dry putty that held the pane in place, and the sill was stained with little drops of blood.

And yet Luìs was a good husband, and if at times, on the road, eluding all control, his gaze still followed a pretty girl, he no longer went to dances and he had no wish to betray his wife.

Once it happened, only once. It was during the Crimean war when cousin Monette arrived with her boy Tomà, who needed the mild air of the hill. She was the wife of a distant cousin of Maria, a naval lieutenant who had to embark for Sebastopol and decided to entrust his little family to his closest relatives, as his wife was a foreigner, from a distant land called New Caledonia. The cousin left almost at once and his wife and child settled in the house.

Cousin Monette had fine blonde hair, which hung loose to her waist, and her muslin dresses required great care in ironing. Ideal for the summer, they exposed her neck and her round, golden arms. She arrived in the house like a gust of an unknown nature, perhaps a land of bananas and coconuts, palm trees rising high into the sky or perhaps volcanoes with black lava, incandescent in the night: nobody had heard of New Caledonia and even Luìs had some trouble picking it out on the map of the world.

She spoke halting Italian, and was often forced to fall back on French; her son Tomà rode the goats, climbed the walnut tree, scrambling along the boughs to the top, and at night he wandered around the house in his nightshirt, popping out from the most unlikely places, suffering from a mysterious illness that made sleep impossible for him. He possessed a voice, this Tomà, tempered, high, deafening, which repeated all the animals' cries and the shouts that commanded animals; but when he became angry he spoke an unknown language, in bursts. Then, repentant, he would kneel at his mother's feet and kiss the hem of her skirt.

Pietro Giuseppe and his brothers and sisters, accustomed to the calm order of the house, regarded him in terror, blinded by awe. Tomà was a beautiful child, but his slender body, which seemed without joints, was frightening, as it seemed every moment on the verge of drooping, withering. Driven into games even by one of the smaller children he would fall to the ground, never hurting himself, he was so light. So light that the day he fell from the walnut, when all were expecting blood and screams, Tomà abruptly stood up. '*Pardon*,' he said, because he had broken a branch.

Cousin Monette embroidered tulle, using her long hair as thread, and she sat at the spinet, mute for so many years. She played old French songs that the colonizers had brought from their distant homeland, and perhaps in France they were no longer sung. Every now and then, with her singing, she mixed different sounds, mournful, obsessive, which drained all pleasure from listening. Only Tomà rejoiced and clapped his hands happily, sometimes joining his voice to his mother's.

But cousin Monette's great passion was the Tarot. She always carried with her an old deck that she said had belonged to an ancestress, a pastry-cook sentenced to death for having tried, with poisoned cream puffs, to take the life of the Grand Condé. She shuffled the Tarot deck, making those greasy and faded cards rattle in her plump hands, so stubby that, at the spinet, to stretch from C to G, she had to jump up. She laid the cards for Maria, but also for Limasa and Marlatteira. For Limasa she predicted a rich, lame husband, with two gold teeth. For Marlatteira a son who would be a general. For Luìs a *fuocco*.

'A fire? What fire?' Luìs laughs in the shade of the walnut, cousin Monette's perfume is a mixture ideally suited to the fine blonde of her hair, to her gilded skin. Perhaps this is the fragrance of coconuts and mangoes, of the flowers that bloom in the tropical forest.

'*Peut-être ici*,' she says, putting a hand on her heart, her round breast gathered in her palm, beneath the pale muslin. Antonia goes by, in her bustling between the children and the house, smiles at the new cousin who has a husband on a brigantine, its sails unfurled towards the Black Sea. She knows little of war, of the Crimea and of Turks, but she knows French well and she grasps immediately that breath of perfume and those gazes in the shade of the walnut.

Antonia will not be jealous, or if she is, she will not show it; and when the evidence becomes all too clear she will look past it. Even on the day of the vintage when they go, all together, up to the Gru farm and the New Caledonia cousin seems to vanish into thin air, and Luìs also disappears, with his little straw hat and the Great Masten's stick, leaving Antonia alone with Gavriel to look after all those children, hopping among the rows of vines, wreaking damage, falling, crying.

When will this wretched war end? Ships that are wrecked, Russians, French, cholera. When, Gavriel? Gavriel smiles at her, soon, he says, soon, and to console her he presses her hand, suddenly unsure, rough from so many children. A child falls, Antonia gets up to tend to him, takes him in her arms, wipes his mouth smeared with dirt, the sun sets, greyish in the pink mists of the day, some leaves of the stripped vines are already crimson, the oxen head off down the road, swaying, the wagons brimming with grapes. The land is so beautiful at this season with the pale green of the reeds along the ditches, the peach trees and the cherries scattered at the edges of the vine rows, the corn that is already straw, and the alfalfa that glistens in the departing day. Down there, among the canes, something moves; it can be a hare, a wild cat. *Peut-être ici*, cousin Monette said, pointing to her heart. But it is late, they must think of going home, putting the children to bed, Limasa is worse than they are and plays hide-and-seek without a thought of the darkness, Marlatteira is all ready, waiting, a basket filled with grapes on her head. Tomà's lips are drained of blood, he leaps like a ghost from one furrow to another.

In the evening Zanzìa comes, who lost all his teeth as a young man and plays a hybrid instrument of his own invention: violin, hand-organ and bass drum. The music it produces inspires an irresistible desire to let yourself go and the children run down from their beds, Pietro Giuseppe is already in the centre of the barnyard dancing, and he turns and turns, his hair dripping sweat, his bare feet black with dust, nobody can stop him, and his brothers and sisters all gather round him and clap their hands, trying to grab him by the shirt. Gerumin's son with a game leg dances, Marlatteira dances, and the women who have come to help with the vintage. Limasa has caught Pietro Giuseppe by the waist and as he dances, she also kicks her heels, she seems a witch who has escaped from the trunk of the walnut. The grapes ferment under the last September moon, never has such an evening been seen, the heat and the dust cloud the air, Zanzìa laughs baring his empty gums and he plays more and more wildly, shaking his head, crazed by his own sound. Fantina and Maria sit motionless on their chairs like two Totems in the mists of the night, for what they have to communicate to each other a few monosyllables suffice and even now they remain in silence as if they were seated at the theatre while the children run off in all directions pursued by Marlatteira with the broom in her hand.

Gavriel has already set off on his horse and will come back only when the sun is high, when Luìs is resigned to doing without him. Antonia has gone to Braida, where the Cavaliera has summoned her because she feels she is dying. She didn't see even the beginning of the festivity, not Zanzìa and the instrument of his own invention, and now kneeling at the foot of the *dormeuse* she rests her head in a lap where all the odours of a fleeing universe are gathered. She rests her cheek against what was once a famous marten cloak in the silent sleds over the snow, among the valets' torches, in the foyers of theatres, and she studies her mother's broad face, white in the penumbra: a melting cake that has lost all recollection of its once exquisite ingredients. A beloved face that she would like to recompose and restore to its lost dignity. Antonia weeps in her helplessness, and the Cavaliera's fingers entwined in her hair slip down. A caress, one more. The last.

And Luìs? And cousin Monette? The candles are alight on either side of the spinet, but the salon is empty, the late September air spreads out, warm, lunar, the thread-like mosquitoes cling to the curtains. No one has heard the old French song break off, drowned out by Zanzìa's music, by the racket of the dancing. Limasa looks in at the window from the garden, Pietro Giuseppe tugs at her arm, he wants to dance some more. She thrusts him away, let go of me, she says, leave me alone, and she looks inside, curious, uncertain whether or not to go in and blow out the candles. And as she looks, she seems to hear a stifled cry, a groan coming from the shadows, and immediately the old stories come to mind about Giai who after his death used to come and play the violin, so she seizes Pietro Giuseppe and runs off, stumbles, falls full length on the lawn. Holy Virgin, what fear! Fear of werewolves that prowl on moonlight nights, of the dead who never find peace. She hugs Pietro Giuseppe tight and feels that he is sweating, overheated. Together, stretched out, they look at the moon with its patterns that seem drawn on ice. Zanzìa wants to marry me, she says, if I marry him he'll buy me a dress and a pair of shoes like cousin Monette's. Do you like him? Pietro Giuseppe asks, holding her tighter still. No, she answers, I want a handsome boy. Wait for me then, when I'm big I'll marry you. Limasa laughs, he clasps her farther down, where he imagines a man embraces a woman, she pushes him away, making him roll on the grass, then she stands up and, crossing her fingers, motionless, she stares at the moon. Heaven only knows what she is asking, what she is promising as her lips mumble incomprehensible words.

Pietro Giuseppe stayed on the lawn and fell asleep, one arm under his head. Nobody knows who, passing by, dropped a handkerchief on his face, for sleeping in the moonlight causes incurable diseases and epilepsy. It seemed to him that it was cousin Monette in her light dress that brushed the grass and he tried to call her but she was walking as if in a dream and she was biting an apple, holding others with one arm against her bosom and she would not turn.

'Cousin Monette!' he cried, louder, taking away the handkerchief. The apples rolled onto the ground and she bent to collect them and her dress allowed a glimpse of her naked body.

Then Pietro Giuseppe remembered what his father had said about the inhabitants of New Caledonia, that they went around with no clothes on and they painted their body. He had also been told how, when they went hunting, those men and women used a curved piece of wood that, after it had been thrown at their prey, came back to them. Little Tomà kept one of these wooden things in his room, with strange signs carved on it. 'Cousin Monette,' he called again, but she was already going off with the apples collected in her skirt. 'Cousin, cousin . . .' But suddenly he thought he could smell the odour of the cemetery when he went there with the Magna Munja and his heart leaped. With excitement, but even more with the desire that, above him, on this night, putting the handkerchief on his face, it had been his Mama passing by. The Maturlins' Teresina.

Maria and Fantina stayed up to the end with their hands folded in their lap and a black umbrella over their heads to protect them against the night's dampness. They didn't budge even when the Magna Munja flung open the window and yelled that they should stop all that racket and those sins: God had recognized them one by one and would punish them all, Gavriel and Luìs, cousin Monette, Limasa and Zanzìa, the farmhands, who were stealing the wine. She yelled so loud that even Zanzìa felt a cold sweat on his brow and it took great courage for him to go on playing. The children, already in bed, hid their heads under the sheets, covering their ears so as not to hear. Only Maria and Fantina did not stir from under the umbrella: they wanted to miss no part of such a festivity, only God knew if they would see another.

Luìs and cousin Monette were the only ones who didn't hear the Magna Munja's cries. The candles at either side of the spinet had burned out and the last bit of wax had dripped onto the candlesticks. When everyone went off to sleep, mindless from the wine and the music, Luìs went to close the window and his steps re-echoed loud in the devastated silence of the house. By now it was dawn and there was no point in going to bed any more; he looked out at the garden and in the first, colourless light that outlined the apple trees he saw Pietro Giuseppe curled up on the lawn, the handkerchief over his face. He tried shaking him but the boy was so sound asleep that he merely rolled over, shivering. Then Luìs picked him up, tall and heavy as he was now, he had never done this before, and as he struggled up the steps he felt at once tenderness and sorrow. Pietro Giuseppe seemed more his child than the others, more his, but at the same time he felt he loved the child less.

Cousin Monette left with the first fogs, news from the Crimea was more and more contradictory, and Tomà's intermittent fevers had returned. The cholera that had circled the area for a year had reached the village through a foreigner who had come to buy livestock. Everybody was seized by a great fear and doors were quickly shut, hens that ran out into the road were called back in loud voices. Cousin Monette had grown melancholy and when Fracin's Rosetta arrived on a visit of condolence after the death of the Cavaliera and offered to take her away, Monette accepted joyfully. From Camurà's house, Rosetta said, she could easily go on to Genoa, where Tomà would have the sea air and she, fresh news from the Crimea.

As a girl, when her father went to Braida to do some job or other, Fracin's Rosetta had played with Antonia, then a small child. They had amused themselves hiding in the maze of corridors, among the tall bookshelves, and often Antonia had gaily climbed on the back of Fracin's only daughter to ride around clinging to the red hair. Now Camurà's beautiful wife sits in the living-room, dressed in laces and taffeta, and becomes acquainted, one by one, with Luìs's children; most of all she likes Sofia, who has her mother's dark eyes and Luìs's pale skin. She takes the girl on her lap and sings her the song of *Pursè Soppin*.

Gavriel stands with his arms folded, looking at her, and his love is so evident in his eyes that her words falter on her lips, and when she is at the door saying goodbye she bursts into tears. They all think it is because of the Cavaliera who, when she went to the castle as a girl, used to give her silk ribbons. But Gavriel knows the real reason and, at first happy because of that visit, he now becomes curt with his sister-in-law because of what she and Luìs have and he will never have. It was then that Fracin's Rosetta mustered her courage, dried her tears, and looking deep into Antonia's eyes offered to take cousin Monette away with her.

Cousin Monette arrived in Genoa in December and there she learned that her husband had been wounded by a cannonball fired from a Turkish barquentine: but the Tarot cards told her he was already dead. She wrote this in a letter addressed to the whole family, the letter was written in a fine hand but made up of so many different languages that it was hard to decipher. She thanked everyone and expressed her sorrow, she wrote *regrette* and only Antonia understood what she meant. The others thought of the grape harvest, the dancing, and the lovely days when cousin Monette in the shade of the walnut embroidered tulle with her own long hair.

Luìs read the letter aloud several times, pausing at each word, the children, sitting on the ground, played with the cat, and Sofia cradled the doll that Fracin's Rosetta had sent, sewn with her own hands. Pietro Giuseppe studied in the room over the barnyard with the tutor and you could hear the poor priest's stentorian voice as he paced up and down, his hands behind his back. Antonia, in mourning, mended a pair of trousers. Through the windows only the fog could be seen and the panes were streaked with water: the grape harvest, the dancing, and Zanzìa's bass drum were lost in the distance, they were sealed by that last image of the two women leaving, one head blonde, one red. So different and yet somehow also similar in their full skirts and cloaks that brushed the bricks of the path. Between them, light as a butterfly, the boy Tomà.

Cousin Monette's husband had died in September in a

hospital at Balaclava. He had suffered thirst and heat, he had been tormented by flies, and fleas had got in under his bandages, he had thought always of that wife he had gone and found in that country at the other end of the world. With her he had been happy for a few years, too few. He dictated some letters to the man in the next bed and he called his wife by the tenderest names, told her how he dreamed of her every night, and as soon as he got back they would take a house in the hills and would live there with their child Tomà, and never leave each other again. His last letter he dictated with a high fever. He was raving, and his neighbour had difficulty writing it all down. Perhaps he forgot a few words, and mixed others up.

At the town cousin Monette was never seen again. She remarried, a Portuguese diamond dealer, and went around the world on a paddlewheel steamboat. She died of smallpox in Athens and to her son Tomà, who had remained in Genoa, her trunk returned with her light muslin dresses and the Tarot deck. And brought by a discreet person of total reliability, a little sack of blue sapphires from Ceylon, which would serve to pay for his education.

The great event of the years that followed was the war of '59, when Vittorio Emanuele II set up his headquarters first at San Salvatore and then, for a few days, at Occimiano, which was not even three miles away.

The war began in spring; the snow was not long gone and in the morning the fog still blurred the trees, Limasa had to come and light the stoves so the children, getting up, would not catch cold.

She hadn't married anyone, Limasa, no handsome boy, no rich and lame husband with two gold teeth. Her loves began in the farmyard in front of the stables and ended in the hayloft with the boy who came to sell carp and pike caught at Pomaro or with Catagrata who passed by with his cart of cheeses. To Fantina's preaching about the virtue of purity she put up a hostile resistance, her eyes darkened; and her nose, in her broad face flattened by her silence, stuck up more pointed than ever. Fantina's virginity did not interest her, and as far as prudence was concerned she knew a thing or two more than the whole lot of them. The old witch Ciapa Rusa had taught her everything when she was still a child, for a bowl of millet, she would go to wash the clothes the woman dirtied with her men.

But that year things went badly for her. It all began with the first French dragoon who appeared on his horse at the top of the high road. His helmet glistened with rain and he looked all around, swinging its plume; finally he made up his mind to ride down, trotting slowly among the puddles. Others followed him and the children ran out to see them and behind the children the women, the youths, the dogs that barked without disturbing for a moment the solemn, cadenced pace of the stallions. Limasa arrived when they were already filing through the square, she was carrying Duardin on one arm, and with the other hand she held Sofia, while Pietro Giuseppe followed her, his little hat limp with rain and his hands in his pockets.

The dragoons went up the road towards the opposite hill, disappearing in pairs, the horses' behinds smooth and plump, the powerful flanks. The last dragoon stopped his horse and dismounted in front of the baker's shop. The shop was small and seemed unable to contain him, and through the door, which he left open, Limasa saw his shining epaulettes. For a dragoon like that she would have given everything, Duardin, Pietro Giuseppe, and the years of her future.

Limasa was twenty-eight and had the soul of a child even if she had passed through many hands, always and only for love. Now it seemed to her she was ready to give away her heart and when the dragoon, coming out of the shop with a package of biscuits, asked her where he could find the *phlebothome*, she felt faint. Duardin slipped down from her arms. 'Who?' she asked in a tiny voice, dazzled by the splendour of the uniform. It was Pietro Giuseppe who explained to her that the phleb-otomist was Bigiot, the leech. Her eyes glued to the scattered crumbs that were sticking to the dragoon's moustache, Limasa had some trouble understanding. '*Phlebothome,*' the dragoon repeated patiently, as he slipped off his helmet and a tawny lion's head shone above the epaulettes.

A flash went through Limasa's mind, she entrusted the little children to Pietro Giuseppe and pointing to herself motioned the dragoon to follow her. Pale, trembling, she crossed the square at his side. She stumbled on the stones and each time she was about to fall the dragoon supported her with his knotty hand covered with reddish hairs. The horse followed, not needing to be led by the reins, and she felt the mud spattering her dress.

They filed through the whole town and, walking, Limasa looked straight ahead as her feet sank into the puddles, and every time she was about to slip she felt as if that hand, prompt to support her, were holding all of her, body and soul. Bigiot was not at home and they sat down outside on a bench to wait for him until darkness fell. The dragoon told her about his country and his life; she knew no French, but she understood everything all the same, and laughed or cried as the story turned merry or sad. When she cried the dragoon would dry her tears with his thick fingers. He did no more than that, he was a dragoon who didn't like women and came from a town in the Auvergne called Le Puy, a town with seven rocks and seven castles, one on top of each rock.

When Bigiot arrived it had stopped raining, the dragoon hoisted him onto the horse, and they disappeared into the darkness. Limasa went home with no fear of walking alone in the night, and as soon as she arrived she made Pietro Giuseppe write down the name of the dragoon and of his town. She hastily sewed a little bag and put in it the strip of paper where, with India ink, was written: Junot Julien, Le Puy. She hung the bag around her neck and vowed never to take it off.

The dragoon Junot passed through the village another three times and each time Limasa was at the side of the road, erect and demure, waving her hand. The rain slid over the dragoon's helmet, dripped from his epaulettes and soaked the cloth of his uniform, the saddle of black ram's fleece; the horse neighed, controlled by the reins, and he passed so close to Limasa that she could have touched his beautiful shining boot.

When the regiment was transferred, Limasa joined the women and children who climbed up every day to San Salvatore in the hope of seeing the King. It was almost five miles, uphill most of the way, through the fields, and Limasa took off her clogs to keep from slipping. Her feet were cut, her heels cracked and bled, but nothing would stop her and the happiness of that month of May seemed to her different from any she had ever felt before. A happiness that went well with the light rain that clung in droplets to her hair, and passed, cool, between her lips. For her the Almighty sent it every day: dewy, fine, green as meadows.

A May that dissolves completely in rain, as soon as the wheat sprouts it slumps immediately on the spongy terrain and the women who go up to see the King at the Poma farm cover their heads with sacks and on the way home their dresses are soaked and cling to their legs. Pietro Giuseppe follows Limasa every time she goes out and walks behind her all the way to the top of San Salvatore and on the return journey he is overjoyed because she hasn't seen the dragoon Junot. He lets himself slide downhill, sings with his lovely voice that was his mother's, the women stop to listen to him, he becomes red with shame but in the dusk nobody realizes it. Only she, Limasa, remains indifferent, doesn't even hear him; she hasn't seen the dragoon Junot but she is happy anyway because surely she will see him tomorrow. And if not tomorrow, then surely the day after that.

But the next day the news comes that the French are at Valenza to stop the Austrians, going up to San Salvatore is not enough for Limasa. She wants to get into Zanzìa's cart, in which he takes wine to sell to the soldiers. There is a grim rumbling under the low clouds, you can't tell if it's thunder or cannon firing in the distance, Limasa gathers her skirts and hoists herself up, clinging to the sides, until she is on the cart in the midst of the barrels of wine. Behind her, Pietro Giuseppe then jumps on, and the two of them take shelter under the broad tarpaulin spread out to protect the load. The cart sets off with a jolt, the rain has begun falling again, harder, it strikes the tarpaulin and Zanzìa curses because he would like to be in Pietro Giuseppe's place, warm, beside Limasa. They go on and on, far beyond the Poma farm; what did you have to promise Zanzìa to make him take you, Pietro Giuseppe asks her; nothing, nothing at all, Limasa answers, drawing farther back under the tarpaulin, I swear. The cart shakes and slows down, the road seems like soap, and now the explosions are definitely not thunder; they come from cannons. Limasa hugs her legs in silence, her eyes full of light and waiting.

Darkness has fallen and there is no news of Limasa and Pietro Giuseppe. Luìs has sent someone to see if they are on the San Salvatore high road, but the last women to come home say nobody is left there, the soldiers have driven everyone off because they need the roads clear for the troops. The Austrians have crossed the Po and soldiers are arriving from all sides to stop them. The children cry in the kitchen where the washing is hung out to dry near the fire, Marlatteira consoles them, hugging them to her bosom, they stop for a minute then immediately begin again.

Zanzìa's cart is stuck in the mud, now he doesn't know whether to go ahead or try to turn back, the rain is coming down so heavily that you can't see anything. The cavalry scouts pass and say the Austrians are advancing, have crossed the Po at Frassineto. And suddenly the soldiers start yelling, cursing civilians, who impede operations, what are that woman and that boy doing here, get out, go home, the horses' hoofs spatter mud, Limasa cries, she's afraid, Pietro Giuseppe angrily clenches his teeth, not him, he says, he's not afraid, and now that they've come this far he wants to go on, to see the French, the cannons, the Austrians. He is almost fifteen, he is tall, sturdy, his hair escapes from his cap; and Zanzìa looks at him, uncertain whether to pay attention to him or not, Limasa doesn't dare say anything more.

Gavriel has had his horse saddled, Maria has woken from the torpor that comes over her towards dusk and she begs him to wait, they're both children, she says, Limasa has become brainless, too, since she began running after that dragoon, maybe they're already on their way home, maybe they've taken refuge at some farm, going out to search for them in the dark is a waste of time. Wait, wait, they'll come back, you'll see . . . she holds on to his sleeve, her fingers clutch him hard, she sees again the winter she spent with Gavriel in Mandrognin's house, she thinks she can smell again the odour of the saddles, hear the sounds of those clear and resplendent mornings. Wait, just a little longer . . . to Gavriel, to his sadness, she is bound in the secret of her heart.

Night has come and the Po has invaded the fields, has lifted Zanzìa's cart, dragging it off, afloat, far away, the cavalry scouts have forgotten Limasa and Pietro Giuseppe and have disappeared in the light of the torches smoking in the rain, the water soaks their ammunition, carries off the horses' straw, drags away bushes and animals. At dawn Luìs mounts the horse behind Gavriel and they struggle up to San Salvatore. At the Poma farm a yellowish light filters from the windows but the soldiers will not allow civilians to approach. Nobody knows anything about Limasa and the boy, and they know little, too, of what has happened down there, at the Po, some soldiers have died, others have been wounded. Still others are missing and perhaps have drowned. The dogs howl on the marshes and the livestock dragged out of the flooded stables impede the progress of the French, who have come to drive out the Austrians.

Luìs is ill and Gavriel leaves him at the inn while he climbs to the top of the tower built by Napoleon at the time of the battle of Marengo. It is day by now and from up there he can see the whole plain as far as Alessandria, the slow curve of the Tanaro, silvery between the banks of poplars. But he sees no cart, no one who might resemble Limasa or the boy.

Luìs has flung himself down on a bench, his beard is ill-kempt, and his hair rumpled. He trembles with cold. A soldier covers him with a cloak and orders the host to bring him something to drink. But Luìs has a high fever and cannot unclench his teeth, the wine spills over the cloak. He is delirious and it is as if, instead of the soldier, he had a woman before him, you're all wet, he says to her, how can you come to bed, your feet, your hands are ice. His eyes are lost in the eyes of the soldier bending over him; and the soldier runs outside to call Gavriel in a loud voice because his brother is dying.

Is it possible to sleep a whole night and all the following day without waking up once in an area being combed by Skirmishers, Sappers, Zouaves, Turcos, Trumpeters and Lancers? In the afternoon a *vivandière* passed by and left a quarter of a loaf beside Limasa, they ate it in their sleep, barely discerning the trousers visible beneath her skirt; they chewed without opening their eyes. Pietro Giuseppe dreamed at length, some of the dreams were terrifying, others, on the contrary, unforgettable because of their happiness.

When he described them to Marlatteira she made many conjectures about his future, but by then many of those dreams had become muddled in his mind and the only one Pietro Giuseppe remembered clearly was a needle of fire that made searing holes in his flesh; but then a tongue passed over his skin, light and cool, it ran over his whole body, and that fire became a warmth like grass in June, and in his delight his skin became covered with feathers. At that point Marlatteira stared into his face, saw his beard still downy, the broad grey eyes and the hollows under them, an Adam's apple that was growing like a chicken bone in his throat; and a smile that was not a smile but a dubious wrinkling of the face passed like a shadow between her and the boy. Then she turned to the stove, muttering something about those who sleep under the open sky. Oaks, she said then, are the meeting-places of witches, never stop at night under an oak. With the witches there is often the devil in the form of a cat, an ass, or even a horse.

What happened was that when the water carried off Zanzìa's cart Pietro Giuseppe and Limasa had jumped down in time and they had seen it bob, slam and finally capsize with Zanzìa, who saved himself by clinging to a bough. Limasa seemed to have turned to stone as the water swirled around her legs and she swore that if she were saved she would do what Fantina wanted. Never again, not with any man. At that moment Pietro Giuseppe had managed to grab her and pull her onto a little mound at the side of the road, and from there, catching his breath, he had run on, holding her tight. A soldier from Occimiano who was passing by there recognized them and shouted at them to stop and he would load them onto his mule. But nobody could have stopped Pietro Giuseppe now; and when Limasa was in no condition to run any more, her feet were so lacerated, he hoisted her on his back. Limasa was solid, inert, but he went on climbing, as he thought of all the tales about the flood of '39. When, exhausted, he dropped her at the foot of the oak it had stopped raining and a few stars were appearing here and there among the clouds. The leaves of the oak were so thick that the ground seemed dry and the two of them fell asleep, hugging each other, as in the days when, a little boy, Pietro Giuseppe would come into her bed to get warm.

Limasa, unlike Pietro Giuseppe, dreamed nothing. She didn't even remember having eaten the bread, and when a Zouave began to slap her on both cheeks to bring her round, she sat up, frightened. Her dress was awry and the Zouave began feeling her legs.

But Gavriel didn't believe the story of the oak and the witches. Luìs was still in bed, ill, and Gavriel assumed the task of punishing Pietro Giuseppe. He went to find the whip and his favourite nephew was whipped for the first and only time in his life.

Not even Sacarlott in his day had ever dared go so far; and Maria and Fantina, distraught, bent over Luìs's first-born and, above him, they embraced and talked to each other as they had in the distant past. Pietro Giuseppe shook off their caresses and went out on the lawn to join his younger brothers and sisters and he started playing with a tame crow, as calmly as if nothing had happened. Every now and then he looked at Limasa, who was taking Evasio for a ride on her shoulders. That face was dear to him: flat, ruined by smallpox, with a nose like the nose of certain bread dolls that they sell at fairs, he saw all its ugliness but it did not make him love it less. He repented nothing and if she had stopped for a moment he would have smiled at her. But Limasa seemed to have forgotten the cannon fire at Valenza, Zanzìa's cart, and the water in the road like a torrent, the long night spent in the boy's arms under the oak. She yelled because the other children were grabbing her skirt, wanting to take Evasio's place; and she kicked them off.

Limasa did not give up the dragoon Junot, and Pietro Giuseppe continued accompanying her every time she went out. The Austrians came as far as Casale and, as they had ten years before, everyone took precautions in case Hussars and Uhlans appeared in the village. But, once again, the Austrians failed to arrive and nobody saw the dread Hungarian Grenadiers: of them it was said that, in possessing women, they tore off the women's ears with their teeth.

Instead, in an open carriage, Napoleon III passed through and they all went to see him, including Maria and Fantina, protected by the black umbrella; but they saw almost nothing, kept at a distance by a great prancing of horses, by dust, flying pebbles. Galloping behind the Emperor there was also the dragoon Junot in full uniform and Limasa tried to pick him out in the midst of the others. It was not easy, but at a certain point the dragoon broke away from his comrades and, riding close by her, dropped a still fresh bouquet of lavender at her feet. It all lasted an instant, then the Emperor's calèche vanished on the Occimiano high road and all that was left of the dragoons was a hazy commotion of men and horses, a horizon flashing like a mirage.

For all the time that the King's General Staff was quartered in the Marquis of Passano's villa, Limasa and the children went to Occimiano every afternoon. It was barely more than two miles, all on the flat, and with them came Marlatteira, who knew a great number of songs. The ground still smelled of rain and they muddied their shoes, the nettles stung their legs, they walked on the grassy verges and Limasa sang, too, the children listened carefully. Pietro Giuseppe, who was unwilling to mingle with them, walked behind, his hands in his pockets. But when some soldier went by and the smaller children turned around, he would say: 'Zouave' – or perhaps, 'Lancer, Gunner.'

At Occimiano Marlatteira took the polenta out of her basket and they ate something, seated on the benches in the square, while soldiers came and went, the wheels of the carriages clattered on the pebbles and aides and generals went by in a great din of horses. The children gaped and watched, their legs swinging from the bench, once they saw the King and they considered him very handsome even if he wasn't. His face was pock-marked and this made Limasa happy. Me and the King, she said, touching her cheeks. The soldiers joked with her, she had forgotten the vow she had made only a few days before. They joked even with Marlatteira and insisted on putting their hands on her to feel her two hearts. Pietro Giuseppe bit into his slice of polenta, standing off to one side, and he was ashamed for them. And along with his shame, he felt anger and contempt.

Before dark they went back home and along the way Evasio fell asleep in Limasa's arms. Marlatteira held the other two by the hand, and they let themselves be tugged along, their eyes heavy with sleep. Nobody sang any more and the swallows

177

darted low to catch the insects at dusk. Spring was suddenly felt, damp, intense.

Montebello, Palestro, Magenta, Melegnano. Too many soldiers, too many horses, too many Frenchmen, eating and drinking and not paying. Even if the battles are won and some cities that seemed so far away suddenly come within reach, in the neglected fields the weeds grow easily and the wheels of the artillery crush the corn that has just sprouted in the furrows. The horses' hoofs destroy the vines. Taxes carry off savings. Gavriel's curls are no longer as thick as they were; looking at him from behind you see a skull appearing that seems carved in chestnut wood, more square than rounded. Now he spends all his evenings in the house and nobody dares ask him any-thing.

For years Gavriel has not dreamed, he has given up imagin-ing, and his thoughts, like the chain of a well, have always the same creak. Fracin's Rosetta has left the house with the big oak and the garden thick with flowers, she no longer lives in the low-ceilinged rooms, crammed with the mementos of Camurà, who would announce his arrival by cracking his whip outside. She has moved to a grand house in Alessandria, where the ceilings are high and frescoed and the furniture has amber glints. Camurà treats financiers and industrialists as equals, and he is himself an industrialist for he has so much money that he can invest it in various enterprises. When Gavriel enters, cloak and hat in hand, Fracin's Rosetta comes towards him in the full splendour of her maturity, her hair with its glints of fire hanging loose around her white neck. She swears that she loves him as she used to, but it is no longer possible for them to meet in the house, two maids, tall in black dresses, cross the great rooms to light the lights and they call her *Madame* in the French fashion, nodding their heads with their crested caps. They look with hostility at Gavriel's muddy boots, at his cloak drenched with rain. Camurà has given up his travelling and he sits in an office across from the station, where six employees

await his orders. On some mornings, seized by a yearning for
the wife he has enjoyed so little, he comes home even before
noon.

They cannot meet at home or outside either, the two dappled
grey horses of Camurà's carriage are familiar to everyone.
Because the former itinerant cloth-pedlar has done things in
style, he wants the whole province, all the way to Turin, to
talk about his money. Where, then? Pensively, she shakes her
head; she concentrates, supporting her brow with her hand,
how beautiful her full mouth is, how beautiful her shoulders,
and the line of her back so made for love. Where? . . . She lets
her hand drop again into her lap, she looks at him with such
sweetness and says, you remember that time down at the river
and that other time, and the first, you remember the first? A
shudder runs through her; but she doesn't say where, that
where no longer exists. It's impossible, you see?

This June is a month of suffering for Limasa too. The King
and Napoleon III have gone and their entry into Milan was a
triumph, the display of candles illuminated the night and
people danced in the squares to celebrate the defeat of the
troops of the hated Radetzky. Alessandria also had its moment
of glory when, at the Teatro Regio, the Emperor of the French
appeared with all his decorations, and the one who applauded
him loudest was Camurà, who as a boy had pulled his cart to
markets and now has a box where he sits beside a wife who
once was the daughter of the anarchist smith.

Limasa looked for the dragoon Junot in the camps, questioned every soldier she met. None of them was able to tell
her anything until one day she met a Zouave from Kabylia
who, at her question, burst out laughing, oh yes, he's seen the
dragoon Junot all right, indeed he has seen him, it's not
everyone who can see a dragoon running full tilt without his
trousers, and a Grenadier chasing him, ready to fire his musket
at him . . . The Zouave from Kabylia is short, stocky, his
drooping moustache reaches his neck and his nose looks

wooden it is so hard and fleshless, big and curved, it casts a shadow on his cheeks, first right, then left. He reaches out to touch Limasa, to see if she is real, so compact, so shapely. She runs off and the Zouave catches her by her apron, Limasa gives it a jerk and the apron remains in the Zouave's hand. It's a new apron, she says, give it back. She weeps. The Zouave flings it on the ground, he feels sorry for her, those pock-marks; without them, the face would be handsome. Your dragoon, he says to her, is . . . Limasa doesn't know the word and she thinks it's a place, a city. She snatches up the apron and asks where is this . . . it's late, she has to go home. Why don't you come back tomorrow, the Zouave says, and I'll explain it to you, I'm not a dragoon, but for some things, I promise you, I'm better. Try and you'll see for yourself.

The Kabylian Zouave drank: beer, wine, cider, anything so long as it tasted of alcohol. And it was all the fault of a bottle of apple brandy, opened to celebrate the victory. A brandy that made Limasa's head transparent, she saw all her dreams pass by as if they were coming true, one by one, and her body was full of endless desire. It was true that the Zouave was good for some things, surely better than the dragoon who didn't like women but better also than Catagrata or the boy who caught carp and pike at Pomaro, and his breath tasted of fire. Limasa forgot what Ciapa Rusa had taught her when she went to do the washing for a bowl of millet; and when she remembered it was too late. Not even the Madonna of the Snows could work the miracle.

The Zouave wanted to marry her but he had no house, not even some land, he had nothing beyond his skill at making love. And for that he was always ready. But he was ugly and had scant acquaintance with soap; even the apple brandy couldn't disguise his stink. Limasa spent the night awake, touching her breasts and her belly, and one afternoon she decided to go to Ciapa Rusa.

When she pushed the door open she saw no one, there was great darkness in the room and a goat was tied to the fireplace, its hoofs scraping the ground. Ciapa Rusa's voice came from the bed. She had become so tiny that she looked like a rag doll, her sparse grey hair standing up in a cock's comb. From the bed she told Limasa what she had to do. It wasn't easy to understand her because she had no teeth, and the smell in the room was so strong that, instead of repeating what Ciapa Rusa had just finished saying, Limasa ran out, leaving two pennies on the bed. And never had sky, fields, the sun setting in a golden dust, seemed so beautiful to her.

That night she dreamed she was in the centre of a room and hands stretched from the walls to grab her; she writhed and was horrified to see that those hands were dripping blood. And when, with a great effort, she opened her eyes she found herself huddled in a corner, her face bathed in tears. The next morning she told the dream to Marlatteira, seated in the kitchen, and she felt a great urge to vomit into her plate. It was a lovely midsummer morning and the light struck the copper pans hung on the walls, Marlatteira took Limasa's hands and held them tight in her own, she closed her eyes, and retraced Limasa's dream. Limasa looked at her forehead where the last hair, grey and frizzy, filtered the sun's rays and in that hair she saw more and more droplets of sweat. Then Marlatteira relaxed her grasp and slowly opened her eyes, round, the irises enclosed in a darker circle: she had understood everything, Limasa was pregnant and it hadn't been the dragoon. Together they remembered cousin Monette, who had predicted for Limasa a rich and lame husband with two gold teeth, and for Marlatteira a son who would be a general. Probably, Marlatteira said, cousin Monette had been mistaken, the rich and lame husband would marry her and Limasa, on the other hand, would have a general for a son. She should keep that baby and send the Zouave packing.

Limasa wept and could see nothing now, neither Marlatteira's beaded brow nor the copper pans reflecting the sun. She wept blindly over the dragoon Junot whom she had lost for ever, because now even if she were to recognize him she would look away in shame. Better to marry Zanzìa, Marlatteira said, than some Zouave who would take her to who knows what Godforsaken place where she would starve to death and the baby with her.

But Limasa didn't want to marry Zanzìa or anybody else, she wanted to remain faithful to the dragoon Junot who, for some unknown misfortune, had been obliged to run off without his trousers.

Antonia had heard other stories like Limasa's in the courtyard at Braida, and when the girl told her she was pregnant by the dragoon and he had drowned in the Tanaro, she pretended to believe it and wiped a handkerchief over Limasa's face, flooded with tears.

Maria and Fantina were told that Limasa was going off to marry a French soldier. In great haste because the Emperor's troops were leaving for home. Gavriel put her in the cart that took the salt cod every Tuesday to be sold at Lu and once again it was Mandrognin who proved useful.

Limasa sat under the fig tree where once Maria had sat and she wove straw to make baskets. The peace treaty had been signed at Villafranca and Napoleon III had embarked at Genoa amid a display of fireworks. The Zouave had gone home and no French dragoons had remained, with their horses, two by two, they had gone back beyond the Alps. From up there Limasa could see the peasants hoe and dig and scythe as they did every year, dark and distant under their broad straw hats. The last carriages went by in a cloud of dust and Catagrata toiled up with his cart on the road as round as a ribbon girdling the hill. Mandrognin never spoke, only at times, as he was kneading the bread, he would sing. It was always the same song: *La povra Olanda / L'è na fumna d'un tamburín / La va girée taverna pir taverna / A sirchée lo soi marí* . . . 'Poor Olanda, a drummer's wife, she goes from tavern to tavern, searching for her husband . . .' The broad hands lifted and slammed the dough and Limasa looked at him with hostility because it seemed to her that the song concealed a sly insult; but Mandrognin had other things on his mind and the lice hopped in his hair. He never spoke to Limasa because his great weakness had always been to love women who were beautiful, and he didn't want even to look at Limasa.

The one who took it worst was Pietro Giuseppe, who didn't believe the story of the marriage with the French soldier, not even for an instant. He had no trouble getting the truth out of Marlatteira; but once he had learned it he would have liked to erase every word of that story; it changed the world for him to learn that Limasa had conceived a bastard with a Zouave while she really loved the dragoon Junot. Limasa had deceived him, she was stupid, lying, unfaithful. He had been able to accept her love for the dragoon because he considered it somehow legitimate, but this monstrosity undid him.

He went out into the fields in the first dampness of autumn, violently trampling on the clods, stumbling, twisting his ankles, his throat dry from too much walking. He sat with his back against a mulberry and looking up towards the hills of Lu he cursed her and babies, born from women's wombs. Aloud he defended the dragoon offended by the nullity of feelings. He banged his head against the trunk of the mulberry, his eyes shut to repress the tears, mourning, for the first time, his orphan state.

One afternoon, coming home, he found Gavriel waiting for him in the drive and when he was within earshot Gavriel began to scold him, he had to stop this, Gavriel said, all this roaming around idly while they were breaking their backs at work. His father, Luìs, after the fever caught in May through the boy's fault, was suffering pain again in his leg, but all the same at dawn every morning he was already outside. Without replying, Pietro Giuseppe continued walking up the drive and as he passed, Gavriel tried to grab him by the arm, but the boy pulled free and stopped, farther on, to stare at him with his broad grey eyes. Gavriel felt his voice rise in his throat and die there, he cursed in dialect, and it seemed to him that he hated this boy, so slovenly and sturdy. Get out, he said, you don't belong to us, you're Maturlin blood.

Pietro Giuseppe barely knitted his eyebrows, the insult struck him in an unfamiliar part of himself, whose vulnerability he had never before considered. He turned his back and entered the house, where the little ones came running to him and Sofia insisted he pick her up. He lay then on the floor in their midst and in the light of the fire in the fireplace, coloured by the air, it seemed to him he was a child again, and stretching out his legs, he let Sofia walk up and down on him, and Evasio played with the buttons of his jacket.

Since the day of his whipping Pietro Giuseppe's adolescence has ended, ended the time of tenderness and abandonment; the time of judgements has arrived, and his judgements are immediate, pitiless. No pity for you, Uncle Gavriel, who have missed, one after the other, the opportunities of life. He watches Gavriel seated at the table going over the accounts with Antonia, and meanwhile his fingers smooth Sofia's hair, the fire illuminates the patched stockings on his feet, patched by Limasa who used to come every evening to turn off the light by his bed. What do they know of Limasa's meaning for him, he, who had no mother and hardly any father; what do they know of her odour of grain and milk that always consoled him for the darkness? Of her laughter like the flicker of a candle when she slipped away, making his throat pulse?

'Pietro,' Gavriel calls him, sorry for his words. Pietro Giuseppe raises his head; so do Sofia and Duardin, and little Evasio. 'Pietro!' Gavriel's voice has become stronger, it is a curt voice but somehow also pleading, and Sofia slips down from her brother's lap, Antonia interrupts her sums. Pietro Giuseppe, seated on the floor, his hair rumpled, now looks like a big puppet with painted cheeks. All wait to hear what Gavriel has to say, and suddenly a sense of the comic overcomes suffering, anger, even pride, and Gavriel laughs. He laughs as when he was a boy; as in the days before Elisabetta went away and his father drove him from the house, before Gioacchino flew down on the wings of his little brown jacket.

Antonia laughs, and the children. And Pietro Giuseppe laughs, too, a light laughter barely edged with embarrassment, his hand scratches his hair dirty with earth and tree bark. But that forgiveness Gavriel is waiting for, Pietro Giuseppe's eyes, as if absent, refuse him.

Limasa's little girl was born at the beginning of spring. The midwife, as soon as she saw the red kerchief Mandrognin had tied to the fig tree as a signal, climbed up the path full of holes. Up there a strong wind was blowing and Mandrognin already had the water boiling and the cloths were spread out near the fire, but the moment the midwife saw Limasa she took fright: the girl's skin was purplish, she writhed and clenched her teeth, and as soon as the woman approached her, she grabbed her, digging her nails into the midwife's flesh. Mandrognin, immobile, waited at the door to be told what to do, indifferent to that scene as if he had witnessed it many times before. The midwife sent him outside because the sight of him made Limasa even more agitated, and Mandrognin went out, slamming the door, giving no thought to the trembling that had seized the girl, and through the clouded windows she saw the big white head go by. If it was true that the devil was at home here then he was surely shut up in Limasa's belly; and instead of helping her the midwife began reciting prayers. Then a gust of wind blew the window wide open and Mandrognin's voice could be heard singing *La povra Olanda / L'è na fumna d'un tamburín* . . . Limasa let out a howl and the midwife didn't have time to reach out before the baby's head had already emerged.

She was a long and thin baby with blonde hair beneath which you could see the veins of the skull throbbing, but her face was round and ruddy, and the midwife couldn't recall such a pretty infant. She immediately set about washing her and wrapping her with great care in the swaddling clothes, forgetting Limasa, who had turned pale again, the pock-marks prominent in her face haggard from suffering, her body shivering violently. Mandrognin looked in at the window and asked what it was, and the midwife showed him the little girl on the sill. Mandrognin had just taken the bread from the oven and he invited the woman to eat some with him under the fig tree. Darkness fell and the evening chill stung the skin, Mandrognin went to fetch wine but after the second glass the midwife remembered Limasa and, frightened, she ran inside. Limasa hadn't stirred, hadn't even touched the baby laid beside her in the bed; and if the midwife hadn't come back she would have let herself bleed to death with her eyes closed, cold as if they had stretched her out on the snow.

Limasa decided to call the baby Olanda and nobody could make her change her mind. At the baptismal font the priest gave her also the name of Maria, but once they were out of the church that Maria was immediately forgotten. Limasa recovered quickly and two days after giving birth she was already at the fountain washing clothes, at dawn so that nobody would see her. For a month she kept Olanda with her and when the baby cried at night Mandrognin would cradle her and give her something to drink because Limasa, once she had nursed the child, refused to touch her. It was Mandrognin, too, who chose the peasant woman to be the baby's wet-nurse, promising that if she took good care of the baby he would work for her one day a week for nothing. Any kind of work.

Limasa came back dressed in mourning: her husband, the soldier, was dead, she told everyone, and she was returning to her job. The children made a big fuss over her and never stopped hugging and kissing her, pulling at her skirt. Some time later she asked the priest if she could put aside the mourning, which was saddening the house. The priest made it clear that she could dress however she chose, it would change nothing, provided she did penance for her sins. And everything was once again as it had been before.

Not for Pietro Giuseppe. When Limasa got down from the cart that had brought her home and the children ran to her, he pretended not to see her and while she narrated, in abundant detail, the death of her soldier husband and her brief, wondrous happiness, he began reading and a little later left the room, irked by the noise. That evening, when Limasa opened his door to put out the light, the room was already in darkness and from that darkness a voice she didn't recognize asked her what she wanted; she hesitated a moment until that same voice asked her to close the door, because he wanted to sleep.

Like Luìs and Gavriel, now Pietro Giuseppe joined the ranks of those people who intimidated Limasa. Only at times the boy's eyes rested on her face and, grey and thoughtful, they seemed to wonder what could have happened so to upset the meaning of events. What negative power had led her to overcome the desires of the heart and sacrifice them to her impulses? To betray when we want to be faithful? To forget what we would like to remember until death? Then, that gaze said, my infancy in your arms, my hand which grew in yours, our life, Limasa: nothing is worth suffering for.

In autumn the oldest of the Maturlin sisters turned up for a visit, the one who had taken away the muskrat coat and the cap and the muff. She had married and she sat under the walnut, elegant like all the Maturlin girls, still beautiful, the big blue eyes and the smile, very beautiful indeed. But her fascination, that sort of challenge in the face at once delicate and brutal, that mixture of vulgarity and grace that was so striking in her manners, that had been lost in the smug serenity of the full cheeks, the relaxed features. She was a mature matron who laughed easily and stroked the children, so pleased with life that she found everything marvellous: the walnut, the house, Marlatteira's cakes. She fanned herself with her gloves and the bees buzzed around her hat rich with flowers, fruit, birds, and if a child laid a dirty hand on the silk of her dress, she betrayed no irritation. She had travelled a great deal, had been in Le Havre, Marseilles, Vichy. She said Vichy drawing out the letters, as if sucking them between her lips. But of all the cities the one she had liked best was Bordeaux. In Bordeaux she had met her husband, a lawyer, a great lawyer. She pronounced this last phrase in a whisper, as if it were part of a secret destiny.

She was invited to stay the night and the hired carriage was dismissed. Excited by the visit, the children didn't want to go to bed and Marlatteira kept coming in from the kitchen so that she too could hear the tales of Bordeaux and Vichy. Though the gaze of the oldest Maturlin in conversation was addressed to all, it kept returning insistently to Pietro Giuseppe. In the course of the talking she asked him about his studies and his tastes. Before it grew dark she asked Limasa to accompany her to the cemetery.

Along the road through the fields, amid the burning stubble with pillars of white smoke, she and Limasa had a long talk. At a certain point the oldest of the Maturlins asked Limasa to pick her some wild mint, which reminded her of her girlhood, and she pointed out the distant hills that had been part of their lands. It was late and the guardian of the cemetery was about to lock up, she gave him a silver coin and told Limasa to wait, she would be quick. Instead, she came back only when you could hardly see, the gravel shone white and Limasa saw she was crying, leaning against the wall where the blue campanulas had already closed.

But that evening at table it was hard to imagine her face in tears, she chatted tirelessly and displayed a great fondness for wine. She talked now about Genoa, where she lived, and she extolled its arcades, Piazza de Ferrari and the Albaro hill, where she went to breathe the pure air, and the ships of every description that berthed in the port.

The next morning, as the carriage was already waiting to take her away, she suggested to Luìs that Pietro Giuseppe be allowed to come to Genoa. If he liked it he could finish his studies there and go on to the University. They had no children, she added, and they would give Pietro Giuseppe a handsome room all to himself, overlooking the square. She looked at Luìs and, awaiting an answer, she smiled serenely but the vein in her neck was throbbing in fear of a refusal.

The request surprised Luìs. He wanted some time to think it over. The oldest of the Maturlins got into the carriage, the door would not close easily and it had to be slammed several times, she leaned out of the window and pressed her nephew's hand at length; then the carriage disappeared down the drive and the children returned to playing with their wagon, Antonia went into the house and Luìs followed her. Pietro Giuseppe knelt on the ground with some crumbs soaked in wine, to train the crow.

That evening he spoke to his father. His greatest desire, he said, was to go to his aunt's in Genoa. He said desire but as he raised his eyes Luìs read in them an unshakeable determination. The low, graceless voice, still hoarse in that transition period, betrayed the effort it cost him to speak with his father. Nothing and no one would ever budge him from this idea.

That winter Antonia's last child was born, Pia, in honour of Pius IX. Even though Luìs didn't share his wife's devotion to the Pope, he was once again in agreement with her, and Pia, known as Piulott, in the space of a week became Limasa's new great love.

She was the never-born daughter of the dragoon and when Antonia held the infant to her breast Limasa stood and watched, ecstatic, unable to tear herself away from the room. She would collect the clean squares of cloth, and fold them, just to hear the gurgle of milk in the baby's throat, to enjoy her every instant. At night Limasa rocked her even when there was no need and what had cost her so much effort with the others became, with Piulott, happiness. The smack of her kisses could be heard from room to room and her voice, singing the *Cavalier*

Franseis, drove Marlatteira crazy, she was forced to hear it so many times a day.

Piulott began smiling almost at once and at a year she talked, to the great wonder of the household. She was a very tiny baby, almost hairless, and she resembled no one. Seated upright in her high chair, she looked all round, her eyes more intensely curious than any ever seen, and she yelled and struggled until they lifted her down. Limasa made a short red dress for her and in it Piulott went all about the house, running the risk of being knocked down if not actually trampled on, she was so small and quick, and she would suddenly be there underfoot. Limasa very soon taught her to sing and the assistant priest, who came one day to call on Antonia, said that there were strange rumours circulating in the town. He wanted to know if it was true that the child who bore the name of His Holiness Pius IX went around singing the *Cavalier Franseis*.

Piulott was sent for and instead of singing when she saw the priest's black cassock she began to cry, in sobs that resembled howls. The assistant priest took fright, blessed her, and advised taking her to the Sanctuary of Crea. And, furthermore, what was the meaning of this red dress? Red was the colour of the Devil.

Limasa burned the red dress in the fire and made another one, pale blue, which was the colour of the Madonna and the Angels. She taught Piulott the song *Santa Maria Maddalena in dal mar an burrasca* about the saint on a stormy sea; but the hair on the baby's head remained a fuzzy down like a bird's, and in spite of the blue dress she ran with the speed of a mouse after the chicks, the rabbits, the hens that squawked as they spread their wings. And Antonia decided to take her to Crea. She was pregnant again and, while she was at it, she would consecrate also the baby still to be born.

But she was too late. Piulott fell ill with German measles and for a month Limasa never left her bedside. At night in the glow of the oil lamp she watched Piulott's head grow smaller and smaller, its down stuck to the pillow with sweat and to her it seemed, dark as it was, the head of a puppy. A bottomless silence, grim, oppressive, grew dense in the corners; for fear of falling asleep she bit her nails till the blood came and meanwhile she thought back over her whole life, from the moment Gavriel brought her home to the day of her meeting with the dragoon, when seated on Bigiot's bench he had told her about the Auvergne and his town Le Puy. She stroked Piulott's hand, now lying without any strength on the sheet, and the little, dark fingers seemed kneaded from earth, ready to crumble. This was not the daughter of the dragoon, nor was she the child of Luìs and Madama; she was the baby born from Limasa's breath and by her breath kept alive.

Antonia went to Crea, taking the other children with her, to implore a special favour. It was an exhausting trip, her belly awkward in the carriage, and the children, unused to being still, wriggling in their seats. A heavy, dusty heat, unstirring, made her temples throb and no fan could make it more bearable. Some black clouds had gathered on the horizon and they stayed there, lightning-flashes piercing them above the yellow countryside. In front of the Virgin Antonia knelt on the floor and stayed there for almost an hour, her insides hard as if they had turned to stone. The children scattered throughout the church attracted by the candles and the coming and going of the pilgrims; and while Antonia became colder and colder they were sweating as they chased one another among the confessionals, pursued by the sacristan who couldn't find out who was responsible for those *masnà*, those little bandits.

What Antonia said during all that time to the Black Virgin of Crea, what she promised on that day of great heat, no one ever knew; she became all icy and to separate her hands clasped in prayer she had to soak them in water. That evening, when Luìs saw her coming back, grey as the dust that covered her dress, he was gripped by a great fear. He didn't even notice the children limp with sleep as they were carried up to bed.

He held his wife tight: her belly pressed against him, she seemed to grow thinner, to be nothing now but that enormous womb, her skin bathed with tears of weariness. Luìs held her tight and felt that if he were to relax his arms for only an instant she would slip away and he would have lost her for ever. She's better, he whispered in her ear, Piulott is better, her fever's gone down, she's sleeping . . . but he felt Antonia's body surrendering more and more as an inner tremor shook her, like a last spring that vibrated still before breaking down utterly.

Maria and Fantina observed his embrace, dumbstruck. Luìs kissed his wife's brow, the eyelids that no longer had the strength to move, he moistened her dry lips with his saliva: life without her, as it had appeared to him in a flash the moment he had seen her dragging herself towards the house, seemed to him unbearable. Every least part of him rebelled at this thought. Go, go ahead, he said to his mother and to Fantina, and taking Antonia in his arms, step by step, slowly, he climbed the stairs, carried her into the bedroom, undressed her and put her to bed, taking an infinite amount of time so great was his care in performing each movement as if she would dissolve at the first careless touch.

Piulott recovered, the Virgin of Crea worked the miracle. The Magna Munja, even if she did not find Piulott particularly sanctified, agreed to paint the picture that would go to Crea in perpetual gratitude to the Virgin.

She painted a little girl so dark that she seemed born in blackest Africa, and Antonia was a little heap of rags on the floor. In one corner, up above, the Madonna of Crea in cottony clouds while Limasa, erect at the foot of the bed, had her braids coiled so many times around her head that they formed a crown. And she seemed the true beneficiary of the miracle, the bastard maidservant mother of a bastard daughter, her pious eyes looking up and two tears, like pearls, on her cheeks.

Limasa kissed the canvas, kissed the hands of the Magna Munja and begged to be the one to take the picture to Crea. Antonia was still in bed because of that baby, born at seven months, who had lived only one day: you can go ahead, as far as I'm concerned, she said. Her gaze was fixed on the walnut leaves that were darkening. That tremor, that inner spring that Luìs had sensed, embracing her on the day of her return from Crea, had stopped, now she was calm. But after the birth of that last baby she seemed to have entered another space, where desires and impulses fell away even before they took shape. I'm happy for you to go, she added, and her gaze shifted from the walnut leaves to Limasa's face: an overpowering nostalgia for the time when, as a girl, she had run barefoot in the Braida courtyard.

Zanzìa offered to take everyone in his cart, all rebuilt after that voyage afloat on the waters of the Po, and Marlatteira cooked and filled a hamper with food. The last stars were shining when Limasa got into the cart with the still-sleepy children and Piulott tried to climb in by herself for fear of being left behind.

It was an unforgettable journey. Zanzìa joked with Limasa, was constantly sighing and hinting, and his toothless mouth looked naked. Limasa answered him back and kept producing sweets from the hamper, figs, slices of warm polenta. As Zanzìa whipped the horse from time to time, it would start galloping to the delight of the children and amid the screams of Limasa, who still grasped this one and that one by their clothes for fear they would be bounced out, clinging herself to the sides so as not to end up on the ground. It was October and at the top of the Alps, in the distance, you could see the first snow glistening, the stubble was burning in the fields and filled the air with the smell of autumn. The more Limasa screamed the more amused Zanzìa was, whipping the horse, and when they turned in among the beeches of the road up to the Sanctuary, the devotees of the Madonna who were climbing up on foot, slowly praying in chorus, stopped aghast at the racket of that cart with Zanzìa standing up, shaking his arse and the whip, as if he were going off to war.

Once they were in front of the Sanctuary the sacristan recognized the children and forbade them to enter, he granted access only to Piulott because she was the beneficiary of the miracle, and the others ran down to the woods with Zanzìa, who was playing his harmonica. Limasa set the picture at the feet of the Virgin and in the church a great silence fell, everyone recognized her as the woman with her braids in the form of a crown and even Piulott, for the first time, seemed an ordinary little girl, her head covered by a white veil, pensive and silent, holding Limasa's hand.

It was night when they came back and the moon was high and shining, Zanzìa had drunk and become melancholy, the dust of the road was barely stirred by the horse's hoofs. The children were asleep on the straw spread out on the bottom of the cart and Limasa kept them covered with an old blanket. Only Piulott was awake and, clinging to the side, she looked at the moon, the tall elms that cast a black shadow on the fields. The pale houses, scattered in the countryside where the baying of the dogs rose as the cart went by. It was the first time Piulott had witnessed the spectacle of the night and her eyes widened in her long, fledgling's face. Limasa had wrapped her in her shawl and at every jolt of the cart the shawl slipped down farther, she was no longer like a puppy or a mouse, she was a little vulture, its talons clutching the wood. Dumb, alert, as if, alone in understanding the great significance of that spectacle, she kept herself in readiness to join her winged brothers. Motionless, among the patterns of the constellations.

In February Mandrognin died. They found him several days later still sitting in his chair: the wind that had piled up the snow against the door had preserved him intact, all white, his hands clenched into fists. Nobody was able to open them, and many made conjectures about gold coins, perhaps marengos from the days of Napoleon's passage.

Neither Maria nor Fantina could give his age, he was already grown up when they first knew him, still wearing a pigtail as the custom had been then. Ninety, perhaps a hundred: his shoulders had never stooped, his mind was crazed but sharp, and even after the last snowfall they had seen him clearing the path with a shovel, the goat that shared his house trotting behind him.

If Luison had been alive she could have told them about his life as a youth, about his nickname that could come from the village where he was born (but they didn't know this either) or perhaps from the rich cloak mentioned in the song *Bel Galant u s'è spartí*. Three hundred silver lire were found in the bread bin, sewn in a little silk bag. On it, Mandrognin had embroidered in red cotton: dowry of Olanda known as Suava.

This, in fact, was what Mandrognin had called Limasa's daughter when he went to see her once a week at the wet-nurse's. He would work and the child would crouch beside him, *suava*, as he said. He didn't dare touch her and was never seen giving her a caress or taking her in his arms. But he made sure she had stockings in winter and that her dress was always neatly patched.

Limasa hid the three hundred lire where nobody would ever find it and went to collect the child. Suava had no clothes, no bundle, nothing, and Limasa led her away by the hand. For the last stretch of road she hoisted the child onto her shoulders. The child had never seen her and kept silent for the whole journey, Limasa tried to tell a story but her voice died in her throat; and when she ventured a song, the child's hands, holding her mother's neck just enough to keep from falling, didn't move. When you're a big girl you'll have a dowry, a real dowry, she kept repeating, and this word filled her lungs, made the road easy; but the child understood nothing of what her mother was saying to her and when they passed through the gate she began to shiver. Darkness was coming on and there was a great silence broken only by the lowing of a cow, and

Limasa took her in her arms. She felt how stiff the child was, alien, and on her face, in the child's breath, she suddenly smelled again the odour of the Zouave.

The day they said the Trigesima Mass for Mandrognin, Maria was found dead in her bed, her head resting on the sheet. Her still dark, thick hair seemed an abandoned scalp, the face had shrunk so. Under the pillow they found the snuffbox that Monsieur La Ville had given her at Casale. In it there was only dust, perhaps what remained of the pipe that Gioacchino had made for himself from the top of a reed. But who could say? And similarly, nobody would ever know which of the three men of her life had been the most important, whether it was Giai, or Pidrèn later known as Sacarlott, or Mandrognin. In her last years she hardly ever spoke and had stopped playing solitaire, she spent long evenings at the window always looking out even when the fog obliterated every shape. She was buried beneath Gioacchino as she had always wanted and Gavriel went to Alessandria to buy a stone cross carved with strands of ivy. Someone, as he was coming home, shot at his back, perhaps to rob him; though there were those who spoke of a vendetta of Camurà's. Gavriel saved himself by crouching flat against the horse's neck and the wounded animal left a long wake of blood on the snow.

That summer, for the first time, the Magna Munja did not come back for her vacation and her room remained empty. Her mother was no longer there and Pietro Giuseppe by now had become a stranger to her, ready to become that man she had feared on the day of Luìs's marriage to Antonia.

Precise, obedient, Pietro Giuseppe got up every morning before daybreak and followed his father, his boots sinking in among the clods, getting soaked if it rained, sweating if it was hot. Never complaining. But if Luìs or Gavriel turned to look at him as he walked behind them, they promptly realized that, whether it was corn or vineyard, alfalfa or oats, he regarded everything with the same detachment. The same, invincible boredom. He passed through cane brakes or along the vine rows in a landscape that constantly changed, light, colour, smell, and nothing, animal or plant, attracted his attention. Without speaking, without smiling. They went up to the Gru farm and he stayed in the barnyard, his hands folded. The only thing he noticed was the cherry tree that, like a big umbrella, was covered with white flowers in the spring and then with purple fruit, almost black. He ate those cherries, absently, spitting the stones far away.

It was Antonia who pleaded his cause. Pietro Giuseppe kissed his brothers and sisters one by one, and lingered for a long time with his head on his stepmother's shoulder; then he climbed into the cart that was transporting some furniture to Novi. From there he would go on to Genoa. In a last fit of pique, Luìs had decided the train cost too much for his son.

That night Limasa lay awake and heard all the sounds of the house, from Piulott's little steps as she slipped into Suava's bed to Marlatteira's snoring. To that faint squeak Fantina emitted in her sleep, like the gnawing of a termite. Pietro Giuseppe's departure separated Limasa from her girlhood, beyond return. It was as if the girl she had been were standing on the rear platform of a train vanishing into the countryside: her girlhood was there, in the shaking of the last car, and it grew dimmer and dimmer. On that platform cousin Monette was going away, and the boy who caught pike and carp at Pomaro, the Zouave and the dragoon Junot, Pietro Giuseppe who had hugged her under the oak. The wind shook the boughs of the walnut and slammed them against the shutters, Suava complained because she couldn't sleep with Piulott kicking in her bed, Limasa pretended not to hear, as the eyes of her mind fixed on that train going faster and faster away and carrying off the dragoon and cousin Monette and also all the men with whom she had made love. Perhaps she had never loved anyone and from that train, for herself, she would have liked to snatch only Pietro Giuseppe.

Zanzìa was killed on the night of February 7th, 1863. He died, smothered in the mud down at the Pontisella, and nobody in the neighbouring houses admitted to seeing or hearing a thing. And yet he must have made a lot of noise because the railing of the bridge had shattered and all around there was blood and scraps of clothing.

This wasn't the first time a crime had been committed in the town, but Zanzìa's death chilled the bones. Nothing had been taken from him and in the water they found his wallet, full, and the watch King Vittorio Emanuele had given him when he had gone to play at Occimiano. But now it was years since Zanzìa had gone about with his instrument, he had become rich and had bought a house on the Barbecana road where he scandalized people by keeping there a girl from the upper Malenco valley.

The girl was sent for and taken to Alessandria, she spoke hardly any Italian and when they asked her how she made herself understood with Zanzìa she burst out laughing. But she was of age and with Zanzìa's death she had everything to lose, so she was sent back until such a time as she could be shipped to the place she came from. The gendarmes turned the new house on the Barbecana road inside out, they searched from top to bottom for some evidence of the contraband traffic in salt that everyone knew had made Zanzìa rich. But they found only empty sacks and that instrument – harmonica, bass drum and violin – which he had invented and had continued to play now and then for his own pleasure.

The night of his death Marlatteira had a dream. Neither terrible nor beautiful, but the road on which she was walking through the red clover flowers led straight to Fracin's old house, where once the smith, tall and heavyset with a flowing moustache, had hammered the incandescent iron. And there it ended. And while the gendarmes were searching the rooms of the house on the Barbecana road looking for God only knows what riches, she sat in the kitchen and searched her memory for a woman because she was sure that Zanzìa's death was the revenge of a jealous man. Or a betrayed one, because Zanzìa had always pestered women.

Limasa is crying, Zanzìa had never been bad with her and they had laughed and joked together, he wanted to marry her. Now she thinks that if she had said yes to him years ago Zanzìa wouldn't have met this horrible end, there wouldn't have been all that blood. The crows light, cawing, on what is left of the snow while through the clouded panes comes the sound of the Tribundina, and the bell that celebrates the arrival of an innocent soul in heaven, poor infants carried off by milk-fever, no voice left to cry with, has never caused her such grief. The children have grown and are studying in the next room, the voice of the tutor is still the same, they have the same shaved heads and trousers to below the knee; they quarrel over a pen, a sheet of paper. Sofia is in boarding school at the Magna Munja's convent, and Suava, even if she has a dowry, sets off, when it is still dark, to learn needlework, taking with her half an apple and a slice of polenta for her dinner. Sometimes a few dried chestnuts to strengthen her teeth.

And Zanzìa . . . Tears fill Limasa's eyes. '*Smettla*,' Marlatteira says, '*al'era in porc*. Stop that: he was a pig.'

Limasa went to visit the girl who had lived with Zanzìa, before they could ship her back nobody knew where, as she had no home. Limasa felt sorry for her because nobody would touch her or talk to her. The girl was beautiful and dirty and ate hazelnuts, cracking them between her teeth. Limasa brought her two sausages along with a bit of bread and she accepted everything, though there was no lack of provisions in the house and Zanzìa had filled the larder with every sort of food. She didn't even say thank you; but when Limasa reached the door, leaving, the girl put in her hands a tin candlestick in the shape of a hen's foot. That candlestick frightened Limasa, that claw seemed the devil's hoof to her. But the girl insisted, she had round and silly eyes, in her village lost in the mountains there wasn't even a road, perhaps the place didn't even have a name. '*Te qui, te qui*,' she insisted, 'Take it,' hiding the candlestick under her dress so it wouldn't be seen by Zanzìa's relatives, who had swarmed like flies to divide up his things.

But the murderer has not been found. Summer has arrived and Sofia has come home from school, embraced her brothers and sisters, and their voices fill the house. In the kitchen the broad wet swathes left by the cloth are not dry before they have to start dirtying everything again for supper. Marlatteira huffs and the girls who have come to help her, children eleven, twelve years old who can hardly believe their luck in eating chicken or rabbit now and then, work hard shining the copper, listen spellbound to her stories about Fantina who embroidered Giai's head on the priest's cope or about Gonda, who died in church and went straight to heaven. Many saw her soul at that Early Mass before it ascended, Marlatteira says, light as a candle flame. Whereas Zanzìa has surely gone to hell because even if the gendarmes haven't found the murderer, in the village they all know Zanzìa was smothered in the mud by Fracin's second son, with the help of his brother.

She can tell those little girls no more than that. She can talk only about her dream that led to the house at the end of the bridge, where the air is unhealthy and the mosquitoes in summer give not a moment's respite. Nobody speaks willingly about what happened to Zanzìa, who got a sixteen-year-old girl pregnant, a cripple, with a cleft palate, but with a pair of breasts as hard as quinces. What was a father to do except crush him like a worm; and nobody has breathed a word to the gendarmes, they are still searching among the smugglers and are keeping Navot in jail, Zanzìa's business partner.

And yet in those houses, greenish with damp, and with windows like holes, more than one woke with a start that night.

More than one heard Zanzìa's screams, the crash of the railing as it fell and then silence while, through the hastily wiped panes, they saw his legs struggling more and more weakly. '*Mi sag nènta, mi sag nènta!*' they say to the gendarmes, 'I don't know anything,' opening the door only a crack, all of them blind and deaf, asleep.

And now the new priest, a bellicose young man who comes from the Biella mountains, thunders from the height of the pulpit against whited sepulchres; against people who see and do not speak, do not warn the father of the dangers his daughter faces. These people look on and enjoy themselves, and then on Sunday they come to Mass and beat their breasts. The girl has drunk almost a quart of a parsley infusion and has nearly died, what sort of world do we live in?

Limasa clasps her face in her hands, she cannot believe this story. It must have been the girl who led him on ... she murmurs to Marlatteira. Be quiet, silly! She knows they followed the whole thing from those windows like holes, they saw Zanzìa slipping into the house as soon as the mother left it to go to the fields. The girl appeared once at the window, she was naked and seemed crazy, Zanzìa immediately pulled her back and afterwards they were heard moaning and sighing. A girl of sixteen ... Marlatteira looks at Suava who is skipping around with her curls hanging down to her shoulders; and what if someone did it to her, she asks Limasa. Limasa starts, Suava is a precious creature, rare, her mother is almost in awe of her, and even if the child were not good and serene by nature, Limasa would never be capable of scolding her the way she scolds Piulott.

In the tangle of bloodlines that has produced Suava there must have been a great gentleman or perhaps an unfortunate Madama with fine features and waxen skin. Even if Limasa really had made her with the dragoon, that child couldn't have been more beautiful. Time and again Limasa has been tempted to dip into the dowry coins and buy her a new dress, a ribbon to tie up her dark, thick hair. but that cannot, must not, be done.

At night, in the darkness, she sees Zanzìa again, she sees him entering the house that once was Fracin's down at the Pontisella and she sees the girl with the cleft palate. A shudder chills her in her bed and she begins to recite the prayers for indulgences because perhaps Zanzìa has some excuse. God must feel sorry for him, toothless since he was a boy; and perhaps after a thousand, two thousand years in Purgatory, he will finally be allowed to enter Paradise.

7

GIAI'S VIOLIN

That summer, when Pietro Giuseppe came home for his vacation, his brothers and sisters would never leave him alone, they followed him even beyond the gate, quarrelling to be closest to him until, exasperated, he raised his voice to send them back to the house. They obeyed reluctantly, following him with their eyes as he went down the dusty road, his hands in his pockets, and his straw hat pushed back on his head. Fascinated and intimidated by that brother who now united the prestige of being older with the further, darker and more thrilling prestige of a city that overlooked the sea and had palaces, theatres, ships riding at anchor.

To them Pietro Giuseppe's life appears like the flickering lights whose intermittence indicates from a distance a life that darkness makes still more fantastic. For Pietro Giuseppe never says anything about himself and when he mentions the arrival of a ship or a performance at the theatre he evades every question that concerns him. His emotions are absent. Where is he, in his long student's coat or in the broad cloak of black wool indispensable on the cold blustery evenings, when the north-west wind blows from the port and rocks the ships' masts?

On the other hand, he is generous with details about Tante Marianne, as he calls his aunt, about the house heavy with hangings, where footsteps make no sound and every afternoon from the pastry shop they bring up the hot brioches that Tante Marianne dips into her chocolate. In her service Tante

Marianne has a *boy*, who accompanies her when she goes out and sits erect on a special little seat behind the carriage.

'A . . . what?' Duardin asks. *'Boy,'* Pietro Giuseppe repeats the English word, laconic. Dazed, Sofia scratches her ear; Piulott, the thin one, goes off somewhere else because she doesn't understand. Pietro Giuseppe calls her back, takes her on his lap; a servant, he explains to her, a little black page whom Tante Marianne dresses in gaudy silk. The others gape with amazement as Piulott leans against his chest as if nothing could amaze her; and from that privileged position she looks defiantly at Duardin, Sofia, Evasio.

Tante Marianne also possesses a keyboard violin, a rare and modern instrument, and demoiselle Ginette plays for her the arias from *L'italiana in Algeri*, an opera that Tante Marianne loves passionately and she listens with her face supported by her hand, her big eyes shining in the reddish shadow of the curtains. Demoiselle Ginette is a 'refugee'; from what and from whom she has fled no one knows, she is a girl with frizzy hair high over her brow and with small, very pale eyes capable of fixing her interlocutor with a disconcerting intensity. Not beautiful, Tante Marianne would say, but of great character.

Tante Marianne flings the window open, and the blazing sun of the winter dusk bursts over the tufted sofas, the *faux marbre* tables, the shawls flung over the armchairs. From the window she signals to someone in the square while that early sunset light shines in her blue and languid eyes. And when she turns and sees her nephew she has a start, her face flushes violet. The face of a girl: down below are the former lovers of the oldest Maturlin. They come to see her from every part of the world, from Vichy and from Bordeaux, from Antwerp; and the first, never forgotten, from Bosco Marengo. She signals to them from the window when the coast is clear because her husband does not like to encounter them and they sit amid the gold and red of the chairs and talk about shared memories, they drink chocolate, enchanted by her smile that still stirs the blood. They bring her rare sweets, essences with exotic names which she orders the *boy* to throw out as soon as the visitors have gone; such is Tante Marianne's love for her husband and her fear that he could be disturbed by some trifle. Unusual flowers like columbines, a perfume different from that *Jasmin de Corse* she has used since she met him in Bordeaux, where, after a week, he carried her off to become his wife.

In the evening she sits beside the fire built on the andirons and with her husband she talks of the pastry shop's bill, of the day's events, her face rosy with powder, her hands stretched out towards the flames, the long string of pearls sliding into the furrow between her breasts. From a corner her nephew looks at her in silence, enthralled by her metamorphoses. Tante Marianne smiles at him but it is as if she didn't see him, as if he had already moved beyond her purview and her smile imagines him outside there, on the stairs illuminated by a gas lamp. Demoiselle Ginette has closed the keyboard violin, a smile dismisses her as well, the girl's feet are soundless on the rug and for a moment, as she goes towards the door, the fire seems to crackle in the hair piled high over her brow, kindle her pale cheeks; Tante Marianne traps an escaping ember and as she does, she glides slowly from her chair, kneeling before the flames in a broad display of shawls.

What could a young refugee do, and Luìs's oldest son, barely twenty, encouraged, driven to leave the room, the house, through the handsome door of heavy oak? They left. They liked those evenings with the smells that came up from the sea, they were both young and didn't feel the cold, the wind stung their cheeks, and demoiselle Ginette slipped her hands into her muff. If Pietro Giuseppe's hands were frozen he could slip them in there, too. The two walked on and they talked, down through the narrow alleys of the port, and if they encountered some drunk Pietro Giuseppe protected her under his broad black cloak. They followed the line of the shore and at times the spray wet that cloak, they watched the lights trembling in the water and the ships' masts become confused with the black of the clouds. From the taverns around the basin they heard the hoarse cries of the dice-players, demoiselle Ginette masked her fear with little bursts of laughter that seemed to well up from the depths of her eyes.

When spring came they began to venture further, towards the outskirts, where demoiselle Ginette had some friends. There in the evening the streets were unlit and they had to take care where they put their feet, people called one another from house to house and the windows were patched with paper, babies could be heard crying. The port was far away and the fishermen spread their nets along the canal, the smell of spring mingled with the smell of the water where refuse rotted. They entered what demoiselle Ginette called the *Milieux*, there they found other refugees like her and the kerosene lamps stank, blackened your nostrils. In the fervour of the debate demoiselle Ginette forgot about Pietro Giuseppe and, standing on a chair, shouted in that hoarse southern French of hers.

Afterwards, if it was not too late, they made love in a boat tied up in the canal, sheltered by some tarpaulin. And with the same fervour she had brought to the debate, demoiselle Ginette participated in those long embraces to the swaying of the boat.

In the summer of '64 Pietro Giuseppe's siblings found him changed. He had lost all desire for society and if some friend came to invite him out, he would refuse on some pretext. He preferred to stay at home, even if only to play blind man's buff, a game he had loathed ever since he was a child.

Often in the morning he collected his books in a basket and climbed up to the Gru farm, where he would sit and read and make notes in the shade of the cherry tree, an overturned keg for his table. He praised the Gru air and even the sultry heat of certain days when everything was still, stagnant, and silence was all around him, broken only by the squawk of the geese going down to drink. The first few times Limasa and the children went up there with him, stopping at a distance so as not to disturb him, but then they stopped because it was hard for the little ones to climb up in that heat, and from the fields the peasants could see him alone up there under the tree, his elbows propped on the overturned keg, as he leafed through the books at a steady pace. A great notebook lay open before him, from time to time he bent his head to write in it, his pen coming and going at the inkwell set on the keg.

Those books, once he is home again, he locks in his room and rarely opens them, though he takes out the notebook occasionally and writes something, no one knows what. To all questions he gives evasive answers. Is this connected with examinations or not? Perhaps not with examinations exactly, there is still time for them. But with his studies, yes, for his studies it is very important. He wrinkles his brow, he scratches his sweaty head. He smiles with his grey eyes.

Demoiselle Ginette he has mentioned only fleetingly and nobody suspects that the letters he receives twice a week are from her. The pale-blue envelopes are addressed in a firm, fluent, virile hand. Pietro Giuseppe slips them into his pocket without opening them as if he already knew what they contained and, at his father's questions or Antonia's, he raises his absent gaze, himself curious at the curiosity of the others.

Often, towards dusk, he stops and talks to the farmhands and sits with them in the stable, bending over to watch them do the milking. But it is not to learn how, surely: he is counting the days that separate him from his return to Genoa and he has made himself a little wooden calendar on which he crosses out those days one after the other. An eagerness to be gone that he never betrays; at evening he sits down at the spinet and with the extraordinary talent inherited from his mother he rediscovers the notes of *L'italiana in Algeri*. His brothers and sisters start dancing, gaily he strikes the keys; Suava also arrives with her arms open wide, ready to take flight.

Through the windows comes the smell of grass and of the evening, and the children, excited by the music, pass and bump into one another, shouting. The grown-ups, more clumsy, also dance. Antonia looks in at the door, and to her, those young people and those children seem to belong to nature, like the apples on the trees outside, and the wild rabbits in the fields. Pietro Giuseppe is at the height of his splendour, at that age where colours are brighter, movements impetuous, and the body has a force that seems tangible in the air.

She looks at him, admiring, not daring to enter. This happiness, theirs and hers, at this moment nullifies anything threatening that exists beyond that corner of garden on which the evening light falls.

Pietro Giuseppe sees her motionless at the door and, turning towards her, without interrupting the music, he returns her smile.

The news of his arrest, in February, hit them like a cannonball. Gavriel would go to Genoa, it was decided. There was snow everywhere, the journey took three days, and when he saw the sea for the first time he felt no emotion. That blue luminescence, distant, wrinkled, seemed insignificant to him. He was too tired; and that beauty, too vast.

They wouldn't even let him see Pietro Giuseppe: he had been arrested along with six other internationalists, and no one could approach them without the permission of the judge. In Tante Marianne's house there was a great silence, and the oldest of the Maturlins did nothing but press her hands to her face in dismay. The keyboard violin was closed: demoiselle Ginette was in prison, also under arrest. No one brought brioches up from the pastry shop, and coffee was served, the only beverage able to fortify the heart at a time like this. The black page sat in the vestibule, offended, depressed, like a bundle of rags. Gavriel found him horrible.

That night he slept on an armchair beside the fire, without undressing, and when he woke in the middle of the night, his bones chilled, he slipped a blanket off the bed and huddled up in it. A blade of light came from under the door and the voice of Tante Marianne could be heard as she talked with her husband, a little girl's voice, all whispers and baby talk. Now and then, at intervals, as if played on a different instrument, her husband's voice replied. A hollow, resentful fuming.

When Gavriel was finally back home, there was much talking behind closed doors. Antonia wept and several times Limasa climbed the stairs to try and catch some word that would reassure her. Had he stolen? she asked. Had he wounded somebody? A brawl? A duel?

A duel was something Tante Marianne could have forgiven more willingly. Even a fight, if love had been involved. But what had happened was beyond her understanding. When she was able to go and see her nephew at last, and after spreading her *Jasmin de Corse* along the corridors of the prison, when she saw him behind the bars, his beard unshaven, the wrath still bursting from the pallor of his cheeks, salts had to be administered to her. She had only to look at him and the whole truth came to her, illuminating every corner that had remained obscure: demoiselle Ginette, the examinations never taken, the books, the walks at night.

Tante Marianne arrived one afternoon at the end of March. The snow still hadn't melted completely and she had taken a long way round to avoid any discomfort. She was fat and it was an effort for her to come up the barc path of the asters. Luìs received her in his study and they talked for a long time, Limasa knocked at the door with some hot chocolate, anxiously looking at the beautiful face of the oldest of the Maturlins. But this year the vintage had been poor and the competition of the French wines had made things worse: Luìs was unwilling to put out a lira, and his long, thin nose pointed at Tante Marianne, indicating her as the one to blame. Tante Marianne concentrated, as in all the worst moments of her life, on preserving her control. She succeeded, but still Luìs would not give in. He would never understand, he said, the reasons for such madness. What did Pietro Giuseppe want? Revolution, kings at the stake, peasants running his property? Tante Marianne looked at him, nodding her head: the grey air, the impossibility of denting that solid refusal, deaf, cruel, oppressed her.

As on her previous visit, she was invited to stay. At supper Antonia was the only one who conversed with her, then little by little the children gathered around her and Tante Marianne forgot her sufferings. She began to tell stories about when she and her sisters had been girls, and the children laughed, the gaps appeared in the mouths of the youngest, where they had lost teeth. Limasa was reassured and made trip after trip from the kitchen to offer Tante Marianne something else to taste: quince jelly, conserves, jams that collected on the table and Tante Marianne distributed them among the children, mouth after mouth, with her coffee spoon. Antonia was seated opposite her: she liked everything about Tante Marianne, even her stoutness.

It had started raining again and the next morning when Tante Marianne left they accompanied her in procession all the way to the square, the children covering their heads with their smocks. Only Luìs barely said goodbye to her and when he saw Antonia come back and read in her face the desire to plead his son's cause, he began limping up the stairs. I don't want to discuss it any more, he said to his wife. Antonia stopped, aghast, her hand on the railing. In her mind darkness had fallen, that man who painfully climbed up, step after step, the man she had loved with suffering and joy, seemed a stranger to her. Stranger in the sense that he was the one to reject any kinship in which he did not recognize himself; it would take very little, she thought with a shudder, to make her, too, slip away, out of his life for ever.

To pay the lawyer, Tante Marianne sold the vermeil cutlery that had belonged to the Khedive of Egypt. She climbed many stairs and she found everywhere sympathy for a boy without any police record anywhere in the Kingdom, who had lost his mother at birth. Tante Marianne's letters moved more than one friend among those who mattered. Pietro Giuseppe himself and his stubborn attitude caused her some concern; but before summer came, in a city streaked by the clear, deep light of the first heat, Pietro Giuseppe again found himself free, still dressed in his winter clothes. Tante Marianne was awaiting him at the corner, in a closed public carriage.

What they said to each other inside it, shielded by the lowered curtains, no one ever learned. Perhaps she asked her nephew for a total capitulation. Perhaps it was Pietro Giuseppe who, faced by that aunt so devoted to legality, shut himself up in a stubborn refusal, without any regrets. It was to be the last time they saw each other; a little later, when Pietro Giuseppe stepped down from the carriage, Tante Marianne watched him go off, hoping he would turn around for one last look. The nephew had taken the downhill road among the clumps of green that spilled over the garden walls, he held his cloak under his arm and was hatless. At the end there was the sea and some children were making their first dives into the corrupted water of the port; he walked briskly, never looking back, not even when he heard the noise of the carriage turning.

To the beautiful house in Piazza de Ferrari he would never return, not even to collect his clothes, they were sent to him, along with his books, to Via Pietro Micca where he had found a room in the house of a rug-mender. Gavriel assumed responsibility for paying the board and lodging.

Antonia sent him more than one letter, none of which he ever answered, then Antonia stopped writing to him in that strange language that had been theirs, halfway between dialect and French. At Christmas time Piulott received the seashells he had collected during his great walks along the shore, when, climbing up among the rocks, every now and then he sat down in little patches of sand that opened out like fans. He sent her others at Easter.

*

In the summer of '66, when the *Re d'Italia* sank, there was a search for the parents of a volunteer who had embarked in Genoa and had suffered a head wound on the morning of July 26th in the waters off Lissa.

The search lasted several weeks and finally they found Luìs; Pietro Giuseppe was already convalescing, and had been taken back to Genoa by sea. There Luìs and Antonia found him, able to walk again, his head shaved, his bare feet in clogs. It was a hot day and all three of them sat on a bench in the shade of an acacia. They talked about the land, about Duardin, who wanted to go into the army as a career, of Sofia now wearing long dresses. Other wounded men wandered around the yard, some on crutches, some still bandaged. Some had had part of their face shot away, and others were missing a hand, an arm; or a black blindfold covered the sockets of their eyes, now empty. When his father questioned him Pietro Giuseppe described the various moments of the battle and what Admiral Tegetthoff's strategy had been from the beginning, when he appeared with his fleet on the horizon at Ancona only to disappear before anyone thought to give chase. Pietro Giuseppe used technical terms and Antonia didn't understand, with the tip of her umbrella she drew in the dust of the yard. She had taken cold during the journey and she moved into the sun.

Pietro Giuseppe described the sea during a storm and the difficulties in rigging sails in the midst of the rain and wind. He described also the fire that had raged after a grenade fell; but of himself, as always, he said nothing; and when Antonia asked him about the wound, he raised his hands to his head as if he had forgotten it. He didn't remember, he said, what had hit him.

Before leaving, Luìs asked him when he would be coming home. This was his pardon; his face still pale and his round head without any hair, Pietro Giuseppe smiled: his father considered he had paid enough. I don't know when they'll discharge me, he answered, for the present I'm still in service.

They embraced and Pietro Giuseppe's head, like his body and his clothes, stank. Antonia left the hospital convinced that her stepson would follow them in a few days. It was August and the war was over; she asked Luìs to take her to see the port. She huddled in her shawl down through the shadowy narrow streets, her hands were frozen and her face grey, almost bluish on either side of her nose.

That visit had comforted her, both of them found Pietro Giuseppe more talkative, more open than in the past, and though convalescent, in good health. Perhaps the wound had not been as serious as they had feared at first. As for the motives that had led him to volunteer, he, an internationalist who wanted peasants and landowners to share the land as equals, Luìs declared his conviction that those motives were to be sought in his repentance. He had realized the mistake he had made and wanted to redeem himself. Antonia thought it was a woman, but didn't say so. They reached the port and the cries, the bustle on the gangways and on the dock, drew them into a dazzling light, almost too intense. Antonia had to sit on a coil of rope. She felt ill. Luìs, excited by the briny air that filled his lungs, would never have left the dock. Both of them had forgotten Pietro Giuseppe; not even Antonia had realized that for Luìs's son the battle of Lissa had represented hell.

Pietro Giuseppe rejoined his companions, he had some breadcrumbs in his pocket and he began distributing them among the sparrows that hopped around under the acacia. Like his grandfather, that Sacarlott who until his death had never mentioned the Cossacks encountered on the Russian plains, he too had kept silent. He had not spoken about when the *Re d'Italia* sailed the first time from Ancona under a sky filled with stars and he thought they were heading for Venice, not even noticing that they had changed course, and in silence he admired the July night, without fear. That had come later, had increased as the days went by, like a seed that had put down roots in his chest. And in the morning, when the island of Lissa appeared on the horizon with the mouths of the cannons turned towards the sea, the wind raised waves and the clouds flew fast. The weather got worse and worse and at dawn the next day the Austrian ships emerged from the rain while the storm twisted the masts and poured torrents of water on the main deck from sea and sky.

There were four battleships that closed the *Re d'Italia* in their grip and one, the *Erzherzog Ferdinand Max*, suddenly rammed its keel against their flank, the steam frigate then split open like a shell amid flying spars and shreds of sail. The memory of that dull blow, like a noise capable of splitting the world in two, would return over the years. Not the waves lashed by the rain, not the fire, not the comrades' bodies tossed around and their screams. But that blow to the heart, to the brain, to life.

Pietro Giuseppe did not come home. Those who thought a woman had been responsible for his going off as a volunteer were not wrong. To escape from a situation that was becoming intolerable to him, he had found no better solution. Gavriel was unable to learn that woman's name and he imagined it was demoiselle Ginette with her pale cheeks and her frizzy hair high over her brow. Perhaps, on the other hand, it was the women in Via Pietro Micca who mended rugs: Gavriel's nephew sent him the new address. A fine room, he wrote, with a window overlooking the port.

In a short time Pietro Giuseppe finished his studies and, passing the competition to enter the Magistrature, he went to take up his first position in Livorno. He was twenty-six and he exchanged letters only with Gavriel. For Christmas and Easter he had resumed sending Piulott seashells that he collected during his Sunday walks on the beaches, sometimes venturing as far as Viareggio and Cinquale. With him came cousin Tomà, who had opened an office in Livorno, importing dates and sultanas from the East.

*

Pietro Giuseppe had been the first. Afterwards it was the turn of Duardin, who was admitted to the military academy. He had yearned for nothing else ever since the long procession to Occimiano, when he had gone to see aides and generals ride by amid the clank of sabres and the rattle of spurs.

Even if there was still no understanding exactly what went on inside Evasio's long, slender head with its narrow temples, he showed a great interest in animals and would sit for hours on a little chair to observe geese and hens, turkeys spreading their tails, their eyes round and yellow. He was delicate, and he too was sent off to boarding school.

Then it was the turn of Sofia, who at eighteen became the bride of the owner of a spinning mill near Biella, who had come to buy the silkworms' silk. It was love at first sight and the portrait her husband had the Milanese photographer Bossi take of her on their wedding trip shows a girl with long, thick hair and an oval face, a strong jaw. She is leaning on a chair, its back tufted, and a mantilla covers her shoulders down to the elbow. She is beautiful and her big, brown eyes stare into the void, a bit dazed.

Her husband would not have his portrait taken; his left eye was missing and he wore a patch covering the socket. He had led an adventurous life even though his name was Tranquillo: at sixteen he had run away from home to join Garibaldi and had got lost in the Comacchio marshes. Sofia was his second wife.

At home Piulott was left, with her inseparable companion, Suava. Limasa had given up thinking about men and even if she wasn't as merry as she had once been, she sang. Her repertory was vast and to her it seemed that each song told some part of her life. Love, betrayal, death, or war. And, after the killing of Zanzìa, crime.

For the land these were the last good years, and Luìs had bought a Sack plough for the new crops, rice and sugar beet. But there was little money circulating, taxes were high because of the debts incurred in all those wars, and boarding schools cost money; so Marlatteira was sent back to her home down at the Pontisella, where the dampness ruined young lungs and the mosquitoes rose in clouds from the stagnant water. Marlatteira had taken up fancy sewing again, but she had little work and almost every day she came up by the aster path and sat in the kitchen with Limasa. She recounted her dreams; and Piulott and Suava, sitting on stools, listened to her, their hands on their knees to hold down their dresses.

After the trip to Genoa, Antonia was ill for a long time with bronchitis and after that, at every change of season, her cough returned. At night when it became more racking she would get up so as not to wake Luìs and would stay a long time at the little window at the end of the yard, looking at the bell tower with the clock face white in the darkness. Through the grille strung with spiderwebs, she stared at it as if she had the tower of Braida before her.

Her walls had been different, thick and imposing, with that grand sensation of ruin that thrills the mind. Not these, which absorb the damp and crumble easily, marked by labile, unknown traces. It seems to her that she has been a guest in this house and that only all those children have distracted her and kept her from realizing it; and now the house slowly rejects her, expels her like an alien body, the rooms no longer recognize her as theirs and she feels she does not belong to them. Even in the direst poverty at Braida there was always a great stir, births, deaths, marriages, in which all had taken part in the shadow of that all-powerful and mournful presence, her mother reclining on the *dormeuse*. Here, on the contrary, silence surrounds her: the silence of Luìs, of Gavriel, of Fantina. And it increases with every season.

At times in summer she goes all the way up to Braida and stops outside the arch of the courtyard. The new owner has repaired the road and the wagons that go in and out no longer risk overturning as in the old days, the peasants are new and they pass before her doffing their hats, never suspecting she is the last daughter of that Cavaliera about whom stories are still told, of her early wealth and then her ruinous passion for the soldier from Santo Domingo.

She takes Piulott and Suava with her and from outside she describes the castle, its rooms, its walls with slit-windows for the blunderbusses. But she doesn't go inside, that she would never do, her pride will not allow it. Under a tree she gives the two thirsty girls a bunch of grapes, and as they eat she closes her eyes with shame at having succumbed to this weakness. Along the road home she will not look back and when, at a curve, the squat spire appears with the copper dome opaque in the sun, she heaves a sigh of relief as if she were rid of a weight. The little girls run ahead, she slows her pace, small and erect under the canvas parasol. Exhausted by the heat and by all that walking.

The winter Fantina died she was written up in the *Gazzettino* as the greatest embroiderer of the entire Monferrato region. The article, signed Giov. Batt. Saletta, listed some of her most beautiful works, including the cope with the head of the Baby Jesus and the dowry for the niece of Signora Bocca, bride of a Viceroy of Carlo Felice. The newspaper also reproduced the pen and ink portrait Giai had made of her when he still played the violin under the walnut. She is seen at her embroidery frame, young and slim. But when she died she weighed almost two hundred pounds and the bedsprings had broken. She hadn't been out of bed for months and Antonia cared for her and combed her sparse hair still the colour of the dust-balls that collected in corners. A colour of which Fantina was very proud; and as Antonia ran the comb over her head, the old woman would look at herself in the mirror, to make sure not even one of those hairs would be lost.

Of her life she no longer remembered anything, not Giai and not even Bastianina, who had then become Sister Geltrude Rosalia; on the contrary, she spoke always of Moncalvo and she called Antonia *Mama* as she had called Luison when she was a child. Every night, when the bell tower struck the small hours, she would begin talking. *'Mama,'* she would say, *'auanda at'a mandà me surela?* Where has my sister gone?' Every night it was the same question, repeated over and over again, always in the same tone until Limasa got up and came to tuck in her blankets.

Piulott heard her from her own bed, and instead of frightening her, that voice comforted her. It was a chant that separated the shadows and seemed to precede the cock's crow, still in the darkness. She would reach out and touch Suava sleeping beside her, but she felt she was alone in understanding what Fantina wanted, like the call of a bird inviting its lost companions to gather round her. It was a sound that carried the vibrations of earliest childhood, when the green of the trees and the wandering of the clouds are still like liquids dissolving one into the other, and words and things, not separated by the perception of the senses, assume forms in constant metamorphosis. And from afar, from its source, that chant dragged with it, like the magic piper, the formless characters of dreams. Things similar to the first years of life, or perhaps the same things.

Pietro Giuseppe's absence lasted twelve years. Even Antonia had given up expecting him; her stepson and Luìs seemed to her to have, even in their opposition, a resemblance that frightened her. And as for Luìs that first wife, dead at eighteen, had become in time the symbol of lost youth and happiness, for Antonia Pietro Giuseppe had finally assumed the same painful image. If in the first months she had so longed for his return, the more the years passed, the more, without even realizing it, she had cancelled his traces, thrown away the forgotten volumes, the notebooks from his boyhood.

The letter telling her he had been named Councillor of the

Court of Appeals in Turin took her by surprise. In the letter Pietro Giuseppe wrote about his transfer to the new post and his intention to come and spend a holiday with them. This way, they would make up for lost time, he wrote; and at the bottom of the page, almost as an afterthought, he added that his cousin Tomà, who had left in November of '55 between his mother and Fracin's Rosetta, in all those years had desired nothing more than to come back. If they had nothing against the idea, Pietro Giuseppe would bring Tomà with him.

They arrived on a June Sunday and Pietro Giuseppe left his cousin to collect their baggage alone: his impatience was suddenly stronger and a boy ran ahead to inform his father. Luìs came down the drive towards him, with his wife and brother, as Piulott and Suava, overcome by a fit of shyness, climbed up to the attic where, amid the fruit spread out on mats, were also the seashells that Pietro Giuseppe had sent for so many years. And when, from the flat windows, at the level of the floor, they saw him arrive, they drew back, frightened by what might happen.

But nothing happened, Pietro Giuseppe wiped his dusty shoes on the doormat and from the stairwell they heard his voice, and the voices of Luìs, Gavriel, Antonia. It was the end of June and Pietro Giuseppe was hot, the journey had been long, and he asked Limasa if it was possible to have a bath.

Piulott came out on the landing and instinctively pulled the bell rope that had once linked Giai's room with the rest of the house. Pietro Giuseppe looked up and glimpsed her as she drew back. 'Piulott!' he called. 'Come down, I saw you.' She let herself slide down along the steps, hanging on the banister, and when she was face-to-face with her brother, she stood there dumb: before her was a gentleman with a bit of a paunch and a thick brown moustache. The eyes looking at her, a uniform grey, seemed to read disappointment in her face. She took his hand and kissed it. 'I'm not a bishop, after all.' Pietro

Giuseppe withdrew his hand and at that moment his gaze met Suava's, as she remained motionless on the stairs, tall, very beautiful. For a moment he continued looking at her, then he bent down and took Piulott's face in his hands, kissed her on the brow. He caught the smell of the attic upon her, a mixture of fruit and dust. Piulott laughed, in her throat, and the laughter ended immediately. She was seventeen and Pietro Giuseppe thirty-four.

He was taken at once to see the shells. In the attic the slanting light struck the hems of skirts leaving faces in shadow, and some wasps attracted by the fruit spread out on the mats circled by those warm bands of afternoon sunlight. Piulott picked the shells up one by one, reading aloud the names she had written with the tutor's help. The nomenclature was absurd and Pietro Giuseppe laughed, beneath his moustache his teeth appeared, irregular, ruined by tobacco. The two of them talked like a brother and sister who have always known each other, but when their eyes met it was as if they were seeing each other for the first time. Suava, in silence, went back and forth replacing the shells in order, her dark braid striking her back between her shoulderblades.

Pietro Giuseppe was tired and sat down on an old armchair abandoned among the mats, near him Suava counted the shells, her white, slender neck bent.

But Piulott crouched in front of him and he took her hands, perhaps to move her, and not lose sight of Suava. The emotion of his return stunned him, Piulott's hands in his were rough, strong. Abruptly, she slipped them free and sat on his lap as when she was a child. An impulsive, instinctive act.

'Now you're grown up, it's not done.' Pietro Giuseppe thrust her off, she went away, shrugging. What nonsense, she said, isn't it all the same? She picked up a shell and polished it with her saliva, Suava turned and watched, dumbfounded. But Limasa was calling from downstairs that the bath was ready and Pietro Giuseppe stood up. When he bowed his head to go through the door, they saw the scar where his hair was thinning.

Later, towards evening, when Pietro Giuseppe sat at the spinet to see if he could remember the old tunes, Piulott did not come over to him, but remained standing by the door. Suava mustered her courage and, resting one hand on the wood of the spinet, asked him if he knew the song *Dona Lumbarda*.

It was a damp evening, almost misty because of the great heat of the day, and when the first euphoria was past, there was a feeling of uneasiness in the house as after a long-awaited occasion whose consequences had not been estimated. In the kitchen Antonia decorated the cake with cream and wondered how she should refer to her stepson when she talked with Limasa. Limasa felt the same embarrassment and so didn't name him at all. The only happy one was Suava, who listened, her chin resting in the palm of her hand, as Pietro Giuseppe sang: '*Sa ve digo dona lumbarda, spusème mí, spusème mí . . .*'

His voice had retained the clear timbre his mother's had had, and that voice, inexplicably, made Antonia shiver, and the cream made a smear on the cake.

That evening they celebrated, word of Pietro Giuseppe's return had spread and little by little the old friends arrived, boys who had once run about the fields with him, tearing their trousers on the vines; adults now, awkward in their Sunday clothes, they looked at him, shy and curious. Pietro Giuseppe drank and made the others drink, too, and in a little while the shyness was dispelled, the talk became freer, Pietro Giuseppe laughed and in his gaiety his eyes seemed to change colour. Later Bigiot's son arrived with an accordion and they started dancing, going off to collect their wives and sisters seated outdoors to enjoy the cool air.

The best dancer was cousin Tomà, and as he danced his fine hair rose and fell, but he was never tired and he asked all the women to dance, young and not so young, and he would have danced with Antonia too if only she had been willing. He held Suava up off the ground and they all wondered where he found the strength, bag of bones that he was. When he put her down again Suava's head was spinning and she ached where her cousin's hands had held her.

Piulott danced with Pietro Giuseppe and he had a hard time holding her at arm's length: she liked his smell of wine, his moustache, the sweat that trickled down his neck. She also liked his teeth ruined by tobacco, clenched in the fury of the dancing.

Enough now, Antonia said to the girls, go to bed. And while Suava was prompt to obey, Piulott went to plead with her father, who had stayed in the living-room with the mayor and Bigiot. Such an evening couldn't just end like this, she said, they would never have another like it, and she twisted her hands in excitement, her face shining in the lamp's cone of light.

Piulott had a mouth that even in her happiest moments held a hint of sadness, enigmatic, unreasonable. Even when she laughed and gaiety transformed her face for a moment, her mouth still held some trace of that sadness. Big, soft, it scored her thin face as if it had been cut there by the depth of her soul. For her, Luìs felt a special fondness mixed at times with a feeling of sorrow, as if the inner tension betrayed by that dark, narrow face, almost savage in its purity, might unhinge her delicate body. Now the greenish-brown eyes, tilted down slightly at the corners, moist as perhaps the soldier of Santo Domingo's had once been, looked at him anxiously. All right, he said, but don't stay up too late. Piulott's smile dazzled for a moment before disappearing again from the cone of light. And in the end she and Suava fell asleep in their chairs and Limasa had almost to carry them bodily up to bed, while Bigiot's son's accordion had been joined, like a bird's piping, by the flute of cousin Tomà.

That night Suava started crying. The tears wet her pillow and her hair spread out around her face. Piulott got up: through the shutters came the day's beginning and she opened the window over the grass covered by the grey light that precedes dawn. It was so beautiful that she rested her elbows on the sill. 'Piulott...' Through the darkness of her hair Suava's face could be glimpsed, even whiter, destroyed by her tears. 'Come,' she said, 'come into my bed, just for a moment.' Reluctantly, Piulott abandoned the window and as she slipped under the sheet, she felt Suava's body tremble, her hands fastened to her like nails. As she wept Suava didn't stop talking, 'Don't leave me, never leave,' she said, 'never, swear you won't.' Then Piulott stroked her, drying her tears with her hair: 'What a silly you are,' she said, 'the ideas you get...' But for the first time it irritated her to feel Suava's legs cling to hers, and she lay stiffly, her feet pressed against the mattress.

Early in July Evasio arrived, too; and a week later, a cart was seen coming up the drive with the baggage of Sofia, on a visit with her two children.

From Biella Sofia had brought some lengths of cloth as presents for all and Piulott had Marlatteira make her a light wool dress first. Every day cousin Tomà organized something, an excursion or a picnic at the Gru farm, where they sat under the cherry tree. Or else they went in the late afternoon along the road towards the Madonna of the Snows and the peasants returning from the fields saw the group of them laughing and joking, Sofia's children running to and fro. The peasants respectfully doffed their caps and were rather amazed that His Honour the Councillor walked along so nonchalantly with that thin, gangling cousin, ready to gesticulate and make everybody laugh.

During the hottest hours, when the shutters of the house were left barely ajar, they played cards and Sofia's voice was shrill, loud. Her husband was a very stern man and he liked to see her with some kind of work in her hand always, sewing or embroidery, and she couldn't remember when she had enjoyed herself as much as in these games with cousin Tomà. To see the passion, real or feigned, as he snatched the cards with his big hands. Games that never ended and were often continued in the evening when supper had been cleared away and from the open windows came the cry of the crickets and the croaking of some frog not far off. And if it wasn't to play cards, they would stay up to play blind man's buff and there was no talk now of sending the children to bed. From her room Antonia heard them still laughing and making a racket, Tomà's voice above all the others. Tomà's cry as Sofia seized him by his checked jacket; and nobody was sure if she had peeked from beneath the blindfold or if he allowed himself to be caught and let Sofia's hands become tangled in his blond hair. The children yelled, excited; and came forward so that their mother could catch them, too.

Cousin Tomà didn't play his flute in public again. Maybe he had played on the night of the party because he had been drinking. Now he played it alone, shut up in his room, and through the open window the notes reached the garden, where Sofia was seated under the walnut tree making the children do their lessons. She raised her eyes to the curtains that swelled into the sun: the music was slow, with long pauses in the melody, and Sofia's mind wandered, she gave the children wrong answers or put her finger to her mouth for them to be silent instead of torturing her with so many questions while her eyes followed the circling of the bees: a move and then the body barely vibrating above the flower, and finally the long flight, far away.

Suava, too, stopped at the foot of the stairs to listen to the sound of the flute, and cousin Tomà's music, so different from what she was used to, troubled her. Evasio appeared at the front door and she saw him reflected in the wardrobe mirror, his eyes seeking hers as if that indirect gaze could express what was directly forbidden him. Suava looked at him for an instant, then turned her head and quickly climbed the stairs, the sound of that flute following her down the corridor.

For Suava's great passion is music and every time Pietro Giuseppe sits down at the spinet she goes to him, tall and straight, her long eyes dark, her face with its strong cheekbones, her lips ready to reinforce the notes. For her Pietro Giuseppe plays *Dona Lumbarda* and sometimes also the song whose name Suava bears: *La povra Olanda / l'è na fumna d'un tamburín* . . .

At times, if asked, cousin Tomà speaks in that strange tongue he had used with his mother, and Piulott and Sofia laugh until they cry; Antonia, on the contrary, has to look away, those sounds hurt her so, recalling a summer now distant. And when they sit at table and Piulott and Evasio get up, when they play with their forks, and the children rock in their chairs, she holds Tomà's presence responsible for that great confusion, the way he treats everything as a game, while Sofia, seated opposite, forgets to eat in order to look at him.

Because Sofia never takes her eyes off him and she likes so many things about her cousin, that she herself would scarcely be able to tell them all. His eccentricity amuses her but perhaps she prefers his sudden gravity, or his acts of extreme sweetness. As when he ties a ribbon for the little girl, or when he removes a minuscule insect from the collar of her dress. And when, in the evening, once the table is cleared, they sit down to finish the card game, and she follows carefully his explanations of *piquet* and *reversis*. For cousin Tomà seems to play with great commitment but he never takes seriously things that, for the others, are grave and important, and even when he sits with Luìs and talks about the Trade Agreement with France, he has to make an effort to maintain his composure, and the pale skin of his cheeks turns red. Shyness or invincible boredom? It's hard to say; and if Gavriel brings up the subject of the battle for the Turkish boundaries, a subject that should be of interest since dates and sultanas are so important for Tomà, she sees his mouth making an evident, painful effort to stifle a yawn.

The truth is that cousin Tomà loathes talking about war and guns, and if the Trade Agreement with France leaves him indifferent, the problem of the Dardanelles turns him to ice. One evening, strolling along the aster path with Sofia, he talked about his father, who had been killed far away by a shot fired from a Turkish barquentine. She listened with sympathetic eyes while from the house came the sound of the shutters being closed, the voices of the children chasing one another for a last time. He talked about that Godforsaken corner of the Crimea where the fleas crawled under the bandages and fever consumed his father. About that letter dictated to his tent-mate when he was already delirious, in which he had put all his torment at being so far from his wife. Between the lank bands of hair, his face looked white as wax, and his long thin hands took the hands Sofia offered him in consolation, while his eyes were immersed in hers. Eyes of water, of grass, that made Sofia's fingers tremble in his.

A summer certainly different from others. Sofia's husband wants to know when she is coming home with the children, she sends word that she can't come just yet, the little girl has developed a fever and the great heat of these days makes the journey inadvisable. The heat is so great that nobody suggests excursions any more and even going up to the Gru farm for a picnic has become wearisome. The blackberries have dried up before ripening and the sun beats down on the shutters, consumes every drop of water. If it doesn't rain soon the clover and the alfalfa will be scorched, the wheat's kernels will be halved, and it will be even worse for the rice, trapped in the dry, cracked earth. Cousin Tomà keeps Sofia company in the sick child's bedroom, he takes the two wooden Cossacks, a bit faded in their uniforms of the Tsar Alexander, and makes them ride over the folds of the counterpane: this, he says, is the snow of Russia, while his big frightened hand is Sacarlott when he was still called Pidrèn and thought he was dying. The child laughs, her lips parched with fever, Sofia tells about the time when Tomà as a little boy climbed the walnut and fell when a branch broke and he said, *Pardon.*

But as dusk comes on and the shadow steals over the yellowish wall of the house, they go strolling in a group along the road towards Lu. Suava is given permission to go too and their feet sink deeply into the dust, as fine as face-powder. A dust that lies on the hedges, on the withered grass of the verge, in the hems of their skirts. Piulott walks beside Pietro Giuseppe so as not to miss a word of what he says and she is irritated by cousin Tomà's voice, constantly interrupting. But she doesn't dare say anything and the greenish-brown eyes disappear under their lids while a sunset that seems dust, too, dust and gold, rises from the earth towards the sky.

In the evening when the darkness comes and Suava lights the candles at either side of the spinet, Piulott remains motionless as her gaze shadowed by her lashes follows Suava's movements, the dark swaying of her braid between her shoulders; and her ignorance weighs on her, she would like to know now about the women her brother has encountered. About demoiselle Ginette with her frizzy hair high above her brow and her pale cheeks.

Pietro Giuseppe sees her and smiles; he likes Piulott's curiosity, her sudden inertia when she sits with her eyes half-closed under the walnut tree, suddenly limp as if she were asleep. He smiles at the anarchy of her body, she is so disarmed and invincible, and when they go out into the fields he watches her walking heedless of the sun that darkens her skin, paying no attention if some bramble tears her already threadbare dresses. But perhaps what Piulott wants is something more and Pietro Giuseppe raises his eyes from the keyboard and in the candlelight studies her long dark face with the slightly jutting chin, lost in listening. He stops playing and immediately her eyelids are raised, her eyes stare at him, uneasy. He can't help laughing: *Donu lumbarda, spusème mí, spusème mí . . .*

Sofia's husband has come to take his wife back. He is tall, sturdy, his face framed by a thick beard, shiny, dark, streaked with grey. Some of his 'merinos' have gone to the Universal Exposition in Paris and he sucks smugly on his pipe, puffing the smoke upwards in little concentric rings that amuse the children. At supper he tells how he ran away from home at sixteen, when he joined Garibaldi in Tuscany and then followed him to Rome. He tells of the arrival in San Marino and how he travelled on a little boat to the shore at Magnavacca, with the Austrian ships after them. His single eye, streaked with red, shines in the light of the lamp, he still has his uniform, he says, the red tunic and the kepi, the shirt bloodstained from the time at Magnavacca when he was lost among the marshes and a branch blinded an eye. Piulott listens, gaping, though she already knows the story, many of the details are new to her and she chews slowly while Sofia, who knows the story and all the details, makes a polite show of attention. Only cousin Tomà irreverently goes on shaping little pellets of bread and threatening the children with them, making them laugh. Now and then he blinks as if the light troubled him, or perhaps the sight of that black patch like a hole on the handsome face of Sofia's husband.

That night, when Antonia went to open the window because of the great heat, she thought she saw cousin Tomà wandering, tall and thin, around the garden. But someone also saw him climb up into the walnut tree like a cat, his body rubbing against the trunk and the blond of his hair appearing at intervals among the leaves. One of the cowmen woke at a slamming of the door of the little stall where they were fattening the capons, and thinking it was a thief, he came out with the pitchfork but saw nobody. Then he heard the sound of Giai's violin, clear, distinct, a sound that one minute came from the well and in the next floated beneath the arbour; and putting down the pitchfork, he went back inside to sleep on the straw.

Only Sofia's husband, with little inclination towards the supernatural, looked out at the window and shouted: who's there? Once, twice. From the bed Sofia didn't tell him of the violin that Fantina had kept, in its case, for so many years and how the termites and the damp had made it as limp as paper; a sound that came back at certain special moments even if nobody knew where that violin was any more. 'Leave it open,' she said to her husband. That sound filled her with a great languor, a lightness in which forgotten desires surfaced. And as her husband was closing the window again because the night air is harmful, she continued to hear those notes through the panes and the curtains, the down of the pillow.

But perhaps it had been the flute of cousin Tomà, who had climbed up among the branches of the walnut, even if the sound of a flute is very different from that of a violin, and Antonia, back in bed, rejoiced that Sofia's husband had come to take her home even though any parting made Antonia suffer. Otherwise who could say how much longer Sofia would have continued taking an interest in the Crimean war, having it described to her in the evening along the aster path, her shoulders covered by a shawl so light she didn't notice when she lost it? Who knows how many more of those endless card games there would have been in the kitchen where Limasa, waiting to put out the lamps, fell asleep on a chair? Fingers touching on the cloth spread over the table, cards passing from hand to hand: wonderful, you've won again . . . It doesn't count, it doesn't count, Piulott would protest, Tomà's cheating, he slips Sofia the cards she needs to win!

Now Sofia has left, her husband carrying the still-convalescent child in his arms, clinging to his neck. Cousin Tomà has left, too, gone back to counting dates and shipments of sultanas. He has promised to return next year and he insisted on climbing up on the box of the post coach; in the square everybody looked at him, with the long cap of lank hair shining in the sun, as he waved his hat in goodbye, his long, gangling legs swinging. Going home then, up the road where the tracks of the wagons dissolve in the dust, Piulott and Pietro Giuseppe are silent, she looks at him, frowning, from time to time. Pietro Giuseppe's face is tanned, spare, every sign of paunch has vanished and from beneath his hat brim he replies to that gaze as if lost in thought. You're sad? he asks her. No, why should I be? His eyes contemplate her, impenetrable, like dust.

Now the four of them are left, she, Suava, Pietro Giuseppe and Evasio, and life has been recomposed in the silence of every day. Evasio has to study and often in the morning he sits and stares through the grille of the study at the two girls picking fruit: figs, pears fallen on the ground unripe, which they set on the sill. In the afternoon the garden is empty, in the first shadows September spreads over the lawn, the two girls have gone out hunting, to accompany Pietro Giuseppe; nothing can stop them. They cross the ditches, are scratched among the bushes, they leap where leaping is necessary, and anyone meeting them in the fields, the dog in the lead and Pietro Giuseppe between the two of them, one thin and dark and the other tall with her lovely head erect, asks himself many questions about the young Councillor of the Court of Appeals and Limasa's bastard daughter. At every shot that strikes home the dog retrieves a quail or a pheasant, at times a hare, and Suava looks away at the sight of the animal twitching in its last spasms while Piulott collects it from the dog's mouth and finishes it off, slamming it against a rock. Blood stains her hands, her dress.

Suava returns from those walks with her face flushed, with a verve unusual in her, Limasa grumbles because she goes out wasting her time instead of learning Venetian stitch and *ardanger*, the little curlicue for fine linen, but the older woman cannot conceal an instinctive pleasure. Suava's beauty is too great for her mother to dwell on the dangers of all that happy wandering, and when she sees the three of them setting out or when Suava comes running past her, breathless, heedless of anything other than catching up with Pietro Giuseppe, who stands and waits for her on the path, Limasa is overcome by a kind of daze.

They were always together. Pietro Giuseppe took the two calling at Pomaro, to visit Sireina, who as a girl had been a great friend of the six Maturlin sisters and now, before dying, wanted to meet the son of Teresina who had become Councillor of the Court of Appeals in Turin.

Sireina's real name was Maria Carlotta and she had married one of the lords of Pomaro but to achieve her purpose she had had to use such arts of seduction that, among the common people, she had been given her nickname of *Sireina*. Now she was old and fat and that nickname pleased her more than the title rightfully hers. She walked along the garden paths in a yellow-fringed mantilla and she called the peacocks that at the sound of her voice spread their tails, their combs quavering, like pistils. The two girls followed her, awed, trampling on the black needles shed by the cedars of Lebanon, so tall that they darkened the sky. At every few steps Sireina stopped and praised aloud the beauty of Suava, her hair, her complexion, her eyes. Later, seated apart with Pietro Giuseppe, she enquired who the girl was and on learning that she sewed trousseaux she volunteered to invite her for a while to the castle, to prepare new bed linen.

The old woman was rather deaf and had spoken in a loud voice; not far away, Suava turned and, red with embarrassment, looked at Pietro Giuseppe to see what he would answer; her small hands, scarred by the needle, twisted, one clutching the other. But it was Piulott who answered: what a good idea, she said, naturally everyone would be in favour of it. Then she broke off, as her nerve failed her.

Nobody had asked her opinion, and Sireina looked at her dumbfounded while Suava's eyes had turned glassy, tears ready to overflow. Pietro Giuseppe said nothing and that silence gave Piulott new courage. Yes, she went on, Suava could embroider very well and besides she would surely be happy to live in a place where there was even a swing! She had used the word *sbalòusia* for what Sireina had pompously called the *balançoire* and now Piulott cast her eyes around seeking further attractions, her face pale with emotion. Leaning against the back of his cast-iron seat, his legs crossed at the calf as Tante Marianne had taught him, his cigar between thumb and forefinger, Pietro Giuseppe looked at her without speaking.

The visit ended in silence. Sireina, suddenly remembering that she was a Marchesa, benevolently patted Suava's head and offered Piulott her hand to kiss. Piulott pretended not to see it and, sketching with her whole body what she presumed was a bow, she went ahead, ready to leave. And once outside she was immediately seized by great hilarity.

It was the evening, the end of the visit, but, even more, it was what she had caught in Pietro Giuseppe's gaze. A blind pardon, an indulgence that went beyond her every hope. She hugged Suava, assured her that nobody wanted to send her away, and took her hand to run together down through the fields, where a light mist swallowed up their feet. Suava let herself be dragged along, a cloud came afire here and there in the sky and the air seemed to penetrate the lungs with those deep colours. Piulott slipped out the pins holding her hair and she would have liked to tear off her belt, the laces of her skirt, in her great desire for freedom. Suava looked at her, at a loss, and as soon as she could, she withdrew her hand.

'*E i pavo, aieru nent bei?*' Piulott has stopped, from that stagnant mist Suava emerges, standing stiffly, her eyes like stars accept the challenge. 'Weren't those peacocks beautiful, and did you see those apple trees? *Ati ha visti al pianti at pum?*'

'Witch!' Suava shouts at her, '*stria, stria . . .*' She runs off as if she were sailing in that cotton mist, a light sail in the rattle of footsteps.

Piulott has reached Pietro Giuseppe on the road, they have clasped hands, her fingers are searing. In the sky all colour is spent and they proceed slowly, they never catch up with Suava. When they turn into the aster path, their hands separate, from the house come notes picked out by an uncertain hand on the spinet: *Dona lumbarda, spusème mí, spusème mí* . . .

Luìs is seated under the walnut tree and he calls them. He offers his son a glass of wine before supper. Pietro Giuseppe tells him of their visit to Pomaro. She had the nasty habit of sniffing tobacco when she was young, Luìs says of Sireina, and her nose was always red . . . but as he speaks he senses something forced in his son's attention as if he wanted to show he is the same as everybody else, trying to be simple when instead so many things prove he is the opposite; and Luìs is silent, pouring him more wine.

But not even Luìs asks himself why Pietro Giuseppe prefers the company of two ignorant girls to that of grown men, people more like himself. And if the thought does cross his mind it is always Suava who prompts it, Suava who has now gone to pick the grapes for supper and in the arbour looks like a pale patch, under the dense shadow of her hair.

Evasio appears at the door. 'Mama wants you inside,' he says to Piulott. Perhaps he was the one playing *Dona lumbarda* and Pietro Giuseppe looks at the boy's hands as he pours himself a drink: hands that tremble slightly, always a bit sweaty. The pale eyes inherited from the lords of Braida are a blue that could be very beautiful if Evasio's were not so bloodshot. Hurry, he says again to Piulott, Mama's waiting for you; his eyes seek out Suava, she has remained motionless under the arbour, not even her scissors make any sound.

Piulott gets up reluctantly and before moving from behind the chair where he is seated, she puts her arms around Pietro Giuseppe's neck, bending rapidly to give him a kiss. It is a kiss of gratitude but her lips press his cheek and slide away slowly, Pietro Giuseppe holds her hand resting on his shoulder, she laughs softly. And everything is so natural, no one is surprised, not even Evasio. For an instant all seems perfect: the evening, the little round iron table, the walnut, Suava's footsteps on the path.

*

Suava fell ill. She, the most ignorant, realized something intolerable was happening. She was moved into Limasa's room and her mother unrolled a straw mattress for herself at the foot of the bed. It was a tedious summer fever; her head on the pillow, Suava stared at the little barred window and any work Limasa put in her hands, even if it was only hemming a handkerchief, she would drop, her exhaustion was so great. When she heard someone going by in the corridor she would turn her head in the hope it was Piulott.

But Piulott came in rarely and her fingers, toying with the sewing abandoned on the blanket, had something cruel in their impatience, they made Suava want to die. The girls exchanged a few sentences and Piulott's replies said nothing: at High Mass the priest had preached a sermon on the Devil. No, they hadn't gone to Pomaro again . . . Her eyes wandered around restlessly and shortly after she had come in she was already at the door, her long, dark face pressed against the frame in a last change of mind.

The summer could have ended like that, with Suava slowly getting better and Piulott out hunting with Pietro Giuseppe and Bigiot's son. A quail flushed, the rifle shot, the dog running and Piulott going to him and taking the animal from his mouth. The fine mist at dusk. The first rains, the evenings growing colder. Pietro Giuseppe playing *Dona lumbarda* and Suava listening to it from her room.

The invitation was delivered by the village clerk and he remained under the walnut tree waiting for someone to offer him a drink. But that note caused such a fuss that they all forgot about him: strictly personal, it invited the Illustrious Fellow Citizen, gloriously wounded in the battle of Lissa, to the inauguration of the Monument to the Fallen in the cause of Independence, which would take place in Alessandria. The town council, to alleviate the discomfort of the journey, was putting at his disposal a carriage and coachman.

Pietro Giuseppe was out and when he came back he walked with the clerk down the drive. As for accepting the invitation, he said, he would let them know as soon as possible. His holiday was almost over and he would be sorry to give up even two days of it. The clerk nodded as if he owed him unconditional approval but when he reached the gate he stopped: perhaps he had misunderstood, was he refusing? The man's eyes looked at Pietro Giuseppe in disbelief and he repeated what had been said about the carriage. A carriage with padded seats, it was all ready and waiting in the shed behind the town hall.

At table Luìs, too, was amazed by his son's indecision and tried to convince him, almost intimidated by such indifference. Say yes, say you'll go, Piulott's voice shrilled loudly, please, then you can take me with you . . . She was changing his plate and her hand resting on the cloth betrayed still her adolescence in its softness. Please. Bold and wheedling.

Luìs looked at her, surprised, Gavriel stopped eating. She turned red, perhaps she had been too daring and now her mother was reproaching her. That wasn't a thing to ask, she said, nobody had invited her. I know, I know, she hastened to answer, but I'm always at home, I never go anywhere. On the cloth, her hand was pleading.

Pietro Giuseppe had said nothing yet and he looked calmly at his father. 'If it means so much to Piulott. . .' he said then; his dusty eyes seeming to leave any decision to Luìs.

'Oh, it does, it does!' Almost ridiculous in her joy.

Nobody protested, even Antonia kept silent, struck by the look Piulott had given them all: in those greenish-brown eyes there was the happiness that none of them had known for a long time. The hand drew back from the cloth, Piulott was motionless again, the plate in her hand, Pietro Giuseppe sensed her behind him. Lost, crazy, because of what she had achieved.

The carriage was a berlin with worn, grey curtains; Barbissa, the man who handled the horses, weighed close to two hundred pounds and as he climbed onto the box he made all the wood creak. People came out into the street to see the carriage that had come for Luìs's son, invited by the Prefect of Alessandria, and Piulott, huddled against the cushions, laughed with wonder, her broad melancholy mouth quivering slightly. She had put on her best dress, of checked wool, and she clenched her fingers in her excitement. When the carriage turned onto the high road, they were already in each other's arms.

They kissed for a long time, for hours, in silence. They kissed each other's face, hair; Pietro Giuseppe's lips were closed in the soft hollow of her throat. But they went no further. And if Piulott had no doubts about the nature of her desires, a kind of blindness prevented her from transmitting them to her consciousness. Her happiness was too great, it had to be lived fully, at once.

Through the curtains they saw the sun sink and then die, and when Barbissa stopped the carriage, his suspicions aroused by all that silence, and opened the door, they were unable to control their emotion. Everything inside the carriage bore witness to what had happened. Barbissa slammed the door: for a moment his big, broad face had reflected, in its amazement, the enormity of what he had seen. But for them it was still not enough and as soon as the horses moved on, Pietro Giuseppe clasped her against his body as when she was a child, so tight, as if he wanted to enclose her inside him.

That evening, in the hotel, they had a very lively supper. For Piulott it was all new and she did not know what to order among the many foods, the table became filled with dishes. The few men supping, their napkins stuck into their waistcoats, looked at the pair with curiosity. They were truly an unusual couple. His well-tailored clothes seemed to conceal a heavy build, a peasant's physique; whereas she, very young, was wearing a dress with which the seamstress's scissors had not been very subtle, but her long, fine features belonged to another breed, to those lords of Braida who could boast of ancestors dating back to the Crusades. And then the excessive intimacy, the fork that went from one's plate to the other's. A Councillor of the Court of Appeals and his young sister, the waiter whispered.

That night, in her little room over the courtyard, Piulott lay awake counting the hours as the clock struck them. She ran her hands over her face and neck, over her hair, to feel what Pietro Giuseppe had felt beneath his lips. Not even for an instant did she have any remorse, the only thoughts that, lightning-like, flashed through her mind concerned Monday, when they would make the same journey in the other direction. Towards dawn she looked out at the window, the air was cold, and a lame scullerymaid was drawing water from the well soundlessly, the chain had been greased to avoid disturbing the guests and the girl moved it slowly, taking care that the bucket did not bang against the sides. Then, suddenly, from one of the arches of the yard, Barbissa came out, still confused with sleep, his grey hair dishevelled; and Piulott drew back, frightened.

It was he, surely, who talked. What he said, and to whom, Piulott never learned: that return in the carriage remained forever confined to the remote corners of her soul. While Pietro Giuseppe was at dinner in the Prefecture, Fracin's Rosetta turned up at the hotel to take Piulott to her house. She had her brother's permission, she said, to take charge of her for a few days and show her the city. Piulott got into the landau lined with scarlet velvet, not realizing this meant a final separation; and she laughed when, at the door of the house, Camurà came towards her, bowing to kiss her hand: an honour, he said, to welcome a granddaughter of the Cavaliera in his home.

All that afternoon she waited for Pietro Giuseppe to join her. She was sure he would arrive and at every sound of a carriage she looked out on the square, where the plane trees were losing their first yellow leaves. Fracin's Rosetta had given her a vast room with few pieces of furniture, and when darkness fell the kerosene lamp illuminated Aurora's chariot painted on the ceiling. She still waited the next day, wandering through the rooms, and at dinner she listened to Camurà tell the story of his life as a poor boy, when he went up to Braida to buy junk and at times, among the rags, he found a sleeve or a *revers* that had belonged to a dress of the Cavaliera: fabrics so fine that the girls made them into ribbons for their hair. When darkness fell again and she realized Pietro Giuseppe would not be coming ever, she flung herself on the bed and in despair slept like a stone. Without dreams, without tears.

Fracin's Rosetta took her to see every street of the city, every church, where the votive lights glowed near the main altar. She took her to see the station and the Tanaro. The landau went down along the scree of the river and the horses stopped at the water's edge, Fracin's Rosetta praised the coachman's skill, the beauty of the poplars, the silver leaves quivering though all that shining seemed to be extinguished in Piulott's dull gaze. One evening, with Camurà, they went to the Teatro Regio, where she took refuge at the back of the box: she was ashamed of her dress and for the whole time she kept her eyes down, deaf to what was happening around her.

The next day Fracin's Rosetta had the carriage stop at the edge of the city, where in the flat countryside furrowed by streams the first factories were rising. Fracin's Rosetta liked that landscape; it had rained and the air was damp, a stripe of sun lit the horizon. She took off her hat and offered her face to the gentle wind rising from the ground: she was still beautiful and the cloak of pale wool like a turtle-dove's plumage shadowed her complexion, sheltered from sorrows. With the tip of her umbrella she pointed out a red-brick building to Piulott: Camurà's future factory. For two days Piulott had hardly eaten a thing, the hem of her dress, always the same one, rumpled, stained, was spattered with mud. What she felt for that beautiful and elegant woman, so concerned to point out with the tip of her umbrella how much she possessed, was close to hatred. The low clouds, brushed by streaks of sun, loured from the puddles. She ran off and hid in the carriage, her face pressed against the seat cushions. When Fracin's Rosetta joined her, she found the girl sobbing. I want to go home, she said, between sobs, I want to go to Mama.

Gavriel came to fetch her and on the train taking them to Giarole he told her Pietro Giuseppe had gone back to Turin. She seemed not to hear and she kept looking out at the poplars along the canals, at the farms, the vineyards where the leaves were beginning to turn reddish. When they were close to Villabella she asked if from the train you could see the Maturlins' farm and Gavriel pointed it out to her, up above, with the tall, twisted elm in front. A lady who had known the Maturlin sisters as girls began to talk of their great beauty: at balls, she said, all the young men were theirs and none was left for the other girls. She also said that the youngest had been the most unfortunate, married at seventeen and dead at the birth of her first child. Neither Gavriel nor Piulott said anything about their connection with the Maturlins and a gentleman seated opposite added that beauty doesn't bring good luck. To the Maturlin girl it had brought mostly misfortune.

Piulott would not go back to sleeping with Suava, for her companion of all her life she had come to feel almost an aversion. One day, as Suava sat sewing, Piulott cut off her plait. Another time she set fire to the dress that had just been sent as a present from Pomaro. On that occasion Suava wept and Antonia made her daughter ask forgiveness on her knees. Piulott obeyed, pale, her teeth clenched, her knees on the brick floor, enunciating every syllable but never raising her head.

A few days after that, Gavriel took her aside and talked to her for a long time. It was winter and the sparrows were pecking at whatever they could find under the trees, the ground was hard, dark, frozen. He said that a nephew of Camurà's had

seen her at the theatre and had been struck by her charm, he
had serious intentions, a good character; he helped his uncle
in the business, one day he would be very rich because he was
Camurà's only heir. Piulott listened in silence, looking outside
at Limasa, sweeping the brick walk. Gavriel said to think it
over because this was a good opportunity, Camurà had bought
his nephew a house just outside Alessandria, where his new
factory was going up, and he would be very pleased to become
related to a granddaughter of the Cavaliera.

Piulott turned then and stared at her uncle with eyes that
seemed asleep beneath her lids. 'Is he old?' she asked.

Gavriel was speechless for a moment. 'No,' he replied, 'I
believe he's not yet thirty.'

'Is he ugly?' She was like a diligent child, enquiring about
her homework, while her face, turned to Gavriel, with the
slightly prominent chin, emanated a sadness almost palp-
able.

'No, on the contrary . . .' But suddenly Gavriel understood,
she didn't consider herself so irresistible, and he had to laugh.
'Don't worry,' he added. 'There are no *buts* . . .' He went over
to her and stroked her hair; she looked outside again: Limasa
was gone and it was growing dark. 'Don't laugh,' she said.

Evasio's love for Suava lasted through the autumn and part of
the winter. From Turin, where he had returned with his books
on anatomy, he wrote home every week in the hope that at
least in taking the letter to his mother, Suava would be forced
to remember him.

He did not know that Suava never even saw those letters,
she was not expecting mail from anybody and in the morning
she got up early to go down to the Barbecana road where the
nuns had opened a new Oratorio for girls. Her hair, growing
back, was a forest around the white oval face and her companions touched it with awe. She was learning a new stitch
called Persian stitch and the nun who taught it to her, sitting
beside her on the bench, talked about the peace of the convent and

the delights that the Madonna had in store for those who offered up their virginity to her as a present. Suava listened with attention, as her little fingers pushed the needle precisely through the cloth; but what she had in her head not even the embroidery Sister could understand.

When Christmas came, Evasio returned. Nobody was expecting him and it was night when he appeared in the drive, the moon high in the sky. He arrived on foot from Giarole and he knocked at the panes of the living-room, where they were having supper. His mother and Piulott hugged him but he immediately sought the eyes of Suava.

A moment, then her gaze, calm and confident, slipped away. Before Evasio had even finished greeting everybody, Suava's skirt had already vanished through the kitchen door.

It was a love without hope, and Evasio knew it. Antonia feared she knew what he was hoping for from the daughter Limasa had had with a Zouave. But perhaps Evasio was not hoping for anything. What was, was. And that evening he sat down at the table, drinking a great deal of wine to get warm, and he told how along the road from Giarole he had been followed by footsteps that stopped when he stopped. And every time he turned around, he saw no one; behind him the road always looked empty, white in the moonlight. Piulott shuddered and she clenched her legs under her chair because she had always feared someone invisible would pull her by the feet. Limasa, on the other hand, thought of Zanzìa, it must have been him, she said, he always took that road at night when he was hauling the salt, hiding from the gendarmes. But Zanzìa had gone out with his cart and Evasio had heard the steps of a man walking. At this point, Piulott was seized with a great horror, and she burst into tears.

Those tears are soon forgotten. Evasio has produced the presents brought from Turin: this is for you, Piulott, and now you will dry your tears. A present for his mother tied with a blue ribbon. One for Limasa. A silver thimble for Suava. A present also for Uncle Gavriel and one for his father. But the waste of money and the futility of these little objects make Luìs suffer, outside the cold cuts the breath in your mouth and in the morning the farmhands' children cannot go to school for lack of stockings, their livid feet refuse to walk, they contract in their clogs with cramps. A blight has attacked the rice and prices have collapsed, the price of corn has collapsed, and wheat and not even the new Friesian cows have been able to improve the livestock. The cowmen are emigrating to the city because nobody has the money to repair their rooms and it rains in on their beds, the walls are green with damp. His son in Turin buys silver thimbles, silk mitts, and for him an embroidered tobacco pouch.

Evasio feels the weight of his father's gaze and turns his light blue eyes to him, eyes of plumage, of a butterfly's wings. Luìs says nothing but his son understands and reacts impatiently, turning to leave the room. Piulott follows him, takes his hand. Thank you, she says, the presents are beautiful.

On the first night of the year much snow fell and in the morning when they got up the bushes were bent under its weight, the brick walk could no longer be seen and the ringing of the bells sounded muffled, useless, because nobody could go to Mass. The snow weighed on the roofs and in the early hours the able-bodied men were already out to knock it down, to avoid what had happened once before, when the stable had caved in. Evasio also went out and with those no-good hands of his, with their network of little blue veins, he grasped a shovel, and for him that was a day of memorable happiness. He felt strong and full of energy, the snow fell on his cap, it slid down his tunic, his face had colour and he kept at it with that shovel, never stopping. Suava, who was big and strong, also helped and carried off barrowfuls of snow, a bright shawl around her head. But then she felt hot and took off the shawl, the snow fell on her hair and melted down over her flushed face, she sucked it between her lips. It was as if she had become a child again and had forgotten any resentment of Piulott;

together they went gaily to empty the wheelbarrow at the end of the garden.

Later, when all the snow had been shovelled, instead of going back into the house, they dragged out the sled and began to pull one another on it. They fell, got up, sank, and ran, the dog leaping around them, barking. Suava forgot the Oratorio and the embroidery nun who was to teach her Persian stitch and she pulled the sled beyond the gate. It was no longer snowing but the sky was low and grey and surely it would snow more, the crows huddled on the boughs, shaking down the snow, their little triangular feet marked the intact and billowing whiteness. They all laughed and cried out, they slid down the Lu slope, clinging to one another; and climbing back up, Suava pulled hard, never tiring. There was a moment when the sled turned over and Evasio found himself hugging Suava, his mouth so close to hers that he could have kissed her: her eyes laughed and Evasio's courage failed him. She slipped away and, still laughing, she ran through the snow, clutching her skirt in her hands.

Limasa came looking for them because it was getting dark, she pulled her shawl around her, and finally she saw them, little spots on the vast white expanse, the dog leaping here and there, disappearing deeper each time; and she began to shout. They were to come home, it was late, and anyway they were crazy to stay out there in all that cold.

When they came into the house they were so wet that the girls were wrapped in blankets and their clothes spread out to dry in the kitchen; they sat in front of the fire to drink hot wine. Evasio's eyes were closing with weariness and his hands hung down swollen and purplish, but he made an effort to stay awake and he kept looking at Suava, her feet sticking out of the blanket in her patched stockings. Suava had never been more beautiful and she laughed, still softly, that wine, strong and sweet, went to her head.

The next day Evasio left for Turin with a basket in which Limasa had put his dinner. His mother gave him the money for the post coach and he set off content, he wanted to study and become a famous surgeon, but his immediate desire was to build, for the coming summer, a great aviary where he could put chaffinches, nightingales, wagtails. But also rarer birds like the hummingbird and the bird of paradise.

Piulott went looking for Uncle Gavriel to tell him she didn't even want to see Camurà's nephew: for the present she wouldn't marry. Maybe, in time, she would change her mind. And she went with Suava down to the Barbecana road to meet the embroidery nun, who knew more than a hundred stitches.

Before February ended, the stationmaster of Giarole sent for Luìs. Lying on a bench in the waiting-room was his son Evasio, who had arrived from Turin with such a high fever that he couldn't stand up. It was almost dark and Luìs sent a message to the stationmaster asking if he could keep the boy until morning. Two men carried Evasio into the little red house overlooking the tracks, and once he was inside they didn't know where to put him; they laid him on a little sofa in one corner. The stationmaster's wife complained because the house was small and God knows what illness the boy had; but Evasio, wrapped in his cloak, no longer heard anything, the voices came to him all muddled together. The stationmaster's oldest girl, who felt sorry for him, kept bathing his temples with vinegar.

Luìs arrived the next morning in a cart covered with an oilcloth. Nothing else could be found on such short notice. It was a fine day and through the last wisps of fog the sky was becoming more and more blue, a rosy light filtered through the leafless poplars, here and there on the dark ground there were big patches of snow. Evasio's head, thrown back, the eyes half-closed, swayed at every jolt of the cart and when Luìs tried to make him drink some water it spilled down his chin over several days' growth of beard, a beard incredibly thick for that face that was becoming smaller all the time, long and narrow at the temples. Luìs took his hand, the veins stood out, livid, on the back, in the fine, cold, white skin, and the fingers clasped his, the only sign Evasio gave. The air was milder than it had been for some time and the crows glistened in the luminous mist, the chimneypots of the houses smoked, white. Gerumin's grandson, driving the cart, sang, a hymn that seemed to him the only thing suitable for a sick man. And so they reached home; it took them almost two hours and when Antonia ran to meet them and looked over the side of the cart, she realized her son was lost.

Evasio lasted three more days. Three days during which Luìs never stirred from the room and held his hand tight. The sickness had reached the lungs and his breathing became more and more laboured. Through the window Luìs watched the day fade and become night and then again the first light of dawn appeared, rarefied, in the room; and every time he tried to slip his hand free, Evasio's fingers would clasp harder. In the silence every sound was amplified: Antonia's steps as she came and went, the sound of the spoon in the cup, of teeth against the glass. And then, a single, set note, now higher, now lower, that frightful breathing.

Three days that created between him and Evasio an intimacy that not even a lifetime of attachment could have created. They understood each other with a pressure of the fingers, an opening of the eyes, a turn of the head. The third day, remembering how miserly he had always been with his son, Luìs slipped beneath the pillow a wallet bulging with money. It was for him, for Evasio, for everything he had always desired. But now it was too late; and Antonia, who was nearby, shifted the pillow, and the wallet fell to the floor. Evasio lay with his eyes closed, he hadn't seen his father put the money under the pillow and was unaware when his mother made it fall. His fingers, yes, they went on holding his father's fingers tight; he needed nothing else. Not Suava any more, not the trees, snow, birds. No more anxieties, desires. Nothing, only those fingers, to the end.

Afterwards, when the gate of the cemetery creaked shut on its hinges, those three days became very important for Luìs; and while, in the house, there was a great weeping and remembering, and the smell of boiling dye for black clothing almost put a taste of death in their mouths, shut up in his study, he felt a great calm. Grief was a block with precise outlines, it did not generate monsters, or horror, or even despair. Terrible to say, Luìs felt superior to the others. He could look grief in the face. Recognize it, test himself against it. Nobody dared open the door, nobody knocked, and while beyond that thin wall the storm seemed to rage with all its thunder, inside an immobile serenity reigned, barely touched by that winter light, clean and cold. His eyes, from the bony hollow of the sockets, grazed the chairs, the table covered with a cloth, the books closed behind glass, the portraits: everything could go on like this for ever. Eternity: a word that revolted Luìs.

Piulott was married in the first week of September. It had just rained and as she set out on foot, her arm in her father's, the whole village stood at their doors to see her and doves flew across the street to light on the roofs. In the air there was a great aroma of cakes, and the baker's wife, who had spent the night making them, was now at her door, her arms white with flour, while the children ran barefoot behind the procession because there was a rumour that Camurà would distribute *pralines* in the French fashion.

Outside the Town Hall the horses of the bridegroom's friends were hitched, the friends had come from Alessandria to celebrate. The priest was waiting in front of the church wearing the ceremonial cope embroidered by Fantina and on the shining head of the Baby Jesus the wasps lighted as if it were honey. When Piulott entered the church the organ began to play and from the pews reserved for the girls from the

Oratorio the shrill high notes of the hymn rose. The altar was snowy with flowers and among the singing girls there was also Suava, a white veil over her hair.

But she suffered dizzy spells and before the groom could slip the ring on Piulott's finger, she felt faint. The crowd, the heat, the smell of the candles. The other girls carried Suava outside and laid her on the steps in the shade of the plane trees. The music reached her even there, she heard it and on her closed eyelids the plane leaves cast fickle shadows.

When it was time for the dinner she had already recovered and, amid the bustle of the women who had come down from the Gru farm, she helped serve the chickens, the sauces, the salamis. Every now and then she looked towards the drive as if she were hoping to see somebody and once she went as far as the gate, where the children, their feet bare in the dust, were waiting for a share of the cake. But she saw nobody and came back on the lawn to serve the bridal couple seated among the friends at a long table with a white cloth. Another table had been prepared in the living-room and there Luìs and Antonia sat with Camurà's relatives and the other *particulari* who had come for the occasion even from San Salvatore and Moncalvo. This was the last daughter and Luìs had done things in style, the courses never ended and the glasses were never empty. Red, almost black Barbera and sharp Grignolino, a ruby colour. And to finish, the muscatel that went to the head, sweet, the colour of tobacco. The blood throbbed at the temples, it throbbed in Antonia's neck as if she had another, tiny heart there.

Duardin had come with his fiancée, a tall girl with a broad straw hat to protect her from the country sun. Her dowry included an apartment in Novara and a villa with a belvedere over Lake Maggiore; thin and jealous, she sat beside Duardin, who was in full uniform. Sabre, buttons and epaulettes flashed in the sun and he was sweating because his wool uniform was buttoned up to his chin. Duardin, too, had been in love with Suava for a summer, but now he could look at her calmly, not feeling anything; and if it had not been for that fiancée seated beside him he would happily have responded to the looks he received from all sides. And yet every time Suava approached with a dish, that fiancée from Novara stiffened, sat up straight, and her cheeks grew redder, while the broad straw hat spread its shadow over the patches of sunlight, for even she was troubled by such beauty.

But the true queen of the feast was Fracin's Rosetta, with a strand of amethysts at her throat and the broad waves of her hair gathered under a high beribboned hat. She chattered tirelessly and when it was time for the toast she made the rounds, kissing all her new relatives. She offered her cheek also to Gavriel, she held it to his face beneath the flutter of the ribbons. There were cake crumbs caught between the amethysts and she smelled, Gavriel thought, as if she had made love a little earlier, all dressed to come here. Gavriel drew back and the kiss did not take place.

To the last, Piulott hoped Pietro Giuseppe would come. She would have liked to tell him many things, how the death of Evasio had changed her, had made her understand suffering and happiness, the emptiness and the fullness on which she had trodden as if blind. And so, seated at the table, between one course and the next, she too would look towards the drive, where the long stalks of the September asters rose.

But Pietro Giuseppe did not come; as a present he had sent her a seashell bound in gold. It was a pendant, he wrote, she could wear it on a chain or attach it to a pin that he would send as soon as it was ready. The note said nothing else, not even best wishes; and before evening the new couple set out in the landau lined with scarlet velvet, placed at their disposal by Camurà.

Nobody knows what went through the mind of the young bride as the door was closed and the carriage turned into the high road. The moon was rising in the sky, which was growing dark, and the first star, the star of shepherds, was fixed up above like a nail of light.

EPILOGUE

They say that, left alone, Luìs and Gavriel never spoke to each other. They sat in front of the fire, old and shrivelled, locked in an inviolable circle of silence. The scuttling of the mice, ever more numerous, the sound of the rain and the thunder, or the flutter of a moth against the pane, were drowned beyond that silence, never crossing its boundary. Not even Giai's violin, if he were still to play it, could have prevailed. Only at the end, when the flame had burned the last piece of wood (logs from apple trees that had ceased bearing, dead branches of the walnut and then, later, also from the pear outside the living-room), Gavriel, the older, would stand. '*Andumma a drommi*,' he would say, 'Let's go and sleep.' '*Andumma*,' Luìs would answer, straightening his leg, which had become pure cartilage. And those words, the only words possible, flared up in the house and ran through it like a wind in the darkness of the rooms. They raised the dust from the furniture, and the whole house creaked like a vessel lying at anchor.

A NOTE ON THE TYPE

This book was set in Janson,
a recutting made direct from type cast from matrices long
thought to have been made by the Dutchman Anton Janson,
who was a practicing type founder in Leipzig during the
years 1668–1687. However, it has been conclusively demonstrated
that these types are actually the work of Nicholas Kis (1650–1702),
a Hungarian, who most probably learned his trade from the master Dutch type
founder Dirk Voskens. The type is an excellent example of the influential
and sturdy Dutch types that prevailed in England up to the time
William Caslon developed his own incomparable designs from them.

Printed and bound by Fairfield Graphics, Fairfield, Pennsylvania

Title page design by George J. McKeon
Title page illustration by Iris Van Rynbach